BLURLINE

CANCELLED

Other books by TW Lawless:

HOMECOUNTRY

THORNYDEVILS

BLURLINE

To East Gippsland Library.

TW LAWLESS

Tom.

CAMPANILE
PUBLISHING

Published by Campanile Publishing
www.twlawless.com

A National Library of Australia Cataloguing-in-Publication entry has been created for this title.

ISBN 978-0-9942651-0-4 (pbk)

ISBN 978-0-9942651-1-1 (ebook)

Cover design by Greg Alex-Vasey
Edited by Linda Nix of Golden Orb Creative
Print typesetting and ebook production by Golden Orb Creative

Distributed by Dennis Jones and Associates

For Kay.

DD

Did you miss me? I haven't written because I didn't have anything much to say. Now all of a sudden everything's changed and I'm so excited! I went to three auditions this week and YOU'LL NEVER GUESS WHAT. They've called me back for one of them. The director wants to see me again. Everyone says I'm really lucky and this could be the opportunity of a lifetime!!! I hope I get the part. Fingers crossed!

Love,
Me

London, 1990

1

He was being followed; Peter Clancy was sure of it. He first suspected it when he left the office in Fleet Street but now he had clear confirmation. He had just stepped onto the train at Temple tube station and his shadow was right behind him. Right up his arse. If Peter had turned and sneezed, his shadow would have felt the blast.

The follower was so anxious to stay close that he had pushed an old man out of the way, just so he could fit into the carriage. He was in his early twenties, hair à la Jason Priestly and wearing a double-breasted beige suit. Well cut. A little too neat.

Peter recalled having seen a young man matching that description leaving the Old Bell Tavern next door to the office, as he passed by. Perhaps he wasn't carrying a Filofax or wearing a Rolex, but the young man had the earthy scent of Paco Rabanne about him. His pedigree might have been unclear, but his aspirations were evident.

Peter stole a glance. *I hate yuppies. Aren't they on the extinction list yet?* Yuppie was now sitting only two seats away, facing him, head buried in the *Daily Mail*. Yes, he was being followed by a yuppie for sure, and by a dumb one at that. Peter caught him peeking over his paper. *They're heading the same way as the Sloane Rangers and it can't happen quick enough.* Peter, the hack journalist, had his own fashion tribe. He was a hackie. His tribe would never die out.

The yuppie shoved his head back down into the paper like a scared meerkat. *So bloody obvious. Okay, who have I upset this time?* Was it wise to confront a yuppie? Yuppies weren't renowned for their fighting prowess. *Shit no.* But then again, as Peter always said, cowards get to run away and show a profit another day. Aside from which, he could probably lose Yuppie at Victoria Station. Or so he thought.

Peter hurried out of the tube station. He rushed past the Apollo Theatre without a rearward glance. He was about to climb the steps leading to the Belgravia mansion of a Colonel Henry Armstrong-Boyd when he next spied Yuppie bolting down the street towards him. *Shit! How the fuck...* It was then that it dawned on him. Yuppie wasn't an aggrieved victim, he wasn't someone out to inflict physical harm for being the butt of one of Peter's stories. No. The prick was a fellow hack from an opposition paper, trying to steal his story.

How did Yuppie find out? Not today, Yuppie Hack; you're not getting my splash. This was the biggest story Peter had picked up since he'd started work at that sleaze rag, that red-top tabloid, the *Star Gazer*—popularly known as the *Geezer* on the streets. *You'll have a fight on your hands, Yuppie. I'm not running away from this one.*

Colonel Armstrong-Boyd, also known as the actor Tom Mortimer, was formerly of the hit British series *The Manor House*, which had run for a decade until it was cancelled three years ago. Tom, or Colonel as he still preferred to be called *(actors are such a strange lot)*, was giving a behind-the-scenes interview about what went on in the upstairs/downstairs department, *if you get my drift.* Unlike the characters they had played, there had been no social distinctions between the actors in this Edwardian costume drama: the coachman and the lady of the manor; the scullery maid and the governess sharing the gardener. And not forgetting the drug use: the vicar high as a kite giving his sermon; the prince taken to hospital with 'exhaustion'.

The Colonel was unburdening himself—all for a handsome fee, of course. It was going to be the best story Peter had scored since arriving in London three months earlier. He had worked hard for this story, but it had been more chance than anything else that had secured the interview. Or possibly the old Clancy charm. Again.

Peter knew well before he had set foot at Heathrow that there were three tiers to the newspaper market in London: broadsheets, tabloids and red-tops. In descending order. The *Star Gazer* was an infant red-top, and it hadn't been his first choice of newspaper—fact is, he had never heard of it. He'd begun his job-seeking at *The Times*. *Start at the top, stay at the top.* Only a fool would have stepped off the plane without letters of introduction or without interviews lined up like ducks. Yet a week later, there he was, still covered in glory, fresh from uncovering a major scoop on Melbourne's underworld, living in London and unemployed. He had, after all, won the Heart of Melbourne Prize for Most Outstanding Contribution to Journalism (Tabloid Crime). Never mind he had been the only nomination.

So, he went out to the new newspaper complex at Wapping, confident that nationality alone would secure him a job at one of the Murdoch papers. Not so. Knocked back there, Peter steadily worked his way down until he found himself pounding Fleet Street, searching for that elusive position.

It all had to do with his references (as he kept telling them, *I can't get a reference from Bob because he's dead*) and his lack of experience working for a major metropolitan newspaper. *What the hell? Melbourne isn't exactly outback Australia.* Stella Reimers would have given him a great reference, if only he'd been able to find her. He'd tried. He'd called up twenty of the biggest newspapers along the USA east coast searching for her. *Stella, where are you? Stella!*

Instead, Peter became a roving reporter of sorts at the *Geezer*, doing whatever and going wherever the news desk told him at a moment's notice. That is, when he was allowed to play outside. He wrote a lot of stories from his desk without ever leaving the building. Most were stories based on press releases sent from agents trying to promote another one of their talentless wonders or just rehashes of overseas celebrity gossip. If he had to do another story on Madonna he would go quietly mad. *Madonna and so-and-so actor will be starring in Coronation Street. So-and-so is the next face of British television, whatever that means. And I care?* It certainly wasn't how Peter envisaged his journalistic career unfolding in London.

Then, in the depths of despair a week ago, he had remembered how Colonel Armstrong-Boyd had been his mother's favourite character in *The Manor House*, her favourite television show. Maybe if he ingratiated himself enough, he could score an interview. Surely, he would be able to get the old Colonel reminiscing with a few drams of whisky. As chance would have it, Peter had then caught sight of a story in another paper that Tom Mortimer's luxury hotel business had just become insolvent. He surmised that Tom would be needing a cash injection to pay for it about now. *A fee-paying story perhaps, Colonel old chap?*

He had consulted the *Geezer*'s secret list of celebrity phone numbers. Peter didn't want to know how it came to be there, but he had even stumbled over the Queen's private number along the way. He had trawled through the list, found Mortimer's home number, rung it and had spoken to the Colonel himself.

'No!' Mortimer had replied forcefully.

'I personally hate discussing things such as money over the telephone, of course,' Peter had hinted.

'I won't lower myself to that level. And I don't discuss my private life with anyone, let alone the press.'

Bugger. 'Thanks, anyway. Just so you know, my late mum was a big fan of yours.'

Peter had been about to hang up when Mortimer casually asked if Peter was Australian. Peter had nearly replied with *I am, you English twit, and no jokes about koalas, please.* But before he could unleash his tirade, the Colonel had jumped in with how he'd served with Australians in North Africa during the war, found them to be tough, cheery men, always good for a laugh, and who could out-drink and out-fight anyone, including the Germans.

Peter had seen daylight through a chink in the door. His uncle had been in the second fifteenth, ninth division. He had told Mortimer as much. *Job done.*

Mortimer agreed to the interview, with the proviso, '...but don't ask me about my private life. How about an exposé on my time on *The Manor House*? That should get the tongues wagging. I could tell you a thing or two about my former cast members. For a negotiated fee, of course.'

Of course. Was it luck? No. It was pure Australian arse, as the saying went. *Sometimes stories are just pure arse.* And Yuppie was going to try and outbid him? *No way on this earth.*

Peter was about to ring the doorbell when Yuppie bounded up the stairs towards him, smiling like the Cheshire Cat and saying some incomprehensible shit in a Liverpool accent. Peter's ear wasn't tuned in. He strained to understand anything Yuppie said. A Scouser-yuppie seemed a contradiction in terms, and Peter had to stop himself from laughing aloud.

'I'll triple whatever you're going to pay,' Yuppie puffed. 'Why don't you bail out? You're wasting your time here.'

'And who the fuck are you?' Peter bristled. He could feel the coward within draining away. This prick wasn't taking his story. *No way.*

'Never you mind who I am, lad. I'm from the *London Morning Courier.* You know, the paper that has double your circulation and twice your budget?'

'Well, well, is that so, junior? How about pissing off back to your crèche for some quiet time and leaving a real journalist to do his job?'

'Australian?' Yuppie doubled over, chuckling. 'You're not...Australian?'

This was too much. Peter grabbed him by the collar, frog-marched him away from the door and pushed him down onto the footpath below. It was surprisingly easy. 'You haven't been eating your Weetabix,' he said.

'Bugger off!' Yuppie cried, as Peter leapt back up the steps two at a time and rang the doorbell. 'Go back home where you belong! You queer bastard!'

Peter might have responded in the same way, but he wasn't in provincial Melbourne anymore. He was in London. London: the most ruthless newspaper market on earth, where newsgathering was a gladiatorial sport. Yuppie righted himself and propelled himself at Peter, just as the Colonel opened the door.

'What's this, then?' the Colonel grunted as Yuppie landed at his feet. 'Mr Clancy?'

Peter stepped deftly to the right and over the prostrate Scouser. 'Colonel Armstrong-Boyd?' It was a risk using his character's rather than his real name, but it worked a charm.

The Colonel's eyes lingered on the yuppie, lip bloodied where his teeth had hit the threshold as he'd landed. 'You brought a friend?'

'No friend of mine, Colonel.'

Yuppie raised his head, clamping a wad of tissues to his face. 'Oi, Tom. Whatever the *Geezer* is paying you, Tom, the *Morning Courier* will up it by a half.'

Peter watched the Colonel's moustache stand on end and knew he couldn't match the offer. By the look and smell of him, the Colonel needed the money to support his habit of cigars, whisky and past days of Empire. The Colonel nodded, looked at Peter and fidgeted with his walking stick. 'Another half, you say?'

Yuppie nodded.

'Well, well. Another half is certainly an attractive offer.'

Peter had nothing more to give. He was going to lose the story. *Madonna, here I come.*

'Think on it. Another half, Tom,' said Yuppie.

The Colonel leaned on his stick, unfolded a handkerchief and blew his nose while Peter was considering retreating into the bushes. Then the Colonel extended his stick and tapped Yuppie on the shoulder. 'You see, whoever you are, bleeding on my front doorstep, I don't deal with gatecrashers,' he paused. 'I am, unlike you, a man of principle. I made a bargain with Mr Clancy and I intend to keep it.'

He invited Peter in with a sweep of his hand. 'This way, Mr Clancy of the Antipodes.' As Peter stepped past the door, he heard the Colonel say to the yuppie, 'And never, ever presume to call me Tom. I'm Colonel Armstrong-Boyd to you.'

Little wonder Tom Mortimer's acting career had dried up at the end of *The Manor House*; he couldn't let the role go. The Colonel lingered at the door. 'And do you really think I would ever deal with the paper that accused Sir Anthony Bowes-Chumley of dressing up as a nanny and begging prostitutes to spank his bottom?' He raised his stick over his head and brought it down towards Yuppie, who ducked just in time. 'For the benefit of your scum-raking editor, Tony Bowes-Chumley happens to be a good friend of mine.' All his airs and graces vanished. 'So you can get the fuck off my property, you piece of shit, before I beat you to a pulp.'

Yuppie was last seen running down the street, still clutching his blood-soaked tissues.

'Journalists,' the Colonel pronounced, 'are the prostitutes of the English language.'

'Only not paid quite as well,' Peter replied.

2

John Devrille had established the *Star Gazer* only three years earlier. He was a media maverick who had the ambition to make the *Gazer* the best-selling red-top. Unfortunately, still in its infancy, the *Gazer* hadn't quite learnt to walk and still hadn't made a great dent on the market. In fact, it had stumbled on a few occasions. It was unique among the red-top dailies in that it was devoted entirely to gossip, both local and imported, with an emphasis on television, movie and sports celebrities. British politicians were on the hit list only because of their interesting sexual habits, and the royals had a columnist devoted to *their* extracurricular activities.

The *Gazer* had mediocrity smeared all over it like sump oil. Devrille said that the *Star Gazer* aimed to be an informative newspaper for all aspirational men and women. 'I don't just want it to be read just by men on oilrigs or in Army barracks. I believe women should be able to keep up with the gossip without having to look at big-breasted women all the time. That's why I have chosen not to have a topless page three girl.'

He paraphrased from *Yes, Minister* that if *The Times* was read by people who ran the country, and the *Daily Mail* was read by the wives of people who ran the country, then the *Star Gazer* was read by people who didn't give a shit about who ran the country as long as they knew who was shagging whom.

Upon arriving in London, confident that he would secure a job quickly, Peter had immediately leased a flat in Hammersmith above a kebab shop run by an Iranian couple, Mr and Mrs Davudi.

They weren't nearly as ebullient as their Australian counterparts, Con and Roula, although their concern for Peter was comparable, and he immediately adopted them as family. In his quiet moments, even Peter saw a pattern emerging. *No*—he had always wanted to live in Hammersmith so he could be near the Odeon Theatre, one of the hallowed venues for rock concerts.

A few weeks later and without a job in sight, his funds were quickly running out. He didn't want to return to Australia with his tail between his legs. It had been a steady downward spiral until he had happened upon the *Star Gazer* while walking up and down Fleet Street one day. It was located in the former offices of the *Daily Express*, in an art deco building nicknamed the Black Lubyanka, so-called because of its sinister, black façade. It did really look like a building where people were tortured. Pulling out all of the charm he could muster without sounding desperate, Peter had managed to secure an interview with John Devrille that same morning.

Once again, Lady Luck rolled Peter a last stakes winner. If he hadn't landed the job he would have been heading home, tail between legs, as his limited funds had begun to dry up. The job was his only because Devrille had worked briefly for an advertising firm in Melbourne a decade earlier, and had liked to read *The Melbourne Truth*, Peter's former masthead. Devrille had remembered some of Peter's stories. Peter had arsed it again. He just wished he had arsed it at *The Times*.

3

The *Star Gazer's* meeting room was painfully small, causing John Devrille's bassoon voice to bounce off the walls like cannon fire. A handful of journalists cluttered the room. Beside Peter stood Nick Georgiou, the chief British gossip reporter, and on his other side, Willy Prager, the sub-editor for that section. Devrille ordered them to sit while he chose to stand. Adopting his usual posture, he extended his six-foot-two rugger-bugger frame over them, his outstretched arms supporting his upper body as he talked, gnarled fingers splayed against the board table like the roots of a Moreton Bay fig.

Devrille liked the higher ground; he liked to gaze down at his inferiors. To Peter, he was Roger Moore, but Devrille's version of Moore was devoid of any finesse: forty-ish, with thick, permanently windswept, sandy-coloured hair, a chiselled chin and a year-round Marbella tan. Devrille had all the accoutrements of success: the Savile Row suits, the fashionable house in Pimlico, the Aston Martin Virage, and the young Italian ex-model wife—his third. He was a right Johnny, all right.

Known in the media circles as the Fool of Fleet Street or Johnny Cowboy, Devrille was considered to be outright crazy for having set up a paper that was pure gossip, funded, it was rumoured, by an Arab prince. Even crazier were Johnny's predictions for the future of the media, since he had also dubbed himself a 'media futurist'. For a start, he predicted the end of newsprint, the advent of television channels entirely devoted to celebrity news, twenty-four hours a day *(they're just not that interesting)* and—wait for it—television shows that were unscripted about people living together, whether famous or not, simply going about their business. *That would be so coma-inducingly boring. It would be like watching paint dry.*

Why would any journalist work for John Devrille? Peter watched him prowl around the office. He wondered if it was Devrille's vision that they shared, or whether they were all a bit like himself. *More of an AOE situation. All Options Exhausted. Stella! Where are you?*

'Put your best fucking thinking caps on, boys.' Devrille punched one hand into the other as emphasis. 'We're onto a winner here, thanks to our latest recruit. What have the rest of you fuckers been up to?'

Peter kept his eyes fixed on the sheet of paper he had strategically placed on the table, pen poised, seemingly ready for action. In his peripheral vision, he thought he saw Nick Georgiou rolling his eyes. His pen met the paper as Devrille continued pontificating.

'Come on, boys, we need something eye-catching. Willy,' Devrille pointed at Prager. 'Take your hand off it for a moment and speak to me.'

'Reefer Manor? Maybe?' Willy squirmed, his hefty buttocks poking in and out of the sides of the chair like a family of badgers emerging from their burrow.

'You wouldn't know what a fucking reefer was, Willy.'

Why would this poor guy want to work here? Willy wiped his brow as Peter wondered how long Willy could hold out before his complete mental and physical disintegration. *As stated: AOE.*

Devrille smirked. 'I want something better than that. It has to jump out of the newsstands, not gather dust. It has to grab them by the short and curlies. Nick?'

Peter had dubbed Nick Georgiou the Cypriot Adonis. Someone, possibly Anne, the nondescript receptionist, had told him that Nick had fled Cyprus with his parents when the Turks had invaded. Sixteen years later, Nick was the whiz kid journalist who Devrille had poached from a major red-top. He was a great bloke; he had helped Peter acclimatise to living and working in London. Today, he was strangely quiet.

'I don't think we should print it, John,' Nick said. 'We could end up sued by the network and former cast members.'

'What?' Devrille exploded. 'Willy can't seem to let go of his and yours appears to have gone missing, together with your balls. We've printed stories with far less substance than this. Mortimer, the old perv, took snaps of some of them rolling around on the four-poster. What more do you need, Nick? What are you talking about?'

'All right,' Nick replied, 'but I'm certain none of us wants another witch-actress-in-the-graveyard fiasco.'

'And that's why I got rid of the moron who wrote that and employed you. If I hadn't run this past the boys at Gray's Inn, do you think I'd be running with it? I don't exactly need to fork out another fifty thousand quid, now, do I? Mind you, I still think the old bitch was a witch right enough, and I should know… I've been married to a few in my time. Come on. We're not getting anywhere here. Nick? Give me something.'

'Stoned Manor?'

'That's your best?' Devrille shook his head, 'Where are your brains today, Nick? Anyone? Clancy? Show us what you've got. Come on, JB.'

Peter gazed at what he had doodled. *Bob*. Bob Connelly. Late and great. Bob had been his editor at *The Truth*, his mentor and the thorn in his side. Right now, Peter felt nostalgic. Devrille's management style was a world apart. Where Bob was laid-back and whiskey-sodden, Devrille was acerbic and combative. Like calling him 'JB', short for 'Joh's Boy', a reference to Joh Bjelke-Petersen, a former Queensland premier; the very same one that Peter's parents had revered and he had loathed, along with this new nickname. And why JB? Just because Peter was born and raised in a characterless country town called Clarkes Flat in northern Queensland.

But his chief annoyance was when Devrille pissed on about modern management practices, always wanting to include staff in the decision-making process. That was where other papers failed, he said. Devrille had read all of the management books. *Was Mein fucking Kampf on that reading list?*

'I like "Mayhem at the Manor. Sex and Drugs with a Dash of Pimms". That'll leap right off the page,' said Peter with a grin.

Devrille thought for a moment. 'I like it,' he nodded, 'It grabs you.'

Nick cut in. 'Doesn't that rather suggest royal involvement?'

'Nick, whatever it is that you're doing or taking, stop it immediately. It's fucking your head up.'

'We're using it then?' Willy piped up.

'It's the splash. Good one, JB. Drinks on me at El Vino after work. And Clancy can drink all he wants.'

'I don't...' Peter began.

'Splash and page three?' Willy asked.

'Of course. Let's give the commuters an easy read. You can't spill the story over onto page two and expect the poor bastards to be able to read it without toppling over somewhere between Plaistow and Upton Park. It has to be *off stone* at two-thirty, all right. And not a fucking minute after.'

'Two-thirty?' Willy stiffened.

'That's right. And I don't want Tom on the front page. He looks too establishment, too boring. It could turn our devoted readers off. I want that old snap of the governess and the gardener having a snog in the bushes.'

'But the quality...' Willy began.

'Just do as I say, Willy. You might know how to sub-edit but I know how to sell a fucking paper.' Devrille walked out and slammed the door.

'Did I hear you murmur something?' Peter grinned at Willy. 'I thought you said something like "arrogant prick"?'

'Maybe it just fell out of my mouth... Got work to do.' He rushed out of the room.

'Congratulations, Peter.' Nick slapped Peter on the back. 'Your first splash. Drinks on the Dark Lord. Let me tell you, that doesn't happen often.'

Shit. Peter hadn't touched a drop since the flight to London, and that was only to try to induce sleep while sitting bolt upright between a large, unpleasant man with a hacking cough and a woman who vomited into a bag each time the plane landed. *Sorry, John, but I don't drink. Given it up, you see*, he rehearsed. *A lime and bitters, please.*

15

Nick stood in the doorway, watching as Peter daydreamed. 'Are you coming?'

Suddenly, Peter was aware of a thunderous noise. 'What is that?'

Nick shrugged his shoulders. 'You'll see.'

Peter followed Nick back to his workspace, to find the other journalists banging their fists on their desks. 'Is this some kind of protest?' he asked.

'You'll see.'

As he watched, one of the journalists that Peter barely knew strolled down the corridor carrying a box of his belongings, winking and smiling as he passed.

'It's called banging up.' Nick yelled over the din.

'What?'

'Banging up. When journalists leave their jobs here, those of us left behind give them a loud send-off. It's tradition.'

'Back home, that's an excuse to have a big piss-up. That's our tradition.'

'The piss-up's coming later. But not for you old chap. You're going to be hobnobbing with the Dark Lord and his minions.' Nick's speech often drifted between Hyde Park and Hobbiton.

'Great. I'll have to sip some Chateau de Shit at El Vino while the rest of you get hammered and have a good time. Great.'

'No good headline goes unpunished, you might say. A tip, by the way, since you're a recent arrival—make sure you take your jacket and tie. El Vino's not your average watering hole.'

Peter was already dreading the prospect of Drinks with Devrille. The thought of having to dress up for it as well was little better than torture. 'Right. I get it. No stubbies and thongs,' he said as Nick looked confused. 'That's shorts and flip-flops to your lot.'

4

Peter had never considered frequenting El Vino wine bar, even though it was located roughly midway between the Black Luby-anka and the Royal Courts of Justice. He thought it uninviting; it bore none of the graffiti that adorned his beloved Tote, none of the posters advertising upcoming attractions. El Vino attracted thirsty journalists and lawyers; it was more gentlemen's club than public house.

He stood at the bar, shifting uneasily from one foot to the other, wondering what was more uncomfortable: Devrille's preaching, the tang of the wine, or the tie that he longed to rip from his neck. Ties were a painful reminder of his schooling and although he always kept one folded into a tight wad in his jacket's breast pocket, he rarely wore it.

The bar was congested and smoky. It reminded him of something. Between Devrille's monologue on Syrah grapes and his sermon on the Montrachet, Peter strained to remember. He'd seen it on a television show, he was sure of it, but which one? His eyes drifted across to a table of barristers, puffing on cigars and celebrating the elevation of one of their number to QC. *That's it! Rumpole of the Bailey.* He almost expected Rumpole himself to wander in fresh from court, and order a bottle of claret.

'So, what do you think of the Châteauneuf–du-Pape?' asked Devrille.

'Mmm.' It was pigswill to Peter's untrained palate. What had he read, somewhere? A hint of tobacco? Freshly mown grass? *I've got it.* 'A big wine.'

Meanwhile, the barristers were quaffing Veuve as if it was going out of fashion. Peter looked around.

The ranks of Fleet Street hacks were thinning, thanks to the departure of so many newspapers. They were either closing down or relocating to the urban sprawl. It could never be the same. The fond and long-cultivated relationship between the hacks and El Vino was drawing to a close. Still, head for head and bottle for bottle, the hacks were easily defeating the legal fraternity and having a wonderful time, by the looks of things.

By contrast, Peter was leaning on the bar next to Devrille and two of his mates, all three looking as if they had drawn in their waistcoats too tightly. He was wishing he was elsewhere. Preferably, the Tote. In Melbourne. Sipping a freshly-drawn Victoria Bitter. *Ah, better.*

'Not a wine connoisseur are you, JB? You're drinking it like it's medicine.'

'It could grow on me, I suppose.' Peter took a mouthful and winced. He wanted to add *like a cancer* but thought better of it. The only time Peter had ever drunk any great quantity of red wine was during a date with an Italian air stewardess, whom he had been trying to impress. Despite feeling like he was drinking cough syrup, he had valiantly battled on through a bottle of Chianti. Unfortunately, it had all ended badly with Peter underestimating the wine's alcohol content, and spilling his glass over her Armani blouse. She had stormed out of the restaurant yelling profanities at him. Even then, Italian sounded sexy.

As Devrille's friends drained their glasses and departed, Devrille looked at his glass and said, 'I've never understood why they don't stock Australian wines at El Vino. Tried a few of them when I was there and they weren't half-bad. Still underrated here, more's the pity. The days of Chateau Woy Woy and the Muttaburra Merlot are long gone.' He proffered the three-quarters empty bottle. 'A top up?'

'No thanks. I'll just finish this off, if you don't mind,' Peter replied, eyeing his glass.

'Well then, either drink it or ditch it, JB. It will end up tasting like vinegar soon.' Devrille caught the attention of the barman. 'A bottle of Chateau La Combe des Dames. None of that non-vintage rubbish. A 1984, I think.'

The bottle arrived with fresh glasses. 'You may think it odd for someone like me, but I enjoyed my stay in Australia. The beach, the women, the women at the beach in bikinis… Oh, and the wine, of course.'

'It's not London, naturally, but it's a good place. A good place to go bush,' Peter replied vaguely, wondering where all this was heading.

'To go native, you mean? Ah yes, of course. Didgeridoo and all that.'

It wasn't quite what Peter meant.

Devrille seemed distracted. 'Are you looking for someone?' he asked, as Devrille glanced at his watch.

'What? Yes. Yes, I am. Must be running late.' He kept looking towards the doorway. 'Good. There she is.' He waved and called. 'Snoddy! Over here.'

'Snotty?' Peter murmured. 'Interesting name.'

Devrille's chuckle sounded like he was gargling razor blades. 'Not Snotty, JB. Snoddy. Short for Snodgrass.'

'Dickensian, either way.'

Winifred Snodgrass was thrusting herself through the crowd, shoulder first. She was a middle-aged woman, with her hair slicked to her head; she tugged at her unbuttoned trench coat. As Snodgrass drew closer, Peter was dazzled by the navy pants, mustard blouse and vermillion cardigan that completed her outfit. *She's part Ealing comedy and part side-show clown.* Obviously, there was no man at home. And no mirror. No woman in her right mind would have let the world see her in such a mismatched ensemble.

'Winifred Snodgrass,' she announced with a flourish, as she drew near. She grabbed hold of Peter's hand and pumped. 'Call me Snoddy.' She raised her hand to check her hair. By the look of the comb trails, it had been fixed in place with an industrial-strength hairspray. Peter doubted it would have moved in a tornado. He was only glad they'd shaken hands first.

'Peter Clancy. Pleased to meet you, Snoddy.'

Snoddy smelled vaguely of lard, alcohol and cigarettes. She stood nose-to-nose with Devrille, only Snoddy's was bulbous and red, jutting out of her heavy-jawed face like a ski jump, whereas Devrille's was regally aquiline.

'Your usual, Snoddy?'

'Please. None of that continental plonk for me. I'll have a straight Dewar's.'

'You're a journo?' Peter asked.

'No. No, nothing like that,' Snoddy laughed as she raised her tumbler in his direction. 'Ex-copper with the Metropolitan Police. Cheers.' She took a large mouthful of her scotch.

'And you two…are mates?' he continued.

'You really like laying on the questions thick and fast. Worse than a copper, you are. Let's just say, we do business together.'

'I say, why don't we grab a booth?' Devrille interrupted. 'Quieter there.'

They sidled into a booth, recently vacated by four barristers. Snoddy drew a packet of cigarettes from inside her coat, tossed one in her mouth and lit up. Then she sat down.

'So what's this all about?' Peter sensed that it was more than a mere social gathering.

'Questions again.' Snodgrass glanced at Devrille.

'Snoddy works for us,' Devrille answered. 'But not as you might think.'

'I thought you were retired,' said Peter.

'Retired from the police. Not retired from life.'

'Snoddy works for us as a private consultant.'

'Private consultant?' Peter nodded slowly several times. 'Nothing to do with being a private detective, is it?'

'You got it in three questions,' Snoddy laughed. 'Bloody good, this lad.'

Peter took a sip of the wine, which tasted like raspberries. It was a revelation. Was his palate acclimatising? 'So you're a private detective. Never had to use one myself, although I've heard of others who have. I don't see the need to use a snoop to look in someone's garbage bin. Doesn't sound like journalism to me.'

'The thing is, JB,' Devrille said, 'I know you did all your own stuff in Australia. *The Truth* may have been good at digging up the dirt, but it wouldn't last a minute here. It's a bloody tough game to sell newspapers in London. The other bastards are fucking ruthless.' He took a swig from his glass. 'So you think it's unethical to use a private investigator. You know that phone book you used to get Mortimer's number? Guess what: you can thank Snodgrass for it.'

'She may have got the number, but I got the story. I know they all bloody do it. I'm not some fresh-faced schoolkid. I hate to burst your bubble. And guess what, some rags don't mind paying a bribe for a good story.'

'We like to think we have some boundaries...' Deville said. 'Explain to Peter what you do.'

'I know you have your sources to turn to for this and that, but we both know that reliable sources can be hard to find, expensive, and sometimes full of shit,' said Snoddy.

'But that's part of the job. You have to get your hands dirty. You have to expect that sources will be unreliable.'

'That's the thing. You don't have to get them dirty. You don't have to fluff around with bad sources. We take it a lot further. For example, you want some information. Something like where someone lives, their phone number, how much they have in the bank, do they have sex toys in the drawer. You ring us. Lionsgate Investigations. Your reliable, high-end source.'

'So how do you get all that information?'

'If I told you that, I'd be out of a job.' Snoddy waved for another Dewar's. 'I have my connections, my feminine ways, you might say.'

Peter had all but forgotten that Snoddy was a woman. 'You pay bribes for information from your former colleagues, in other words.'

'Bribery is a filthy, insulting word. That doesn't merit a response.'

'You're a bloody saint, Snoddy.' Peter sighed. 'Let's call it charity, then—charity to your lowly-paid former colleagues. Who else do you offer charity to? Lowly-paid government officials? Fifty quid for an address wouldn't hurt anyone.'

'We have our connections: people in the right place to get the information.'

'This isn't the place for a discussion on ethics, JB,' said Devrille.

Peter shook his head again. 'And why are you telling me all this? Is this why you brought me here tonight?'

'I telephoned your former editor,' said Devrille.

Peter tilted at his glass. 'You couldn't have. He's dead.'

'The current editor of *The Truth*, then. Bill Symes?' Devrille paused. 'He told me that you'll do anything for a story. Says the bottle and women got in the way of you becoming the best. The *Gazer*, on the other hand, needs you at your absolute best. So I'm introducing you to Lionsgate, to Snoddy.'

'Bill Symes wouldn't know what alcohol or women were. I don't remember putting Bill Symes as a reference. Why ask that prick? We're not exactly mates.'

'I know this stuff is just your thing, Clancy, and Snoddy's damn good at her job. Today's article shows you have the makings of a fine journalist. I could make you the top journalist in London. All your ambitions and dreams realised.'

'Okay, so *The Truth* may have been a sleaze rag but we still had a few standards. We never used private detectives.'

'Ah, the innocence of youth.'

'All right, I'll admit I used disguises; I had fake IDs. Once or twice I might have broken into a mansion. I paid sources. Okay. I got some bloody good stories though. Ground-breaking ones.'

'The difference being?'

'The difference being... Where's Nick stand on all this?'

'Nick worked at a newspaper that handed out payments to coppers like boiled sweets. He knows how it all plays out,' Devrille replied.

'They all bloody do it,' Snodgrass added. 'Not worth getting upset over. It's just business.'

'The thing is, Clancy,' Devrille said, 'it's not up for discussion. From now on, you'll be consulting Snoddy. You're in or you're out. Otherwise, I'll get someone who has the vision. There are plenty of damn good journalists out there willing to do it.'

Devrille had made himself perfectly clear. *You're in or you're out.* During the entire train journey back to Hammersmith, to the Davudis' kebab shop where he regularly bought dinner, and to his flat above their shop, Peter thought about the evening's events. He'd really only just arrived in London; he wasn't ready to return to Melbourne. So, he would now use Snoddy to get his information. Was it all that different from getting information from his sources back home—his *puppies?* He'd always been careful not to delve too far into how they secured their facts. All he'd be doing would be substituting a professional for an amateur, a Snodgrass for a puppy. Was it really a step too far?

Ethics was just a word, an outdated concept dreamed up by a Greek philosopher thousands of years ago. *It's a medical term isn't it? It has something to do with turning off people's machines. Or is it the name of an English county?* Ethics in journalism had always been as malleable as wet clay and Peter Clancy had certainly slopped them around during his career. *Less saint, more sinner. Ethical dilemma.* Those words were still bouncing around his mind, even after he had gone to bed. It was one-thirty before those words finally went away; when he finally came to a decision.

5

'JB, you're back, I see.' Devrille leaned back in his leather chair, laced his hands together and smiled.

'I've thought about what you said. I'm not here just to write stories about Madonna's fucking bra. I could make good use of Snoddy.'

'Amen to that.' Devrille's chair squealed as he leaned forward and took a piece of paper from his desk. 'This one's right up your alley. I was going to give it to Nick, but he's working on something else.'

'What is it?'

'Just came in. A girl, crossing her street, run over and killed by a drunk last night. Turns out the drunk's a football player and his club's in the first division. Talented striker he may be, but not much of a driver. Apparently tried to get away in his BMW, no less, but he crashed it down the road. The other papers will be all over him and his family, but I want a story on the girl and hers. Make it tug at the reader's heartstrings. And take a snapper with you.'

'Are the parents willing to talk?'

'Use that considerable charm of yours and, when that fails, give them five hundred pounds. But not at once, mind. Only if they push you. And I want a photograph of the girl. Something sweet. At a birthday party, perhaps.'

'I'll need an address.'

'Here.' He pushed the piece of paper towards Peter. 'Courtesy of Snoddy.'

'Okay.' Peter slowly picked up the paper and his stomach turned.

'I know it's not everyone's cup of tea, Clancy, but it'll sell. Sales make me happy and they justify your continued employment.'

It was Peter's first death knock in London. Arriving on someone's doorstep and interviewing family members about their recently deceased was the hardest, most thankless assignment a journalist ever had. *Heartless arseholes excepted.* Devrille ought to have been a master at it. Even worse, Peter had to ask for a photograph of the departed for the public to ogle over breakfast. *Poor little girl. Poor parents.* He'd understand if they got angry and lashed out.

He had once gone to a house in Melbourne to interview the parents of a teenage girl who had been found dead from an overdose in a rock singer's hotel room. Unfortunately, Peter had got there before the police. He regretted being the one who had inadvertently informed them of their daughter's death. He never wanted to do that again.

Now here he was standing at the door of a council flat in South London at nine in the morning. The snapper stood behind Peter, camera to his face, poised to catch the bereaved parents' reactions. There was no answer. Peter knocked again, guts tightening into a ball. The door cracked open.

'If you're from the newspaper,' the girl's mother said, 'I'm not telling you anything. You've got a hide turning up on my doorstep. You can just piss off. I don't want to talk to you. Go and annoy that bastard what killed my daughter.'

Peter's eyes were drawn to her dishevelled hair and red-rimmed eyes. She was probably in her twenties, but looked twenty years older. He could hear people sobbing and wailing inside. He stealthily slid his foot between the door and the jamb.

'Of course, you're right and I'm sorry to trouble you at this difficult time, Mrs Wyler,' he began softly. 'I'm Peter Clancy from the *Star Gazer*.' He expected her to slam the door on his foot, but instead she looked up at him blankly.

'Are you all right, love?' an older woman's voice called from inside.

'Fine, Mum, fine. Be there soon.'

'I'm sorry to hear of your loss,' Peter continued. 'I don't want to cause you any more grief, so I completely understand that you don't want to tell our readers your side of the story.'

The woman started to sob. She removed a tissue from her dressing gown pocket to dab her eyes.

'I bet no-one from the papers has even asked about you? About Millie?'

'No. No they haven't.'

'Of course not. Everyone wants to hear from the driver because he plays football. Meanwhile, Millie's forgotten in the rush. But what about poor Millie? Millie should get to tell her story, and you and your husband are the only ones to tell it.'

'Her dad? Now, there's a laugh. He left us six months ago. It was just me and Millie. She was only eight years old, sod 'im.'

'It'd only take a few minutes of your time. You can tell the story straight, before the others twist it.'

'Okay. You seem nice,' she softened, 'but maybe you could come back another time when things have settled down a bit? See, the police were here last night and then there was another officer here just now, going over it all again. I told him the exact same thing. You think they'd write it all down.'

'They do. Was he uniformed?'

'Not this last one. It was just a male detective, by himself. This time, he asked for a photo of Millie.'

'A photo?' She wasn't a runaway. Why would the police need a photograph? 'Just left, you said?' Peter scanned the street.

'I watched him leave. You must have crossed him. He got in that Escort over there,' she pointed to a beige sedan about a hundred yards up the road, with its engine idling. 'Is there something wrong?'

Peter tapped the snapper on the shoulder and backed away from the doorway. 'No, no. Why don't I pop by later?' He sprinted to the road, waving at the Escort as it slowly accelerated towards him. *That bastard isn't a copper!* He recognised the man sitting in the passenger seat, waving at Peter and smiling. Yuppie!

Peter threw himself towards the car and grabbed hold of the passenger door handle. He held on tightly while rapping on the window with the other hand. He felt his feet falling from under him as the sedan sped up. He punched the window once, before his legs gave way. He fell heavily onto the road, on one arm. The Escort drove away, its horn honking, Yuppie laughing aloud and projecting a raised middle finger out of the window.

Peter struggled to his feet, supported by the snapper, who took hold of his right arm.

'Not too hard,' he winced.

'I don't think it's broken. You'd be in worse pain.'

'Believe me,' said Peter, 'my arm's my least concern right now. I'm more worried about the pain I'm going to get from Devrille when we get back.'

Mrs Wyler and an older woman were standing on the footpath, watching the scene play out. The older woman sucked on a fag. 'He wasn't a copper, was he?' she asked, dropping ash onto her dressing gown.

'No. Afraid not,' Peter said quietly. 'Another paper.'

'Bastard,' said Mrs Wyler. 'Mum...'

The older woman placed her arm around her daughter's shoulders. 'He's pinched the last photo ever taken of Millie. It was only taken last week. We won't be seeing that again.'

Mrs Wyler sobbed. 'Bog off and don't come back. You're all the fucking same. Sell your souls to the devil for a fucking headline.'

Peter couldn't argue with that. Instead, he found himself assuring her that he'd get the photograph back. How, he didn't know.

'Oh yes, of course you will. And Santa fucking Claus really lives in the North Pole.'

6

Should I go to ground? I hope I'm not in the line of fire.

Peter braced and held his painful right arm tighter to his chest as he watched Devrille pick up an empty coffee cup and throw it at the wall of his office.

The coffee cup smashed into several pieces, luckily none hitting Peter. It was soon followed by one of Devrille's executive toys that had pride of place on his desk: a Newton's cradle. It was thrown in the same direction as the cup. Peter expected it to be sturdy enough to survive the impact but instead the metal balls broke away from the frame and scattered like shrapnel around the room, again not inflicting injury on Peter.

Duck and fucking cover. I'd hate to tell him really bad news.

Out of breath, Devrille fell into his chair and whipped his sweat-stained hair away from his eyes. 'You should have jumped on the sodding bonnet and stopped them. It's a fucking war, a fucking war!' he yelled. He sat forward and dropped his shaking head into his waiting hands.

'Could have,' Peter said calmly, 'but I'd probably in the bloody morgue by now. It would have been a good story if it had happened. *Journo Dies for Story.* Would have made the front page.'

Devrille looked at Peter. He wiped his hand and straightened himself up. 'Front page? Really? Here's some news for you. Nobody would have given a fuck. You're strictly page twenty material.'

Peter feigned a smile.

'Hard game running a paper. Ruthless.' Devrille shook his head.

'They got tipped off for sure. This is the second time it's happened to me.'

'Nothing happened to you. You're still walking and breathing, still have a job. So, you missed out on a by-line… Not worth dying for,' Devrille continued.

'I'm glad you see it that way.'

'Be quiet. I haven't finished yet.' Devrille sucked in a lungful of air. 'Yes, it's a big fucking deal!' he shouted. 'It's a big fucking deal to *me*. It's a big fucking deal to this paper. It's life or death, Clancy, and don't you ever forget it. You miss out on a scoop and it's a matter of life or death. That's how fucking a big of a deal it is.'

'Have you thought that Snodgrass might be tipping off the other papers?'

'I own Snodgrass. She doesn't take a shit in the morning without running it past me first.'

'The desk?'

'They only get part of the information; names only, no addresses, no contact details.'

'That just leaves the other journalists,' said Peter.

'Bravo, genius,' Devrille replied. 'Include yourself on that list also. Now get the fuck out of my sight.'

Later that afternoon, after the day's edition had been put to bed, Willy Prager informed Peter that he was wanted in Devrille's office.

'He's given me an earful about Millie Wyler,' said Willy.

'He did the same to me. Any idea what he wants now?'

Willy shrugged his shoulders. 'Got your passage home booked?'

It's been an interesting ride. If it's over, it's over.

Peter trudged the length of the corridor to Devrille's office. He had no illusions about the summons; he knew how the industry worked. As he turned the corner, he thought about home. How he missed Collingwood, watching a Saturday afternoon contest at Victoria Park, a sweet victory over arch-nemesis Carlton. Today, he'd been Peter McCormack to Yuppie's Warren Ralph. He'd been robbed. There was a traitor in the ranks. Someone had handed the yuppie a free kick, right in front of goal. It wasn't fair, but neither was life. And neither was football.

Devrille was unusually composed—stony-faced even—when Peter entered his office.

'Ah, Clancy,' he said. 'Despite everything that happened today, I have faith in your abilities. Call me a hopeless optimist, if you must.'

Peter sat down and shuffled his feet. He'd been so certain that the summons was going to be his last that no words came to mind.

'So much faith, in fact, that I'm going to give you the scoop of a lifetime. How about that?' Devrille removed a set of keys from his pocket, turned his chair and opened a heavy wooden cabinet behind him. He removed a bulging manila envelope, turned and pushed it across the desk.

'What's this?' Peter asked as he viewed the package.

'As I said, the best scoop of your career.'

'I don't get you.'

'Ever heard of David Tucker?'

'David Tucker, the Member of Parliament? The bloke married to the Deputy Prime Minister?'

'The same.' Devrille opened the package and removed a cassette tape. From one of the desk drawers, he retrieved a cassette player. He placed the cassette into the player and turned it on. Amidst the crackle and whir of the tape, Peter detected a woman's voice. Devrille turned up the volume. Peter sat forward.

'It was all getting rather hot and heavy,' she said. Despite the distortion, it was evident that the woman wasn't very old—late twenties at most—and the beneficiary of a top public school education. 'Passion overtook the both of us. Then he pushed me onto the bed and had… Well, he had his way with me.'

The woman was surprisingly dispassionate.

'After we'd done it three times, he said that he loved it when Marjorie was at a cabinet meeting. It meant he could play up more.'

Devrille switched off the cassette player. 'Meet David Tucker's mistress.'

'You're joking?' Peter laughed. 'You're having a go at me.'

'It's the real thing. I've had it all verified.'

'Who is she? She could be some nutter or maybe a con artist.'

'Lady Pamela Moncrieff, second wife of Lord Moncrieff. Young and aristocratic. She looks a little like Princess Caroline of Monaco. But with bigger tits,' said Devrille.

'David Tucker?' Peter shook his head, 'He's not exactly a looker, is he.'

'She was apparently turned on by his charm and his bedroom eyes; her words, not mine. His staying powers were the icing on the cake. Again, her words not mine. She had a screaming orgasm the first night they made love. David the Dynamo.' Devrille pulled out the tape and shoved it back in the envelope.

'Or Tucker the Fucker? Not the first thing that comes to mind when you see him. I guess women fuck Keith Richards for the same reason. Why else would they fuck him, if he didn't have money and power? Aren't those two the ultimate aphrodisiacs? But why would she come to you? Surely, she wouldn't need the money.'

'Lord Moncrieff is divorcing her and she is going to be needing an injection of cash soon to maintain her lavish lifestyle.'

'Sounds like bullshit to me.'

'Not to worry, old chap,' Devrille replied as he reached across to his intercom and pressed a button. 'You've lost your nerve. I'll give it to someone else.'

'Hang on a minute there, mate. Not so fast.' Peter held up his hand.

'Right. Yes or no. Give me a decision,' Devrille demanded. 'Has to be now.' He took his finger away from the intercom.

'All right, but I want to interview Lady Pamela myself.'

'Certainly. I'll arrange it.'

'I want to listen to the tapes. You have transcripts too?'

'All there.'

'Can I take them?'

'Not bloody likely. You listen to the tapes here, with me. You read the transcripts here, with me. I must have total secrecy on this. I'm paying a lot of money for this story and I don't want the other tabloids getting it.'

'Okay.'

'Only you, Lady Pamela and myself know about these tapes. If this gets out there'll only be one name on the list of suspects. I'll assume you've leaked it. After I've sacked you and removed your balls, I'll also make sure you never work in London again. Get it?'

'Got it.'

'What are you waiting for then? Get cracking.'

Peter spent the next fifteen minutes in Devrille's office listening to the tapes and reading the transcripts.

What is it with the English upper class and bottom slapping? Constantly tying each other up? It must have something to do with their boarding schools.

Devrille forbade Peter to take notes, in case they fell into the wrong hands, and Peter was fine with that. He had a photographic memory, which had improved along with his sobriety. You could have asked Peter what he had eaten the previous day and it would have registered a blank. Ask him to recall the details of an hour-long interview, though, and he had no problems. A mind for journalism. Or possibly spying.

The plan was that he would interview Lady Pamela, then they'd review the tapes and transcripts again, this time at Devrille's house. Once Devrille approved the content, tick one for newspaper scoop. Await infamy and stand on the peak of the slippery slope of London journalism, albeit briefly.

*

'You're looking chipper for a man who's been copping it in Devrille's office for over half an hour. Most journos either look pissed off or relieved after Devrille's given them the sack,' Nick remarked as Peter passed his desk. 'I was going to come in and rescue you earlier, when I heard him yelling and things breaking. Do you need a hand to clear out your desk?'

'I'm looking chipper, as you say, because I didn't get sacked.'

'Really?' Nick replied. 'I thought you were a goner when you lost that story.'

'I told him, short of killing myself, I did all I could to stop the pricks. He must have felt sorry for me when I said I got run over by a crappy Escort.'

'We are talking about the same John Devrille, aren't we? The Dark Lord and all that? Never known him to feel sorry for anyone. You must have given his cock a right old suck. I shouldn't expect any more reprieves from old Johnny boy.'

'I know. He's no Mother Theresa.' Peter winced as he moved his right arm.

'You might want to get that checked out,' Nick suggested.

'It'll be right. I need to catch a good story to impress the boss. Starting now.'

'Let's celebrate your stay of execution tonight. I've just been on the phone to my ladylove and we're off to the American Bar at the Savoy. Why don't you join us?'

'I'll have to dry-clean the top hat and tails and give the Roller a wash first,' Peter laughed.

'Just come as you are, and be ready to meet a load of new people. I'll see you there at six-thirty.'

7

At six-twenty, Peter wandered through the Savoy's checkerboard marbled foyer, looking for the American Bar. He was a little early, but it gave him a chance to drink in the atmosphere. The Savoy was definitely at the top of the top end of London. He was a long, long way from Clarkes Flat.

Nick was already sipping a cocktail when Peter found him. He'd heard of the bar's reputation for exotic cocktails and famous patrons. So famous that even the head barman was a London celebrity.

'Ah, there you are,' said Nick. 'Peter, this is my wife, Elise.'

Elise was beautiful. Far too beautiful for heavy-featured Nick, whose thick eyebrows sat like a pair of hairy slugs over deep-set eyes the colour of kalamata olives. She motioned Peter to sit next to her in a leather tub chair. The bar was a modern expression of New York art deco, complete with Cole Porter tunes playing on the Steinway.

'I think I'll get myself a beer first,' said Peter, standing up again. 'Can I get you anything?'

'We were sipping on White Ladies,' said Nick, shaking his head. 'There's one there, if you'd like it.'

'You can't come here without having a cocktail,' Elise purred. She swept her thick black hair away from her face with a clang of bangles. Peter immediately pictured her in a bikini. *Those curves...* Yes, he did need a woman. Yes, he had to do something about it. *No, leave Elise alone. That will create a problem.*

34

Peter took a sip of the cocktail and placed the glass back on the table. 'I think I would much prefer a beer. What's in it?'

'Gin, Cointreau, lemon juice and egg white.'

'Sounds like something you'd have for breakfast to get over the night before.' Peter took another sip. 'It might be a good meal replacement, if nothing else. My shout. What will you have?'

Peter ordered a Wolfram for Nick, a dry martini for Elise and a Foster's for himself. He nearly choked at the cost, but figured he was buying himself some local goodwill. That, and he'd order a Hennessy XO when it came to Nick's turn to pay for the drinks.

'So this is the place?' Peter said, looking around at the patrons, most of whom appeared to be tourists who had wandered in to buy one expensive cocktail, savour the ambiance and, with luck, catch a glimpse of someone famous. His eyes finally fell on a group of three young women seated near the piano, giggling as they drank their cocktails too quickly. What caught his eye was the incongruity. They were all bohemian: hippies for the nineties, dressed in a clash of bright colours and bangles. One of the girls, a blonde with flawless olive skin, was possibly the most beautiful woman that he had ever seen in his life. Even more beautiful than her... Even more beautiful than Poppy. *Shit, there I go again. Control yourself, Clancy.*

'You know, this is the place where the Savoy hacks hang out,' Nick said, pulling Peter's gaze away from the girls.

'What was that, Nick?'

'Can't you see that you're interrupting him, dear?' Elise laughed as she tapped Nick on the arm. 'Seems that blonde girl near the piano has caught his attention.'

'I'm just a keen observer. I like the way she dresses. It's all right. I'm concentrating on your every word now,' Peter said. 'Something about a Savoy hack?'

'Hacks from the various tabloids hang around the foyer, trying to catch a celebrity as they pass by.'

'Including the *Gazer*?'

'Of course,' Nick replied. 'I noticed Tommy Sorenson loitering by the lifts when we came in. It's a good gig if you can get it. You really have to suck up to Johnny to get this one.'

35

'Sounds too easy to me. I've always been more street than foyer.' His eyes wandered back to the blonde. She appeared to be looking his way. *No. It was just coincidence.* Then she smiled in Peter's direction; perfect white teeth with a small gap. *So cute.* His heart jumped and heat surged through his body. *Haven't felt like this since...*

He looked away and then back again quickly. She was talking to her friends. It was all a fluke.

'You're having trouble concentrating, Peter,' Nick laughed.

'Okay,' he admitted. 'It's the blonde. She's very distracting.'

Nick looked in the direction of the three girls.

'She's been looking at you since you came in,' Elise observed. 'So what are you going to do about it?'

'Nothing. I don't need her,' Peter replied. 'I'm happy just to sit here with you two and enjoy your company. I'm only focusing on you two from now on. Tell me about yourself, Elise.' His lips were moving in one direction, but his eyes quickly darted back to the blonde girl.

'Funny,' Elise laughed. 'If I danced on this table you wouldn't even notice. Go over there and introduce yourself.'

'You know who she is, don't you?' Nick said.

'I know she's beautiful,' Peter replied, as he looked over at her. She smiled back and held up her glass as if she were toasting Peter. 'Shit. She's forward.'

'That's Ruby Manzanoni,' Nick said.

'Ruby who?'

'She's a fashion designer. She has a posh boutique in Knightsbridge, probably all thanks to Daddy's money,' Elise added.

'Daddy?'

'You should know these things by now,' said Nick. 'Her father is Dick Manzanoni. He was a seventies rocker... What was the name of his band?'

'Not *the* Richard Manzanoni? Of Marquis Fission?' Peter's mouth dropped open.

Nick nodded.

'Shit. They were my favourite prog rock group. I thought they were even better than Pink Floyd. I had all of their albums.'

'He now composes West End musicals. *Children of the Dark* was one of his.'

'Thanks for telling me, Nick,' Peter said, picking at a hangnail. 'How the hell am I going to go over there and act suave when she's famous?'

'I'm only trying to help. I thought you'd want to know all about your interview subject before you meet her. You'll be thanking me tomorrow.'

'Look, she's doing little waves at you. How sweet,' Elise interrupted. One of the other girls reached over and whispered in Ruby's ear. They both laughed.

'See. She thinks I'm an idiot.'

'One way to find out,' Nick said, before finishing his cocktail and tapping Elise on the leg. 'Come on, love. Let's get out of here. We're cramping lover boy's style.'

'Don't go,' Peter stiffened. 'I've forgotten how to do this.'

'I'll see you tomorrow,' Nick replied. 'Have a great time.'

'Nice meeting you, Peter,' Elise said.

'By the way,' Nick whispered, 'You might not want to let on that you're a hack. The Manzanonis don't have a lot of form, but they do occasionally turn up in the tabloids. She'll probably think you're after a story and stab you with her stiletto. You're anything but. Say you're on *Neighbours* or something.'

'Thanks.'

As Nick and Elise left, Peter glanced over again at the trio. A guy in an expensive suit had just snuggled in next to Ruby and was trying to gain her attention. *But she's still there, looking over at me. Okay. Be daring, be calm, be... She's only a rejection away.* He pushed his drink away, did a safety check to ensure his fly was done up (yes, he had been caught before), slowly lifted himself out of the chair and strode over. Ruby's radiant smile grew brighter, the closer he got. The man was trying to talk into one of her ears, but she wasn't listening.

Hey, you're not interviewing the Prime Minister, so why the nerves? The old Peter Clancy had been destroyed in Melbourne, and what was left was the shy guy without the booze. *Hang on. Poppy didn't* destroy you emotionally; she only tried to kill you. Peter never went away, so stop fucking acting like he did. Get back in the saddle again, Clancy, or breed Persian cats. He smiled back at Ruby. His was a smirk, hers was luminous.

'I was wondering if you were brave enough to come over,' Ruby flirted. Her accent may have been posh and clipped, but her voice was a sun-filled lagoon. Peter dived in.

'I was...in the area and thought I should drop by.' He wished he had not said it.

That smile again. It seemed to emanate from her Mediterranean-blue eyes. He couldn't help but stare at her. He had never met a woman so beautiful. Not ever. Beauty that could cause a man to stare open-mouthed. *I hope I'm not open-mouthed.* She swept back a long strand of hair that had fallen across her face. Her skin was the colour of milk toffee and immaculate except for some freckles on the end of her nose that made her look cute. She was beautiful and cute at the same time.

'I...' Peter looked past her face, thinking his way. He wasn't a pick-up line type of guy. Pick-up lines were tacky and sleazy. He was more a total charm-offensive that eventually won over all opposition. *Most times. Fucking lame. All over. Go home. Cat man, here I come.*

'That's truly awful,' Ruby giggled. 'That's so bad, it's hilarious.'

Her two girlfriends, who had been listening, joined in on the giggle-fest. The man next to Ruby laughed like a braying horse. In fact, he resembled a horse, from his large, soft nose to his mouth, which sprang open like a trap every time he laughed. Ruby squirmed as she copped the brunt of his horse-laugh in her face.

'Positively wau-cous,' Horseman said.

Peter was stunned. Was he Ruby's boyfriend? *Why do upper class twits mispronounce their r's? A genetic defect? Inbred twit, Hooray Henry, dickhead; he's probably the rich boyfriend. The Duke of Poof-ingdom, or whatever. Time to exit via the nearest window.*

'Shut it, Tristan,' Ruby said angrily as she pushed him away. 'You really are silly sometimes. You can buy me another drink.'

'Sorry. I didn't want to cause any argument between you and your boyfriend,' said Peter.

'Oh, you must be joking! Tristan and me? You are joking, aren't you?' Ruby laughed. 'Tristan's just an old friend. More like the annoying brother. He thinks he's my business advisor, don't you, Tristan? Now be a good boy and move over.' Tristan vacated the seat obediently, and Ruby invited Peter to take his place with a flourish. 'He's not my boyfriend. Good God, no.'

'Well, that's a relief,' said Peter, recovering his composure. 'I'm Peter Clancy.'

'Sowwy old chap. Only a little fun, you understand,' Tristan interrupted, holding out a fleshy hand.

'That's all you had to say,' Ruby said. 'It's a solid name. Peter Clancy. I like it. On second thoughts, you can buy drinks for everyone, Tristan. Peter, what would you like?'

He opted for beer, but made it German this time.

'I'm Ruby and these ladies are Penny and Eugenie, my business partners.'

Peter nodded and smiled. They were pretty, but not a patch on Ruby.

'We don't come here very often but this is a little work celebration. You're very welcome to join us. The more the merrier,' she continued, her eyes widening.

Those eyes are either undressing me or looking straight through me.

'Congratulations,' Peter replied. 'What are we celebrating?'

'Our collection is going to be shown at London fashion week.' Ruby smiled at Penny and Eugenie. 'We're hoping Naomi Campbell will agree to open our show.'

'We're wearing some of our designs now,' said Penny, flashing a look at Ruby. 'How do you like them? Would you buy this for your girlfriend?'

Ruby smiled and nodded with satisfaction. 'New decade, new look. Death to the shoulder pad!'

'Well, I don't have a girlfriend, but if I did I would love to see her in your designs. Love the vibrant colours. They remind me of home.'

'Are you Australian?' Ruby asked. 'Only your accent's not very strong, if you are.'

'Actually, I haven't been in London very long. But yes, you'd make a great detective.'

'I hope I'm not insulting you, but I've noticed there are three types of Australians. There are the tourists who want to come here, see a few sights and get drunk. There are the ones who want to work here for a while, make some money and spend it all getting drunk. Then there are the others who want to live here permanently who don't want to sound Australian, but they still like getting drunk. Which do you fit into?'

'None. But that's because I'm a writer,' Peter swallowed hard. 'We don't belong in any category or anywhere really, except at a typewriter.'

'A writer? That's exciting,' Ruby said. 'Penny and Eugenie thought you were a businessman, but not me. You look too rugged for that.' She looked Peter up and down.

He took a drink and continued. 'I mainly ghost-write autobiographies for famous people in Australia. You know, sports personalities, politicians, pop idols.' The thought flashed into his head already formed and he had no problem expressing it. He had no idea where it was all coming from. 'It pays well but... My name doesn't appear in the book, which can be unsatisfying. I'd rather have a success in my own right.'

'Of course. I'd hate to design clothes for someone else to claim. Peter Clancy deserves recognition. Writing for people who can't write, or probably even spell. What a drag. So that's why you're here?'

'The two people I was meeting with before, well, they are...my publishers. I'm...going to get an advance and write a book here. I need to be here to do research and concentrate.'

'What's your book about?'

'It's a thriller,' Peter replied. 'MI5, Cold War, East Berlin.'

'Exciting. Congratulations.'

Tristan interjected. 'We have a big day tomorrow, girls. We have to be at our best.'

'Not yet,' Ruby put down her glass of champagne.

'Tristan's right, Ruby,' Eugenie said. 'You have a load of work to do.'

Peter wasn't about to let the moment pass. 'Maybe we can meet up again?'

'I'd like that.' Ruby downed her drink and flashed Tristan an angry look. 'I thought you might have suggested I come home to your place and see your manuscript.'

'I haven't started it yet,' Peter replied. 'But perhaps you'd better give me your number so I can contact you when I have. I'll do a reading for you.'

'I'll think about it,' Ruby teased. 'How about I call you? I'm going to be very busy for a while. Write down your number and I'll give you a bell. Do you have a mobile?'

'I have.' Peter was trying not to sound too disappointed. *She won't call. A woman never calls a man. Never. I'll never see her again.*

He took a pen from his pocket and wrote it down on a coaster. 'All the best with fashion week. It was really nice meeting all of you.'

'Liar!' said Ruby. 'Let's face it, nobody thinks much of Tristan.' She smiled quizzically. 'You don't think I'll call, do you?'

'When you write a thriller novel, you have to add twists and turns. You just never know what's going to happen sometimes. I'll wait for the unexpected.'

The tube wasn't congested by the time Peter arrived to catch the train, and he drifted away into his thoughts. The ease with which he'd created his author alter ego had taken him by surprise. Had it always lived inside him, just waiting to burst out? In his line of work, lies were stock-in-trade, but not in his private life. In his love life, one lie always led to more lies and the creation of an emotional avalanche that eventually, inevitably, came crashing down. Attracted to Ruby or not, he eventually concluded he was glad he'd most probably never see her again. Avalanches were painful.

8

Lady Pamela Moncrieff wasn't at all what Peter was expecting when he finally met her. Her butler left him waiting in the entrance hall of the lavish Kensington terrace house, only a stone's throw from Kensington Palace. He could only imagine what it was worth.

From a darkened corner, Lady Pamela approached in a blur. 'Would you care to follow me?'

Peter had imagined her as the head prefect type, preachy and pushy, but she wasn't like that at all. Her voice was pure sexpot. Where he'd imagined ironing-board flat, Lady Pamela was all curves. What was a busty, lusty package of sexual energy—a Nell Gwyn for modern times—doing with an old battleaxe like David Tucker? With Pamela's looks, the story was certain to go ballistic when it came out. Head now clearer, Peter saw Lady Pamela in a different light. *Catherine Deneuve with chestnut hair.*

She sat on the chaise longue, tanned legs stretched out to best effect, and gestured for Peter to sit on the opposite sofa.

'Peter—now I may call you Peter, mayn't I? Please make yourself comfortable.'

Peter smiled. He took out a pen and notepad from inside his jacket and sat down. The smell of her perfume, deep and spicy, was intoxicating. He was doing his best not to stare at her breasts that threatened to burst out of her designer dress. *Stunning.*

'The dress is Azzedine Alaïa,' she said, leaving Peter to wonder if he'd expressed his thought aloud. He could definitely see what old David saw in Lady Pamela, but the other way around remained a mystery. David was no oil painting, not even a Picasso at his most surreal. If there was a secret to Tucker's appeal, then he was definitely going to uncover it.

'Would you care for a drink? Something refreshing, perhaps? It is so awfully warm…'

'Well, I wouldn't normally drink before an interview, but I'd kill for a beer.'

'Well, we can't have you committing murder now, can we?' She buzzed the butler. 'Henry, a beer for Mr Clancy and a Dubonnet and gin for me.'

'Lady Pamela,' Peter began, 'I've listened to your tape and read the transcript but I have to say that I am incredulous about your affair with David Tucker.'

Lady Pamela gave a faint smile, shifted her legs and inched forward. 'Are you doubting that a woman like me would have a sexual liaison with David Tucker?'

'Well, Lady Pamela,' Peter hesitated, 'he isn't exactly a movie star.'

'Ah, that's where so many of you men have it all wrong. Good looks don't mean anything to me. I'm attracted to a man who overpowers me with his charm, his sexuality and his confidence. Women aren't looking for a pretty face to please them. That's what most men look for in a woman, but not the other way about.'

Henry returned with a tankard of beer for Peter. Brewed by Cistercian monks, no doubt. Peter took it and had a sip. Lady Pamela slid next to Peter and grasped his knee. A jolt of electricity ran through his body. Becoming aroused would be a massive faux pas. Peter deliberately thought of David Tucker. He imagined his stained teeth and tufts of nostril hair. It worked a treat.

'You're undeniably handsome,' Lady Pamela cooed. 'Most women would be attracted to your dark, brooding looks.'

'Well… I don't know…'

'False modesty. I'm sure you know the way into a woman's bed. I'm sure you know how to please a woman.'

'That's not the issue here, Lady Pamela. I'm more interested in David Tucker's appeal.'

'Ah, but you see, looks aside, I'm really not attracted to you. My sincerest apologies. There's an element missing. You can easily bed women who frequent pubs and nightclubs, but you'll never bed a woman like me. You and most men don't have what David Tucker has.'

'So what is that? Would you really be attracted to him if he was David Tucker the grocer and not David Tucker, MP, the Deputy Prime Minister's husband?' Peter asked.

'You've touched on something. What makes men like David Tucker attractive to women like me is that they have that aura of power about them. I can smell it. Most men have an animal smell which they try to disguise with colognes and aftershaves.'

'But body odour turns most women off...'

'I don't mean going around unwashed like a derelict, Peter, I just mean allowing your natural pheromones to come through.'

'So David had that animal smell, for want of a better term?'

'Yes he did,' she smiled, 'but he also had something extra.'

A wave of nausea passed through Peter's gut. *Oh, God. Tucker the Fucker stinking like a ripe Camembert? What else now?*

'It's the smell of power. That's it. As if he were the king of the beasts.'

'But I thought Marjorie Tucker was the king of the beasts,' Peter said.

'No. David is definitely the king at home.' She smiled enigmatically. 'He made me laugh,' she continued. 'It was his humour and the smell of power. And he was an amazing lover. Sadly, it ended far too soon.' She dabbed at invisible tears. 'It ended after only three months. You might say it was a blur of passion. You may quote me on that.'

'Why did it end?'

'It's very painful for me to recall.' Lady Pamela sipped her drink.

'I'm listening,' Peter said, trying his hardest to sound sympathetic. *Hurry up, Lady Pamela.*

'She found out.'

'Who did? Marj did?'

'Yes. Her. That witch Marjorie. She told me that she would destroy me if I kept seeing David.'

'And? Did you see David again?'

'No. I wasn't even able to say goodbye,' Lady Pamela started to sob. Peter had a drink of beer while she composed herself.

'Then my husband found out and now he is going to divorce me. She has destroyed me. The Dragon Lady has destroyed me. I miss David so much. My body and mind ache for him all the time.'

I like that. 'The Dragon Lady destroyed me.'

After a second Dubonnet, the interview concluded. He had enough information to write his story. Lady Pamela showed him out personally.

'Thank you, Peter.' She caught his eyes with her own and held them there. 'You know, you have many qualities that I'm attracted to. You have only to work on that one, elusive quality.'

'I know. I don't have the attraction of power.'

'It's not too late. If you want the women of your dreams to yearn for you, you must cultivate power.'

'Thank you for the interview, Lady Pamela. And for your advice.' Peter descended the stairs to the street.

Cultivate power? Is that what Ruby Manzanoni wants? He feared he had 'peasant' written all over him. He wasn't certain how he would acquire power, but the first thing he was going to do tonight when he got home was throw out all the aftershave and body lotion. *That's a start.*

9

It was to be a top, top-secret operation. 'Don't even trust your fellow journalists. It's only between you and me.' That's what Johnny Devrille had continually reinforced. There would even be security guards posted at the printing press to check identification. No-one was going to talk their way into the printing press and pinch the copy. Peter had heard about journalists from opposition tabloids disguising themselves as cleaners to get into an opposition's printing press. It was indeed a filthy game in London.

Under the pretence that he was ill, Peter was permitted to stay in his flat and type up the story. He hammered it out on his trusty Olivetti. *An old-fashioned typewriter instead of those word-processor computer monstrosities. Floppy dicks, hard fucking drives. They won't last.*

The copy was delivered to Devrille at the office by courier in an envelope with a tamper-evident seal. Devrille was going to handle all the editing and layout himself. He wasn't trusting anyone. Peter was instructed to stay home until called.

The story was coming out the next day and would cause a sensation—most likely scoop of the decade. Devrille warned Peter to prepare himself for scrutiny by the other papers. 'They'll go to town on you. They'll question your credentials, try and ruin your reputation. Question everything about you. I'll take most of the flak. But you'll be in the firing line too. Are you prepared for the storm?' Peter calmly replied, 'I'll enjoy my time in the sun while I can. If I have to go through a hailstorm to get there, I'll give it a go. Someone has tried to kill me once or twice. This won't faze me.'

It was a lonely way to celebrate impending success. Here he was, sitting in a flat that hadn't been renovated since 1960-never, looking at a mind-numbing game show on television. Or was it a talk show? It was worse than Australian television, if that was possible. He looked at the bottle of whisky still standing on the kitchen bench, which he had bought from the off-licence days ago and still hadn't touched. This had been his longest dry spell and he was going to celebrate tonight, with one very weak scotch and ginger ale. He opened the bottle and poured himself one.

Peter drank to his impending fame, or infamy, and thought of his late parents. Would they be proud or ashamed? His father probably wouldn't have understood. Biggest story of his life or no, his mother would have been ashamed, had she been alive. He imagined her lying to her friends in Clarkes Flat that he was a royal correspondent for *The Times*. Would anyone congratulate him? Peter poured his second whisky, feeling increasingly maudlin.

Bob would have been proud of him, of that he was certain, but he would have been the only one. Bob Connolly would have understood. Printer's ink, rather than blood, had coursed through Bob's veins. He was a reporter's editor. *Printer's ink and Jameson*. It was a shame he'd died. No-one else understood how hard Peter had worked towards this. How he'd risked himself to get the scoops. He finished off the second glass, put the cap back on the bottle and returned it to the kitchen bench. Ruby flashed into his mind. This self-pity had to stop.

Why hadn't Ruby called? *She isn't calling. I'm still maudlin.*

He got off the chair, switched off the television and put on a Whitesnake cassette. He leaned back on the chair and tried to distract himself by singing along to 'Still of the Night'. Or was it 'Bad Boys'? His last day of anonymity. *Yes, I'm celebrating. Really I am.*

10

Early next morning, Peter found himself running to the news-stand nearby, even though he had promised himself he wouldn't. Remaining dignified had gone out of the window along with a good night's sleep.

There was already a small crowd gathered around the stand. The news vendor was holding a stack of papers, exchanging coins for copy faster than he could count. 'David Tucker beds Lady Mon-crieff. Dragon Lady not amused.'

Peter watched as the crowd pushed forward. *What a beautiful world I've created. I feel so powerful right now.* He listened in to their murmurs as they read.

'Well, I never...'

'David Tucker, I can't believe it. He's ugly as a hatful of arse-holes.'

'Dirty old bastard.'

Peter caught a glimpse of the banner as he got closer. *David Beds The Lady.* Yes, he wanted to shout out that he was the author, but thought the better of it. He could get mobbed. Then he looked at the poster again.

No! Not true! This isn't true!

Above the headline was the *London Morning Courier* news-paper's masthead. The *London Morning Courier?* They'd pinched his scoop again. The *Gazer's* newsstand poster didn't have any story about David Tucker's affair at all. How had the bastards got hold of it? Peter pushed a woman aside, snatched a paper out of the ven-dor's hand and dropped his loose change into it.

'Settle down, guv'nor,' he growled, 'It's not the start of bloody World War Three.'

Peter wandered away from the newsstand, eyes fixed on the story. *Yes, it's my fucking story!* It was his, except for a handful of embellishments. Lady Pamela had never mentioned to him that she and David had planned a holiday together in Spain, or his penchant for wearing women's knickers. How was it leaked? He found a bus shelter seat and flopped onto it with head in hands. He felt like crying. The story of his career had gone to the opposition.

It was a leak from within. *Had to be. Who? Suspicions. Only Devrille. It was that cowboy, Johnny Devil, fucking Johnny Devrille. But why?*

He had to get into the office, pronto, and sort this out. He tossed aside any idea of catching the tube. That was too slow. Peter jumped up, threw the paper on the ground and hailed a passing taxi.

Devrille was standing at the end of the corridor as if he was waiting for something or someone. Peter stormed up the corridor towards him.

'What happened to my story?' Peter shouted at Devrille. The other journalists peered over their cubicles like rabbits to see what was happening. Most lowered their heads again, sensing an imminent storm approaching.

'In my office, Clancy,' Devrille called back. 'Now!'

'Where's my story?' Peter shouted at Devrille's receding back.

'Settle the fuck down, Clancy. My office.'

Devrille shoved Peter through the open door of his office. A stony-faced Nick and another journo called Ron Fullerton were already there. He stumbled towards a spare chair and sat next to Nick. Devrille stood, as per usual.

'Okay. Let's get right down to business,' Devrille growled.

'What fucking lowlife stole my story? Did you, Nick? Did you, Ron?' Peter continued. The other two didn't answer, choosing to not even look at Peter.

'Will you shut up,' Devrille yelled, 'before I throw something at you? And I won't miss this time.'

Knowing Devrille's propensity for throwing missiles around, Peter decided to fall quiet.

'Yes, there has been a leak,' Devrille lowered his voice as he spoke. 'In response to other leaks that have occurred far too frequently, I decided to set up my own…deliberate leak.'

'Deliberate leak? What's that?' Nick asked.

'For a while I've suspected three hacks at this paper were leaking stories to the opposition newspapers. And they were you three.'

'What the fuck?' Peter bounced out of his chair.

'Let me finish,' Devrille said calmly, pushing Peter back down. 'So I set up an operation. A sting. I had been given the David Tucker story by a source, and I knew, despite all our best efforts, that it would be "borrowed" by one of our unscrupulous competitors. It was going to be leaked. I knew it. It was just too big.'

'What are you bloody talking about?' Ron asked. 'You said I was the only one working on this story.'

'Me too,' Peter added.

'Ditto,' Nick replied.

'Clever cunt, aren't I?' Devrille smiled. 'I astound myself sometimes. I should work for MI5.'

'What are you talking about, Devrille?' Ron asked.

'I gave each of you the story but with different versions.'

'To what end?' Peter asked.

'So I could work out who had leaked the story to the *Morning Courier*. You see,' he continued, 'only two people knew David Tucker and Lady Moncrieff were going on holiday to Spain and that he liked wearing women's knickers.' Devrille moved closer to Nick and stood beside him. 'Those two people were me,' he said, tapping Nick on the shoulder, 'and the boy wonder here. And I'm fairly certain I didn't leak the story to the *Morning* fucking *Courier*, which leaves…'

'So, don't you think you're a Clever Johnny,' said Nick, as he pushed Devrille's hand aside. 'But you can hardly blame me for it. The *Morning Courier* must've got their scoop the same way you got it.'

Ron Fullerton was smarting. Peter could see it written on his face. 'You bastard, Nick,' he said, 'all those leaks came from you.'

Nick was the last person Peter would have suspected.

'Ah, no. The gig is well and truly up, Nick. Nobody else in this world knew those two juicy tidbits.'

'My version said that Tucker liked threesomes followed by high tea,' Ron added.

'You really think I'd choose to work for a paper such as this?' Nick pushed past Devrille and headed for the office door. 'I'm loyal to the *London Morning Courier* and I'll do whatever it takes to get a scoop for them. Even work here. I'm actually glad you found me out, Devrille, because I don't have to be here any longer. I've wiped you out as any opposition to us and most of all, we have the scoop of the decade.'

Devrille pushed the door shut.

'Right. What are you going to do, Devrille?' Nick smirked. 'Hit me? I'll enjoy the lawsuit that'd follow.'

'I'll hit the prick,' Ron offered as he leapt off his chair.

Devrille pushed Fullerton away. 'No-one is about to hit anyone.' He continued to block the door. 'Before you go and celebrate with your chums at the *Morning Courier*, there's just one more thing I want you to know.'

'What's that?'

'The celebration might be short-lived, Nicholas my old friend, because right about now David Tucker and his lovely wife Dragon-Tits are probably sitting in the plush offices of a QC; one that specialises in litigation. I can't imagine how much they'll sue for.'

'That won't get them anywhere. I checked my sources. It's a legitimate story.'

'Interesting you should say that. Ah, it's such a burden as well as a pleasure being the Dark Lord!' Devrille watched Nick's face pale. 'I have a confession to make. Lady Pamela Moncrieff isn't any lady. In fact, she's no lady at all. She's actually Sheila Parry. You may have heard of her from such delights as *Sunday Afternoon* on BBC4. She's an out of work actress, whom I employed to play Lady Pamela. Snoddy is full of great ideas. The scam cost me a few bob, but it was well worth it. Clever, don't you think, Nick? Are you all right, Nick? You look unwell. Do you need to sit down?'

'What...what...did...' Nick stammered.

'You fucked us up the arse a few times. Ask JB here. He nearly got run over by one of your hacks. But what you did to the *Gazer* pales into insignificance compared to what's going to happen to you… What's the saying? You'll never work in this town again. Or should I add, in the whole fucking world.'

'I don't believe a word of it,' Nick said.

'Believe it or not, it'll be real enough once the writs start flying about. You have five minutes to gather your belongings before security throws you out on the street. I'd like to throw you out of a window myself but I don't want to go to jail. Bye, Nicholas. Enjoy your miserable life. By the way, I've already rung your missus and told her. Just in case it slips your mind.'

Devrille stood away from the door and Nick stumbled out without looking back. Peter was paralysed with shock. He felt as if he had witnessed a major trauma. Devrille came over to him and had to tap him several times on the shoulder before he realised.

'Ruthless game isn't it, JB?'

Peter tried in vain to shake himself out of his stupor.

'Ruthless game,' Devrille repeated.

'What do you think's going to happen to him?'

'A lot of fucking pain. But don't worry about him. Concentrate on yourself. There's a paper to run. And the good thing is that there'll be no more leaky boats.'

'I thought he was a mate.'

'Where you're from, you may have mates, but here in London, your colleague could be the one slipping the knife into your back to get the story. Isn't that right, Ron? You have a few holes in your back.'

'One or two. Add this one to the list,' Ron muttered as he attempted to light a cigarette with his shaking hands.

'You'll be happy to know, Clancy, that Sheila thought you did the best interview of the three. She said she nearly broke.'

'That's a compliment?' Peter answered.

'She thinks you're a bit of all right too. She wouldn't mind meeting up with you sometime. Bloody Aussies coming here and getting our women…'

'Another compliment? Don't know if I can take any more,' Peter said dryly.

'How about you both have the day off,' Devrille announced, 'and start fresh tomorrow. I have big plans for you two. I have big plans for this paper.'

11

Peter came out of the Black Lubyanka desperately needing a drink, lots of them. He was done with London. *If you have to cheat, back-stab and step over the dead bodies to get at the next opponent, they can shove a large wad of their tabloid newspapers up their stuck-up English arses. The weather, the people, the whole fucking set-up. Fuck them. I'll get a job back in Australia even if it is at the Wagga Wagga Chronicle. No. I don't need a drink. I need a ticket home. Where's the nearest Qantas office?*

He got as far as the Old Bell Tavern before he snapped out of it. Trying to imagine it was an icy glass of Victoria Bitter instead of a pint of barely cool English lager, Peter settled in as best he could into a corner booth and took in the pub's ambiance.

Yes. Soon I'll be having a VB in the comfortable and shabby sur-roundings of my real home, the Tote Hotel. I'm not going back to The Truth, *not with Slimy Symes at the helm. Crawl to Gavin Jenkins for a job? I'm a proud man. Try the other papers in Melbourne? No. I'd be going backwards. Then again, the footy and the Tote would be a good reason to go back. Maybe I could try working interstate but not in Queensland. No way. There is no such thing as investigative jour-nalism in the Sunshine State.*

The field was steadily narrowing. *Maybe I should try and work in America. A good reference from Stella Reimers will get me over the line. Don't I need a Green Card? If only I could find her.*

Peter had rung just about every newspaper outlet in America using the pay phone in front of his flat (thus avoiding the office phone). Transatlantic calls would attract attention on the expense account, as one might expect. He had decided. He was resigning tomorrow. He removed the mobile phone that had been issued to him by the *Gazer* from inside his coat.

Hate it. A grey fucking brick with an aerial on top. They should definitely make a holster to carry it in. It drags your coat down. Hang it like a fucking six-shooter off your belt, pull it out and throw it at someone. I'm going to run this baby into the ground before I have to hand it back to Johnny the Fool.

Peter removed a piece of paper from his jacket that contained the list he'd compiled of the major newspapers in America that Stella might be working at. Many of them had already been crossed off. He was running out of options.

Maybe Stella had given it all away. He wouldn't blame her for that. If she had, he would run a small beef farm in the Victorian high country. *Yes. I'd like that but where's the money going to come from?*

Peter was checking the piece of paper when the mobile rang.

'Is that Peter? Peter Clancy?'

'No. I'm not talking today,' Peter snapped.

'Oh, Peter, it's me,' a soft female voice chuckled. 'I said I'd ring. Am I interrupting something?'

'Who's this?'

'You've forgotten already?'

'Ruby?'

'That's right. You seem surprised. Have you forgotten me already?'

'I'd just thought...' he stumbled.

'Shame on you,' Ruby laughed. 'You really didn't think that I would ever ring.'

'I'm glad you did,' he replied. 'I was having a discussion with my...research assistant... I thought you were her. Hey, this is a pleasant surprise. Can I make up for my transgression by buying you dinner?'

'Cheeky. Okay. Forgiven. Where?'

'I don't know many restaurants in London. Can you suggest one?'

'I like Harveys. Have you heard of it?'

'That's Marco Pierre White's restaurant? Isn't that hard to get into?'

'Not when you know people.'

'Is tomorrow too soon? I'm an impatient man.'

'My thoughts exactly,' Ruby replied. 'I've already booked for seven tomorrow.'

'Great.'

'Sometimes you have to put in a little extra to achieve what you want,' she paused, 'especially when booking at Harveys.'

Suddenly, London and the *Gazer* were starting to look good. *What a fickle creature I am. Amazing what a woman can do to change a man's mind.*

Suddenly, the tail was wagging the dog.

12

'Don't turn around but I think I've spied Oliver Reed. And he's sober.'

'Oh, really?' Ruby's head spun around. 'Yes, that's him.' She looked bored. 'So, tell me about yourself.'

'What's to tell? I was brought up on a cattle station...' Peter began.

'You're a rancher? Now that's interesting.'

'I prefer to say grazier. No, I'm not a grazier myself, but my father was. I come from a long line of graziers. Rancher's very American, by the way.'

'I stayed at my father's friend's ranch one summer. In Wyoming. So, I guess they're the only kind I've ever met before.' Ruby sipped her champagne. 'Continue. I'm listening.'

'Well, the family sold out and moved into town when I was a kid. I was brought up there. I guess my early isolation fuelled my imagination.'

'And that's how you became an award-winning author?'

Peter laughed. 'Award-winning? Hardly. Ghost writing for celebrities...'

'Well, when your novel becomes a bestseller, everyone will want to know you. You could have Hollywood beating a path to your door. You're on the brink of greatness, you know.'

'I'm really only thinking about writing the book at the moment.'

'So, do you have an image?'

'I beg your pardon?'

'How you dress, how you project yourself. You have to have an image.'

'I'm not an aspiring fashion model or movie star. I'm a writer.'

'Hmm. Most writers look, sound and dress like old professors. You can smell the mothballs a mile away. That's not an image you'd want to project.'

'You're not suggesting I'm an old professor?' Peter feigned insult.

'Hardly. I haven't met that many thriller writers, to be perfectly honest. I met Jeffrey Archer once. Does that count?'

'I'm impressed.'

'Oh no, please don't be. I think you're the most appealing writer I've ever met.'

'Thank you,' Peter sipped his burgundy. It was his concession to a first date. He was out to impress; he'd forgo the beer and preserve his image.

'Better looking than Harold Robbins,' Ruby laughed.

'What?' Peter laughed out loud. 'That old sex-boiler? Although, I wouldn't mind selling as many books as him.'

'Ah, now that will depend greatly on your image. Jeffrey is impeccable. You could go grazier-chic and wear a checked shirt and ten-gallon hat. Or you could go all-out in a Savile Row suit and GJ Cleverly shoes.'

'Enhance my image but decrease my bank account?' Peter smiled. 'Unless you know a charity shop that sells Savile Row suits, I'll have to dress a little closer to Oxford Street. I didn't get the biggest advance in the world.'

'I know people. They'll get you a good price.'

'You seem to know a lot of people, Ruby,' Peter said.

'Manzanoni,' she interjected. 'That's my name. Ruby Manzanoni.'

'Oh. Wow.'

'By the look of you, you know who I am.'

'Well, I'm hoping to get to know you much better. Isn't that why I'm having a beautiful dinner with you?'

'You're very funny. I guess I'm used to people knowing exactly who I am and what I do. I keep forgetting that you don't follow celebrities and that you're not from here.' Her eyes dropped and she twisted her hands. She looked embarrassed. 'My father's Richard Manzanoni.'

Peter bit his lip. *If you had any idea of the kind of work really I do, you'd be gone in ten seconds.* 'I...think I've heard of him. He was in a rock band in the seventies? King Crimson?'

'No. It was Marquis Fission. I'm his one and only daughter.' Her eyes lit up. 'Do you have any idea how refreshing your ignorance is?'

'I guess, when you live halfway around the world, news travels slowly. Or it gets lost on the way.'

'You are the first person I can remember who hasn't asked me five minutes into the conversation if I'm related to the great Richard Manzanoni, and then proceeded to bore me about my father.'

'And you're the first person who hasn't asked me if I descend from the Great O'Neill.' Ruby looked perplexed. 'It's an Irish joke,' he explained. 'Sorry. So tell me about yourself.'

'I have a fashion boutique called Hoboh and I design clothes. Apparently, I'm an emerging designer; a designer to watch.'

'That's very impressive.' *I'm bloody good at this game. Maybe a little too good.* 'You're famous in your own right, Ruby Manzanoni. A young Vivienne Westwood.'

'To be honest, I don't really mind all the trappings that are attached to being the daughter of Richard Manzanoni, even if I do tire of it at times. I hate the annoying questions, the ones who want to know you just because of who you are. Yes, I want to be famous in my own right but I also want to be respected for what I do.'

'Same here,' Peter replied. 'Step out of the shadows and create your own sun.'

'I like that.' Ruby emptied her glass. 'Is that in your book?'

'No, but I'll write it in somewhere.'

'What's the title of your book, by the way?'

'At the moment the working title is...lots of titles. I particularly like *The Shadowed Man*.'

'I like that. Good thriller title; sounds ominous.'

'It's going to be a good book. I'd like to think I have a great future, writing books.'

'I admire anyone who wants to carve a career for themselves.' Ruby smiled and waved to a passing brunette with a tall man in tow, part rugby player and part model.

'Who's that?' Peter recognised the woman, but she seemed slighter and prettier in person.

'Koobie Sans and her husband, Tom Jaffre.'

'Didn't she have a fling with one of the royals a few years back? They were pretty close, but Mother didn't approve?'

'Yes, that's her.' She leaned over the table and whispered, 'Do you want to know some gossip?'

'Only if it's really filthy.'

'They're breaking up,' Ruby paused, 'tonight. They're going to do it here.'

'But they look happy. How do you know that?'

'Koobie comes into my boutique and likes to tell me what's happening in her life. She said not to tell anyone but I hardly think it's fodder for a thriller. By the look of it, she hasn't told him yet. Apparently she found out he was having an affair. Another one. Tommy just can't control himself around pretty models.'

'Just as well I'm a writer and not a journalist,' Peter joked. 'Same words, different attitude.'

'I don't know how anyone could be a journalist,' Ruby said. 'They don't bother to get the facts right. They just make it all up.'

'That's...' Peter took another sip of wine. 'It's so dishonest and invasive.'

'But isn't it just? My father was supposed to have been in a punch-up with Sir Talbot Weiner because he was jealous of him. It was all made up. They're actually great friends.'

Peter swallowed hard. 'Lies are damaging. Has it ever happened to you?'

'I'm too busy working to get in the papers. I avoid those sorts of parties and nightclubs. I'm a quiet girl really.'

'That's the best way to avoid unwanted publicity.'

'Oh, but they create it anyway. One of the papers once said that my boyfriend was cheating on me—with another man.'

'Extraordinary.'

'It was absurd,' she replied. 'Sebastian wouldn't have... Sorry. That's the past.' Ruby was lost in the moment. 'It was the *Star Gazer*. Don't ever buy it. It's full of lies. It must be the worst rag in London.'

'I haven't heard of it,' Peter stammered. 'Sounds trashy. I'll stick to the *Guardian*.' He glanced at her face. Ruby was downcast and he unexpectedly felt a pang of guilt. 'Sorry for delving, Ruby Tuesday.'

Her face shot up immediately, her brows knitted. 'How did you know?'

'Know? Know what?'

'About my name? My mother loved the song, so I was named after it.'

'Fantastic song. Great lyrics,' Peter said.

'I love it too. It reminds me of my mother. I've met Mick once or twice. Jerry comes into the boutique every so often.'

Suddenly a commotion erupted from the direction of Koobie and Tom's table. They both turned to look. Tom had thrown down his cutlery. He stood up and his plate and napkin followed suit. Peter heard him mutter *bitch* and, without looking back, he stormed out. Koobie leaned back in her chair, glanced over at Ruby and shrugged. She was unusually wan.

'Oops. Looks like she's told him.' Ruby grimaced. 'Poor Koobie. Tom's such a cad. She'll meet someone nicer one of these days. Hopefully someone who isn't a celebrity.'

'Should we do anything?'

'It's okay. She'll tell me all about it when she comes into the boutique tomorrow. She'll be going on a buying spree for sure. The ups and downs of the rich and famous are always good for our business. Of course, I don't tell them that.'

At the end of the evening, Peter escorted Ruby back to her car, a velvet-red Porsche 911. 'Very nice,' he remarked, as she reached into her handbag to retrieve her keys.

'You think so? Why, what do you drive?'

'Taxi usually. I don't know if I'll buy a car here. The traffic looks unbearable. I drive a Triumph Stag back home.'

'British! I'm impressed.'

You wouldn't be if you ever met it. It's definitely more Snag than Stag.

She continued, 'Can I give you a lift?'

'No. It's fine. I'm afraid that if you invite me into your car I might never want to get out.'

Her eyes glittered under the streetlight. He'd never met anyone like Ruby before. She was exceptional. He reached out and hooked his hand behind Ruby's neck. He gently pulled her towards him and kissed her. He felt no resistance.

A drunk staggered past, pausing briefly to watch. 'Get a room!' he yelled.

Ruby broke free and giggled. Peter briefly glimpsed the schoolgirl she would have been some five or six years earlier. He traced the smattering of freckles across the bridge of her nose with his finger and kissed her again. 'I guess you'd better go.'

'I suppose I should. I had a wonderful time, by the way.' She reached into her handbag and handed Peter her business card. 'My number's on it,' she said. 'Be sure to use it.'

13

'You're unbelievable, JB. I really can't believe it.' Devrille leapt out of his chair. 'Ruby Manzanoni told you all that? I can't fucking believe it.' He was rubbing his hands together. 'Tell me you're dating her. Tell me you'll be seeing her again.'

'Well, that's my intention.'

'A prick like you dating an English rose. And an Australian to boot. You shagged her?'

'I'm not dignifying that with a response.'

'Which means you shagged her.'

'No, actually, I haven't.'

'What a shame. I could make something of that. Still,' he said, 'we'll be able to get Koobie into today's edition. And Ollie Reed's on the wagon, although I must say, he's more fun when he's on the piss. We'll mention it. Koobie's dumped Tommy? Love it. That will be today's splash for sure. If we can get around to Tom's place and get him punching the snapper… He hates the snappers especially when he's been caught with his fingers in the jar. I'll send that new kid. He needs some fucking experience. Brilliant result.'

'I don't want my by-line on the stories.'

'You're fucking joking. You, of all people, should know how hard it is to get good stories like this.'

'She thinks I'm an author. She thinks I'm a budding novelist called Peter Clancy. She wouldn't have touched me with a ten-foot pole if I'd said I was a hack.'

'This gets better and better,' Devrille laughed. 'Too stupid to use an alias. If you can stick with this dollybird for a while, we'll have one of the best gossip sources this rag has ever had.'

'There's a bit of a conflict of interest here, don't you think?' Peter sat in the chair behind him while Devrille hovered.

'The only conflict will be if you don't continue to see her. Then conflict will come from me. Get it?'

'Look, I'm prepared to share information with the *Gazer*, but I draw the line at doing anything that might hurt her. I'm not going to use her to fill pages. We go out somewhere and something interesting happens, then fine. She tells me something openly about someone, then fine. I just have a few demands,' Peter said.

'Demands? What is this? Since when has the *Gazer* become a democracy?'

'Well, I have to look the part. She wants me to buy a Savile Row suit and wear handmade shoes. She has contacts, so I'll be able get it cheaper, in case you're worried. And I can't take her back to my place. It's a shithole. So, I'll need a few quid in my pocket to impress her.'

'All right. It'll be stretching the budget but your girlfriend knows everyone in the London celebrity world. All of the young actresses go to her boutique. You know who her dad is, don't you?'

'Of course.'

'Great band, pity they broke up, but I don't like his musicals much. Too dark.'

'What do you know about her?'

Devrille pursed his lips. 'Unfortunately for us, she's a clean-living girl. She doesn't have much form; she doesn't sleep around or take drugs, like a few of them do. A real go-getter. I think she wants to prove herself in own right.'

'And boyfriends?'

'You jealous already, Clancy? Ruby's had one or two celebrity boyfriends. One was an artist who dressed like a New Romantic. Sebastian… Looked like a total fucking poof. I remember we did something about him having a fellow on the side. We didn't have enough proof and Daddy got all upset, so we dropped it after one outing.'

'She mentioned the *Gazer*,' Peter said.

'Not a fan I bet.'

'Hence my dilemma.'

'We're not here to stroke fragile egos, are we? Just enjoy yourself while you can and don't get caught.'

'I have one other demand.'

'Another? I'm getting very tired of this...'

'I absolutely, positively don't want her or her family in the paper. They're out of bounds. For a start I don't want to get found out and I...'

'They're people, Clancy, but they're celebrities, first and foremost. We deal in people who are celebrities. As such, they're fair game.'

'Not negotiable, John.'

'Now, if that's not a case of the horse riding the jockey!'

Peter wasn't budging. He stared Devrille down.

'Well, fine,' said Devrille after an age. 'Fine. But you break up with her and it's all fair game.'

'I just don't want to hurt her.'

'A word of warning, JB. Don't get emotionally involved with these people. Don't defend them too much. Celebrities always look after celebrities. Celebrity is a closed shop, a Masonic Lodge, if you like. You might be feeling guilty right now, but, mark my words, pretty Ruby will still work out a way of using you.'

'I'll have to figure that out. We're agreed then. We don't touch Ruby and her family?'

'I'm not happy about it,' Devrille sighed, 'but fine. Did she happen to tell you that her mother died from an overdose seventeen years ago?'

'It wasn't the topic of conversation on the first date.'

'Rickie Manzanoni must have got randy very quickly—Randy Ricky, I like that—because he married again within four months. Then he divorced pretty soon after that. And now he's married again. To some pin-up girl.'

'He's not into grieving, by the sound of it.' Peter stood up to leave.

'Just one more thing,' Devrille said. 'I'm afraid I received some bad news earlier. I wanted to tell you first.'

'About?'

'It's about Nick Georgiou.' Devrille stared at his hands.

Peter felt uneasy. 'What about him?'

'I'm afraid Nick killed himself.'

Peter fell back into his chair.

'The police called to see me this morning.'

'Shit. It never occurred to me that he'd do this. The police?'

'Wanted to know about his last day.'

'Not suspecting?'

'No, no, nothing like that. They're just dotting i's.'

'And Elise?'

'I telephoned her. She was surprisingly lucid. Said she didn't blame us for what had happened. Seems she blames the *Morning Courier*.'

Peter frowned. 'Surprising.'

'She wants to do an interview about it,' Devrille said. 'I think you should call her and arrange a time. I'd say, from the sound of her, she's more angry than grief-stricken. It seems Nick had many demons. Invisible ones.'

'What? Today? Isn't it too soon?'

'That's apparently what she wants. The other thing: she suggested you.'

'Me?'

'Why not? You're up to it. It'll be a great way to get back at those bastards once again.'

14

Peter felt uneasy for the rest of the morning. He called Elise just before lunch and was surprised when she suggested they meet at her house. At three.

At two-fifty, Peter was bounding up the steps of Pimlico station and down Bessborough Street. Elise met him at the front door. She looked like she had been crying, but was otherwise composed.

'I'm so sorry,' Peter said, as Elise showed him into the hallway.

'I wish it could be in happier circumstances, Peter.' She led him down the hallway, to a conservatory tacked to the back of the house. There was coffee already brewing on a table.

'I'm sorry about Nick, we all are. Despite everything, he was a great friend.'

Elise didn't reply. 'Coffee?' she said as she lifted the jug.

'Please. No milk.'

She poured a cup, handed it to Peter then poured herself one. 'I know I don't have to do an interview,' she said, taking a sip of coffee, 'but I want to clear up a few things.'

Peter took out a pen and notepad. 'You knew that Nick was working for us and leaking information to the *Morning Courier*?'

'Yes, I did.'

'You could have told me. I might have been able to do something.'

'I would never have jeopardised Nick's career. He was going places at the *Morning Courier*.'

'Why did he take the job with the *Gazer*, then?'

67

'He was ambitious. He wanted to be an executive and play with the big boys. Neither he nor the *Morning Courier* ever thought that he would be caught. Devrille was the Fool of Fleet Street.'

'It's a dangerous way to go up the ladder.'

'He was promised editor if he destroyed the *Gazer*.'

'Promised? By whom?'

'The owner, David Morton, when he flew in from America on one of his visits. He pulled Nick into the office and told him.'

'Why Nick? I know he was a good journalist but Morton has hundreds of journalists working for him around the world. They'd all be as hungry and ambitious as Nick.'

'Morton told Nick that he could see the same fire that he'd had when he was younger. Once Nick agreed to get on board, he became like an adopted son. We were invited to his house, to his parties. Nick was going places.'

'He was grooming him?'

'Morton trusts very, very few people. He doesn't even trust his family. Nick was one of the few.'

'That would have been a huge compliment.'

'You have to put it into context.' Elise took a thin, black cigarette out of a gold case and lit it. 'Nick's family lost everything during the war, not that they had much to begin with. He meets Morton. Suddenly, he's no longer the poor refugee; he's become the anointed one. He's offered all the spoils—drugs, money, influence. Morton put so much importance on destroying the *Gazer* that he persuaded Nick to work there, undercover. It's not that Morton thinks the *Gazer* is a major threat, but he hates Devrille. He thinks John Devrille's an upstart.'

'That's astounding,' Peter replied. 'I didn't think anyone took the *Gazer* too seriously.'

'Make you feel any prouder to work there?' Elise butted out the cigarette. 'I'd stopped, but all the stress, you see...'

'*The Times* or the *Gazer*? No contest, is there?'

'Nick didn't want to do it,' Elise continued, 'but I guess at some point greed and ambition took over.'

'A way to prove his loyalty. Pity you have no evidence to show that Morton told Nick to do it,' Peter said.

'But I do.'

'Someone like Morton would never incriminate himself. Morton's a ruthless man but he isn't a stupid one.'

'Nick taped it.'

'He was wearing a recorder? Did he usually do that?'

'Only when he was dealing with the big bosses or if it was something really important. Don't you?'

'No. Maybe I should.'

'Funny. Morton trusted Nick, but Nick didn't trust Morton. He always said that he liked Morton's drive, but that Morton had no soul. He could tell by his dead eyes. Nothing there.' Elise smiled faintly. She slowly removed the recorder from a drawer and placed it on the table.

'You've listened to it?'

'Nick brought it home from wherever he'd hidden it the day before he died.' Elise blinked away tears. 'He played it to me. I thought he was going to take it to a newspaper… I didn't think he'd do this. I didn't pick it.'

'Perhaps he felt too ashamed to keep going,' he suggested.

'He was proud. He loved being a journalist. He was proud of everything he'd achieved. He knew his career was over, and it killed him.' She pushed the recorder towards Peter. 'It's up to you now.'

'Do you want this released? You know all hell will break loose. They'll be coming after you, Elise.'

'I want Morton to burn in hell. I want him destroyed. I curse him. I curse that evil man.'

'Do you want me to leave it until things settle down?'

'No. The sooner, the better. I'm taking Nick's body back to Nicosia to be buried. I'm not returning. My parents live in Athens. I'll live with them until I can get back on my feet.'

'I understand. I'm really very sorry, Elise.'

'I never want to see another English newspaper again as long as I live. I asked for you to come because I could tell you are a good person. Like Nick said, it's in the eyes. I can see your soul, Peter. I just don't know how you can work in this filthy business.'

'I became a journalist to uncover corruption and the bastards who take advantage of good people. When I first started, things were more black and white. There was a line you never crossed. The older I get, the more blurred that line seems.'

'Please don't end up like Nick.'

'I'll get out of it before that happens.'

Elise paused momentarily. 'Did Devrille mention anything to you about a fee?'

'Yes. He said he's fine with twenty thousand.'

'Please don't judge me, Peter,' she said as she poured two more coffees.

'I would never judge you. You lost your husband. You didn't deserve any of this.'

'You are too kind.' Elise feigned a smile.

'In Melbourne I was regarded as a ruthless arsehole with a drinking problem. Now I'm in London and you think I'm kind. What's happened to me?'

'Kind people can't do the job. One day you'll get out of journalism.'

'I want to hang in a little longer in London. I guess I have something to prove.'

'Don't be a proud man. You'll only end up dead.'

15

Life was perfect. Peter closed his eyes and drank in the air. The Cotswold countryside passed in a rolling green haze as Ruby pushed her Porsche 911 harder. For the last hour, she had been passing traffic along the M40 as if it was all standing still. Now they were belting along the A44, way too fast. He glanced at Ruby, her chin lifted, jaw clenched.

'What?' she said playfully, turning briefly to look at him. 'What are you staring at?'

'You.' He could hardly believe that it had been a month already since their chance meeting at the American Bar. So much had happened since.

Moments later, she slowed the car from light speed to supersonic and turned into a narrow country road edged on one side by a stone wall and on the other by a thick hedge. He felt claustrophobic. She was still driving too fast but Peter didn't dare check the speedometer. Any second he expected they would have a head-on with an oncoming car veering around a blind corner. *No way to enjoy the beautiful surroundings*. He placed his hand on Ruby's knee and gripped it for reassurance. Then he tried closing his eyes.

London was an hour and a half behind, and a bustling, cacophonous world away. It was good to be back in the country. The last time, he had stared down several gun-toting members of the Russian mob in the Yarra Valley. A drive through the Cotswolds should have been a welcome return to the place Peter felt most at peace. If Ruby would only slow down, so he could breathe it in.

'We're nearly there. I do so love coming home.' Ruby slipped down the gears to get around a tractor travelling along the edge of the road.

'Can't wait.' He let go of her leg and gripped the dash instead.

'Not nervous, are you?'

'A bit. I hope your parents won't be too disapproving of me.'

'Why should they be? Megan couldn't give a toss. And don't be too intimidated by my father. He's never liked any of my boyfriends at first. He looks dark and gothic but, underneath all that, he's really a teddy bear. I know he'll like you once he gets to know you. Just be your usual, charming self.'

'I don't know if my charm will work on your father.' He placed his hand on her thigh again. This time, he pushed her skirt up, just a little.

'Hey, hey, hey,' she said, 'you don't want to cause an accident, do you?'

'Why don't we go somewhere else instead? We could stay at an intimate little hotel, spend the weekend fucking and licking chocolate off each other's naked bodies.'

'Afraid not. This party is very important. It's the launch of my father's new musical. A lot of influential people will be there.'

'I can wait. How about a quick shag in a haystack?'

'Later.'

'You've driven all the way from London. I think you need to rest. You look very tired. I'll give you a massage by the side of the road.'

'Behave yourself, Peter. We're nearly there.'

Ruby decelerated into a driveway surrounded by an imposing wrought-iron gate attached to two stone columns with stone eagles perched on top. She stopped the car at the gate, leant out of the cabin and pressed a button on the security panel. She waited while the gates slowly parted.

'Shame there has to be so much security these days,' Peter remarked as they drove through the gates.

'My father has always attracted religious nutters because of his works. The odd one has hopped the wall over the years. The Dobermans usually get them.'

They drove along the estate's private road, past sheep grazing in a paddock. *It must be the greenest, lushest grass I've ever seen.* He was trying to think of something other than the weekend ahead. He was failing. As if it weren't overwhelming enough to be spending a weekend with a beautiful girl in a sprawling Georgian manor, he'd soon be meeting her father. One of his all-time heroes. Page, Hendrix, Blackmore, Manzanoni. Their posters had adorned the wall of his bedroom in Clarkes Flat. Now he was going to be hobnobbing with one of them. Not even in his wildest dreams... Peter suddenly felt nauseated.

'Are you all right? You're looking pale.'

'I'm fine,' Peter lied. 'Just feeling a little carsick.'

'My father's lovely, really he is. He's never set the dogs on anyone I've ever brought home.'

'How comforting.' Peter caught his first view of Haydon Manor. It sprawled across its parkland setting like a gilded Playboy centrefold.

'Beautiful, isn't it?' Ruby smiled. 'Welcome to our humble abode.'

'Like *Brideshead Revisited*.' Peter was awestruck. 'I'll need help not to get lost in it. It's enormous.'

'There are fifteen bedrooms, eight bathrooms and two ghosts— that we know of. You're not frightened of ghosts?' She stopped the Porsche on the gravel driveway in front of the manor. She revved it several times and switched off the ignition.

'No problem, as long as they're friendly,' he said. 'What are the sleeping arrangements by the way?'

'Separate bedrooms, I'm afraid. My dad may be an ex-rocker but he's a little old fashioned.'

'That's fine.' Peter was crestfallen. 'Draw me a map and I'll come to you in the dead of night.'

'Don't worry, we'll find a way to have a shag. We don't have to confine ourselves to bedrooms.' She brushed her lips against Peter's. 'More fun that way.' She glanced out of the car's side window. 'No-one to meet us,' she sighed. 'They must be in the garden getting ready for the party.' She swung the door open.

'We can give them a hand.'

'They'll have caterers doing all that. You won't want to be around Manz when he's organising one of his parties. My father likes to control everything.'

'Okay.' He slowly opened his door. *Stop being nervous, Clancy. You're only meeting a parent, not the Prime Minister. I think I'd rather meet a Prime Minister.*

'Just one more thing.'

'What's that?'

'Manz doesn't like people asking him about his days in the rock band. They didn't part company on good terms.'

'No worries. I'd heard of them, but I wasn't a fan.' He thought of the worn-out Marquis Fission album he'd replaced with his first pay.

'He doesn't want to be remembered as just an aging rock star, he wants to be remembered as a serious composer, whatever that means. Maybe he wants a knighthood? He already has an OBE. Come and meet the family.'

'Sure.'

Ruby led Peter around the back of the manor to a vast, French garden. It was a mini version of Versailles. A squadron of workmen, all dressed in black, were struggling to erect a giant black marquee adjacent to a huge marble fountain. Above the din was a lone voice, their commanding officer, yelling instructions, imploring them to charge the French at Waterloo, all said with perfect, rounded, English vowels.

Peter first glimpsed Richard Manzanoni's back. Even from the rear, Manzanoni looked imposing and flamboyant. He was taller than Peter had imagined, with a nest of jet black hair resting on the collar of his salmon-pink, pinstriped suit like a plume. Manzanoni looked like a colourful cockatoo—the back of him did, anyway.

Manzanoni was throwing his arms around wildly, as he shouted his instructions. Gone were the days when he wore wizard cloaks on and off stage. He was now playing the conservative country gentleman in his own gaudy way.

'That's Manz,' Ruby said, taking hold of Peter's hand, 'as you can probably tell. He's very dramatic when he's playing to a crowd, even if it's a bunch of workmen.'

Peter could feel his guts twisting tighter and tighter, as they drew closer to the marquee.

Ruby must have sensed it. 'You'll be fine. Just imagine you're researching one of your novels.' Then she yelled out, 'Manz, give those poor men some peace.'

Manzanoni spun around like a ballet dancer and laughed. He strode towards them with his arms outstretched and grabbed Ruby in a tight embrace. 'Darling. Darling. It's so good to have you home. It's been just too, too long.' He kissed her on the cheek. Ruby blushed.

'It's only been three months. You really should go easy on the workmen, by the way,' Ruby said as she slipped out of her father's embrace.

'They're four rashers short of a bacon butty, Ruby,' Manzanoni moaned. 'They'd have taken a piss in the roses bushes if I hadn't hired Portaloos for the caterers. It's so exasperating. I have to tell them everything.'

'Do you really?' Ruby exhaled with frustration. 'But they're only putting up a marquee.'

'The best words of advice I've ever given you—' Manzanoni started, looking Peter over as if he had just discovered an intruder. He eyed Peter up and down and then continued, '—is to control your own fate. I wouldn't have got anywhere if I hadn't been master of my own destiny.'

'So I've heard. I've been doing my best to follow your advice, as you may have noticed. London fashion week?'

'Yes. I heard. Very good,' he replied vaguely, his dark, luminous eyes still fixed on Peter. 'We'll talk it over later. And this is? You're not from the caterers.'

'This is Peter, the Australian writer I told you about. He's very funny. He's writing a thriller novel at present.'

'Is that so?'

Peter held out his hand. Manzanoni sniffed. For a man in his fifties he had flawless skin, lightly bronzed with a neatly trimmed van dyke beard bordering his mouth. He wore a hint of rouge on his cheeks.

Is this how seventies glam, prog rockers age? It's too scary. He looked so much better as a poster on my bedroom wall.

Manzanoni looked down at Peter's outstretched hand as if it were a loaded nappy.

'The only Australian book I've ever tried to read was that dreadful one about the priest. It might make a good musical, though. If you could just train kangaroos to sing and dance.' Manzanoni found the concept amusing. He brushed Peter's hand with the tips of his fingers and immediately withdrew them into the pocket of his colourful suit. Peter noticed his nails were lacquered black.

'Very nice to meet you, Mr Manzanoni,' Peter stammered.

'You can call me Sir Richard. Sir Richard de...'

'Don't be silly, Manz,' Ruby chastised.

'Fine. Call me Richard,' he grimaced. 'My daughter must like you if she's already defending you.'

Ruby was exasperated. 'Can't you just be normal for a few minutes?'

Peter felt sorry for Ruby. He remembered wondering, a long time ago, what it would be like to be the son of a famous rocker. Peter Page? Peter Jagger? He was now actually glad he had been brought up by an alcoholic mother. She seemed normal by comparison.

'Normal, normal. Tell me, Ruby, what's that when it's at home?' Manzanoni clicked his fingers. 'I see Sebastian has a couple of pieces on show at the Saatchi gallery. I told you that boy was going places.'

'Please don't mention Seb,' Ruby fumed. 'You know we broke up a year ago.'

Manzanoni exhaled dramatically as he swept back his hair. 'I'm not delivering my fatherly lines very well today, am I? Must be the stress these wretched workmen have caused.'

'I like Peter. Could you please try to like him too? Is that too difficult?'

'Apologies,' Manzanoni said. 'I'll be more civilised after I finish here and slip into a few martinis. It's the launch party. I haven't slept in two days.'

Ruby kissed Manzanoni on the cheek. 'Can I suggest you play the cute, middle-class dad for a little while? Consider it a reprise of your failed acting career.'

'Why don't you go inside, get comfortable? Megan's in the drawing room,' Manzanoni said. 'She's really looking forward to seeing you. She's desperate to ask you about fashion week.'

'That's nice,' Ruby said coldly.

'Now, Rubes, my darling daughter,' Manzanoni lowered his voice, 'it cuts both ways.'

'Okay.'

'We're going to have a fabulous weekend. Aren't we?' Manzanoni raised one eyebrow.

'Of course we shall. I'm looking forward to it. Do you need any help?' Peter offered.

'That's what I'm paying these bloody workmen for. Go inside. I don't want to shout in front of you.' Manzanoni spun on his heel and returned to berating the workmen.

Peter and Ruby wandered back through the ornate garden to the front entrance. Ruby grabbed hold of Peter.

'Are you all right?'

'I'm fine. He's your dad. Of course he's going to wonder who this new bloke is. It's natural. I'm fine. Don't you worry about me.'

'I'm glad you're here.' Ruby kissed Peter. 'You make everything normal.'

'Richard's right. Nothing's normal. I don't know what normal is. Staying home and watching television? Going to a soccer game?'

'Whatever it is,' Ruby replied, 'sometimes I wish Manz was more common man, less celebrity.'

'Your dad's been a celebrity for a long time. That's all he really knows.'

'Do you think it went well?'

'His career?'

'Don't be silly.'

'I thought it went well. He didn't set the dogs on me.'

'You keep me laughing,' Ruby smiled, 'and I may find a place in my bed for you tonight.' She took Peter's hand and they continued walking until they reached the portico. 'We have to see Megan, otherwise Manz will think I'm mad at her.' She opened the heavy oak door.

'It sounds like it's going to be a chore.'

'Megan's okay. It's strange having a step-mother who is only five years older than you. We don't dislike each other, we just feel awkward around each other. I guess that's normal for a step-mother and step-daughter, isn't it?' Ruby walked casually through the entrance hall, while Peter stared at the walls. *Is that a Turner? Bloody hell!* Taking pride of place among English impressionist paintings was a portrait of Richard Manzanoni himself. A sweeping marble staircase further enhanced the room's opulence.

'I'd say so,' Peter replied vaguely. He was staring goggle-eyed at his surroundings. *The old rocker has certainly earned himself a few bob.* 'Nice painting of your father.'

'It's by Maria Gabankova. It's my favourite one.'

'There are others?'

Ruby peered into a room to her left, leaving Peter's question hanging. 'I wonder where she is? Let me guess. She won't be in the kitchen. She never goes there. She might be in the solarium, the indoor swimming pool or the gymnasium. Or she may be getting her hair done upstairs. I'm not turning over the entire house to find her. Let's go upstairs and get unpacked.' Ruby winked. A vision of taking Ruby into a dark corner of the mansion entered Peter's mind.

'Ruby, darling.'

Peter and Ruby spun around in unison. A young, skinny, bleached-blonde woman sidled through the door behind them.

'Megan.' Ruby winced as Megan embraced her. 'We were looking for you.' She air-kissed Megan on both cheeks and then pulled away. The performance was more dead grandmother than beloved step-mother. Megan wore a leotard and leggings topped with a loose white cotton T-shirt. It draped over the awkward angles of her body, but she still looked stick thin. A pink headband held back her hair and her face was covered in a thick layer of make-up. Megan might have been pretty scrubbed clean, but Peter certainly wasn't attracted to her. She looked too artificial, like a bustless Barbie doll. She also looked somehow familiar.

'Megan, this is Peter. Peter, Megan.'

'Hi,' said Megan, waving at Peter as if she was farewelling some-one on a train.

'Nice to meet you,' he replied. *Yes, it's her.* He realised where he had seen Megan before. She was Megan Woolf, a one-time model in the 1980s, who then had a brief singing career.

'New boyfriend?' Megan looked at Ruby.

Poor Megan. She definitely has an IQ to match her bra size.

'I was gutted when you broke up with Sebastian...'

'That's old milk,' Ruby interrupted.

'Ooh, hit a raw nerve? Sorry. I'm happy for you.' Megan giggled, crossed the floor and patted Peter on the chest. 'Really I am. Not bad. He's quite handsome, really. Lovely blue eyes. You could really make them pop with a bit of eyeliner, you know.' She emphasised the 'pop' with a matching gesture. 'So what is it you do? For dosh, that is?'

'A writer. I write novels.'

'As in books? You must be smart.'

Peter smiled. *Poor Manzanoni. What can he possibly see in her? The sex must be transcendental.* 'I'm even smarter when I'm with Ruby.' Peter took hold of Ruby's hand.

'So happy for you both. I'm clairvoyant, you know. I can see great things happening.'

'Where's Seamus?' Ruby said impatiently. 'Do we have to get our bags out of the car ourselves?'

'Seamus and Maria are in the kitchen. It's all feet on desk at the moment.'

'Or hands on deck?' Ruby corrected.

'If they're busy, I'll get the bags,' Peter offered.

'You're from Australia?' It was the first insightful thing Megan had said.

'Sydney,' he lied. 'But I'll be living here for a while.'

'I think I went to Australia once, when I was singing. Or possibly modelling.'

'You don't remember much about it?'

'I went all over the world. It was all long trips on planes, then hotel rooms. Lots of people... That's right, I did go there. I remember I went to a zoo. I held a koala. It peed all over me. That's Australia isn't it?'

'Certainly is.' Peter smiled at Ruby who was now tapping her foot. *Megan would need instructions to boil water.* Yes, it wasn't the intellectual stimulation that kept Manzanoni and Megan a happily married couple. *His fame and wealth, her vibrating vagina perhaps?*

'What's the time?' Ruby asked.

'A bit after one o'clock,' he replied, looking at his wristwatch.

'Got to get ready.' Ruby looked panicked.

'But it doesn't start till four, does it? That's three hours away.'

'I have to get ready. Fashion designers can't look like scruffs.'

'Of course not.

'Oh my God,' Megan cried as she ran up the stairs. 'I have to get ready too.'

Poor Megan, she probably can't even tell the time.

'You're evil, Ruby Manzanoni,' Peter said as he grabbed her around the waist.

'I can't help it if I want to spend some alone time with you. I couldn't stand listening to her anymore. Megan starts to sounds like a screeching bird after a while. You have to be a bitch sometimes to get what you want.'

'I'll get the bags out of the car right now.' Peter hurried to the front door.

'Meet me at the top of the stairs. You'll get lost in this pile otherwise. You'll probably end up in Megan's bed instead of mine.'

'No hope in hell of that happening.'

16

Ruby checked up and down the corridor before opening the door of her bedroom.

'What are you looking for?' Peter asked

'Seamus and Maria.'

'I thought they were helping in the kitchen?'

'Those two are like the ghosts in this place. They have an uncanny habit of appearing out of the walls.'

'I take it they're the family retainers? Let me guess: old, Irish and Catholic.'

'They're like a priest and a nun. Manz loves them. Don't know why. Come on!'

She flung open her bedroom door and pushed Peter inside. She followed quickly, closed the door behind her and then locked it. 'I give it thirty minutes before they start to hunt around, in case anyone's having fun.'

'That's still a good start,' Peter said, looking around Ruby's bedroom. It was soft and chic, like a high-end French hotel. A large, white, four-poster bed took up half of the bedroom.

'Stop talking, we don't have much time.' She locked her lips onto Peter's.

Her lips felt like a garland of fresh roses. *Soft, rubicund, I could kiss those lips until my mouth goes numb.* He pulled away and smiled. *Take me to a manor house and suddenly I'm Lord Byron.*

They clung onto each other, moving together in the direction of the bed. Ruby unbuttoned Peter's shirt as they went, and he shrugged himself free of it. She watched him as she slipped the spaghetti straps of her dress over her shoulders and let the silk slide off her body. Then she stroked his bare chest. 'I want you,' she whispered.

A moment later, Peter was naked. 'You're so beautiful. So intelligent. So…fuckable.'

She stepped out of her knickers. Peter's hands slid down her body and gently between her legs. 'The bed?'

'Fuck the bed.'

They sank to the floor. Peter lay astride her, kissing her face and breasts. She reached across and pulled his hips towards her.

'No time for foreplay. I'm so fucking horny already.'

She pushed him up into her, as she threw her head back and moaned.

'Oh God, yes.'

It was urgent, fast and exciting and they both came in a rush.

Later on, when they finally made it to the bed, they lay their heads together on the same pillow. Resting beside them on another pillow was a large, white, fluffy toy bear.

'We have company,' Peter whispered.

'What?' Her eyes followed Peter's. 'Oh, that's my lifetime friend, Maynard,' Ruby smiled. She took hold of the bear. 'I'll put him on the floor. This may be too shocking for you, Maynard.'

'You think he's had his eyes shut till now?'

'I think he may have peeked. Good for his education. Although, I should warn you, he does have a tendency towards jealousy.'

'I was starting to think that we were going to have some sort of weird threesome.'

Her mouth searched out Peter's and they hung onto one another. Her kisses were intoxicating. 'Time's ticking, Peter. You're hard again. I'm dripping. Let's fuck.'

He was exploring every inch of Ruby with his hands.

'I totally agree.'

He tossed Maynard under the bed as he eased himself once more into her welcoming body.

17

Peter arrived at the garden party at quarter to four, resplendent in his cost-price Savile Row suit. Ruby really did know someone. Taking a flute of champagne from a waiter, he gulped it down nervously then took another before the waiter was able to move on. *Hurry, Ruby, I need saving. I feel like a prostitute in an Amish house.*

He took several canapés from another waiter. Despite his nerves, he was ravenous. He'd had a quick nap and a shower. He felt refreshed, shielded by sexual afterglow and charged with energy. *Sex, sex, sex on my mind. Already.* There would be more Ruby Time later in the night. *Another quickie will not be near enough time with her. I'm not a schoolboy.*

Richard and Megan were already welcoming the first of the guests: a pack of middle-aged men and a woman who looked and dressed like a young Princess Margaret. Peter immediately guessed them to be the invited entertainment reviewers from the broadsheets. Certainly no tabloids would be invited here. *Good God, no.* How did he know they were hacks? They had arrived first and they were knocking back the champagne. *Yes, they're still hacks.*

Megan was all air-kisses and bleached toothy smiles for the columnists. She was wrapped in a low-slung floral gown, like a bonbon in cellophane. Shame she had no curves to fill it out. Manzanoni, as always, was his own fashion installation: a purple sharkskin suit with a plum red shirt underneath.

Ruby had said she was going to be thirty minutes late as her sex hair was going to need a lot of restyling, thanks to their rigorous love-making. Peter was happy to hang in the background until her arrival, listening to a string quartet playing something that sounded like Brahms' Lullaby and watching the staff setting up tables. Megan spotted him and waved him over.

Bugger.

'You look very handsome and dapper,' said Megan, kissing Peter on the lips. He wondered if she'd meant to do it, or if he'd just turned at the wrong time. Her face defied scrutiny.

'Thanks, Megan. You're looking...very radiant.'

'You're nearly part of the family. I'm so happy Ruby brought you home,' Megan breathed.

'She's a great girl,' Peter replied inanely, waving to a hovering waiter for another glass of champagne.

'Did she tell you much about Sebastian?' she continued.

'Not really. I always think past is past,' Peter replied.

'What are you saying to the poor man? He's squirming like a worm,' Manzanoni interrupted, turning away from the reviewers, who were now leaving to take their allocated seats in the marquee.

'Oh, not much. Talking about...history.'

'But you know nothing about the subject.' He turned to Peter. 'She tried to read the Domesday Book once. She thought it was a prediction about the end of the world.'

Peter chuckled. 'I'm fine,' he said.

'Megan, darling, why don't you greet Sir Thomas and Lady Ashley, there's a good girl. Tell them I'll be there very shortly.' He watched her sashay away and added, 'They're throwing in a few quid for my latest venture. Sir Thomas loves ogling her arse.' Manzanoni sniggered. 'It is perfect, isn't it?'

Peter couldn't see the attraction but kept the thought to himself.

'You're settling in? Enjoying yourself?' Manzanoni said.

'Yes, of course. Thanks for inviting me.' Peter sensed that it was going to be one of those father–boyfriend lectures.

'Well. I didn't do the inviting, but Ruby was very persuasive in stating your case. She's quite taken by you. To be honest, I said no, but she became so angry that I gave in. She has a very strong personality.'

'I only have good intentions for Ruby. She's very special.'

'I haven't liked anyone she's ever brought home, Sebastian aside.' Manzanoni took a sip of champagne.

'I've heard a lot about him in a short period of time.'

'Frankly, I was shocked when they broke up. They were going to get engaged, you know. They were the talk of London: a beautiful, artistic couple going places. I was quite attached to Seb.'

'Forgive me for saying that Sebastian is none of my affair.' He was getting sick of the mention of his name. *What was he? The second coming?* 'I have the feeling that you think I'm going to hurt Ruby on the rebound.'

'I need to know that you're worthy of her affection.' Just then, Manzanoni looked up and smiled. 'Speaking of angels,' he said, 'you look ethereal, sweetheart.'

Peter glanced over his shoulder. He was right; she looked exactly like a pre-Raphaelite angel, clothed in a filmy, white dress, hair curled in tiny ringlets. She seemed to float. *She looks so beautiful that it hurts to look at her. I'm the luckiest man on earth.*

'You look stunning, my darling, stunning. All the women are going to be jealous of you. Especially Megan.' Richard kissed Ruby on the cheek.

'I don't care about them,' Ruby smiled at Peter. 'I only care about one person's opinion right now.'

Manzanoni was distracted. 'Darling, must go.' He waved at a throng of arriving guests. 'They're all coming at once. Must press the flesh... Ah, there's Ruggles.'

'You know, I'm just going to stare at you all night. Like staring at the sun; I won't be able to see anything else,' Peter said once Manzanoni had left.

'If you do that, you'll miss out.'

'I don't know what you mean,' he replied. 'As far as I can see, there's nobody here but us.'

Ruby laughed. Her voice sounded like a rainforest stream trickling over rocks—one of Peter's favourite sounds. 'It's all a bit ho-hum for me, given that I grew up with these people, but it might be an opportunity for you to make some useful connections.' She pointed to a few of the guests being welcomed by Richard and Megan. 'Florence Baker and Jeremiah Lord. Hmm. I thought they'd broken up. There's Reggie James and his entourage. And Kellie Dougherty. Oh, she's brought…whatshisname with her. That lead singer of that Australian band…'

'You mean URme? The one who does that great impersonation of Jim Morrison? I know the guy. His name escapes me…'

'See that man next to Megan, the man with the really bad wig? He's Solly Wiseman, one of the biggest publishers in Britain. He's someone for you to know.'

'I'm not looking.'

'Well, you should.' Ruby took a glass of champagne from a waiter and sipped it. 'Oh, my giddy aunt,' she spluttered. 'Olivia Michaels! I didn't think she'd be coming. I heard she was in rehab. We'll steer clear of her. She's a mess at the moment.'

'I don't care and I'm still not looking.' Peter peered at Olivia. 'Besides, she has nothing on you.'

'I hope she behaves herself. As you can see, my father knows lots of famous people and you're not looking.'

'I couldn't care if the Queen was here. I'm hopeless, aren't I?'

'You're soppy,' she laughed. 'Shagging's supposed to be serious, yet you make me laugh.' She nudged Peter. 'Come on and meet everyone. I want to show you off.'

'I'm only looking at you.'

'I have plans for tonight,' she whispered into Peter's ear. 'We get everyone liquored up. No-one will notice where you sleep.'

'Great idea, Ruby.'

'Come on. The show's about to start.'

At last, the long summer evening surrendered to the night. *Is that the time?* Peter glanced at his watch. He'd found the evening's entertainment mind-numbing. If anyone else belted out another arpeggio about witches and warlocks, he was ready to leg it.

It had taken several hours of solid Cristal for Manzanoni to begin to yield to its effects. *Old Rockers have extraordinary livers. Must be all the years of training.* Peter looked over at Ruby—still radiant, if a little tired. *Hurry up, you're all interfering with loving time.*

After the launch was officially over, Reggie James hit the ivories and gave an impromptu concert to the remaining guests. Peter found himself singing vaguely along to all Reggie's hits, although he usually couldn't bear his music. How did all this happen? *Here I am standing around a grand piano with beautiful Ruby by my side, the who's who of British entertainment gathered around Reggie, as if we're at the local pub singing around a pianola.*

Manzanoni kept saying that the night had run like a lucky charm. First, there had been afternoon drinks on the lawn, followed by the launch of Manzanoni's new musical, *Merlin The Wizard*. The cast members had sung excerpts and Manzanoni himself had conducted the small orchestra.

Despite his inner disdain, Peter had clapped along, like everyone else, while he tried to distract himself by thinking about things other than Merlin. Or sex. If he had thought about Ruby, he might have become aroused. And that might have proven embarrassing.

As he listened with half an ear to Reggie James's megahit 'The Son Always Shines', he decided that Manzanoni had definitely done his best work in Marquis Fission. The *Wolfen* album was one of the best albums ever. 'Wolf Clan' one of the best songs ever. *Okay, I'm supposed to be singing along to Reggie. Muzak. It's all muzak.*

Now it was time for the next stage of the plan—Ruby had to feign a migraine. Then she'd leave, Peter would wait half an hour (so as to not arouse suspicion) and he would quietly slip away through the French garden like a predatory cat. By the look of Manzanoni, he wouldn't notice a thing. Reggie's playing was good but Manzanoni's singing was slurry and pitchy. *Not long to go...* Megan was distracted, flirting outrageously with upcoming actor Jeremiah Lord who was so drunk he could barely talk. His sometimes girlfriend was nowhere to be seen.

'Are you okay?' Peter turned to Ruby.

'I don't feel well,' Ruby replied loudly, rubbing her forehead.

'Not a migraine is it, darling?'

'Could be. I'll go inside, take something and lie down. I'll see you in the morning.'

'Okay. Take care. I'll see you in the morning.'

Ruby gave Peter a peck on the cheek. 'No longer than thirty minutes or I start without you,' she whispered into his ear.

She excused herself to her father, gave Peter a final come-hither look and left. Peter checked his watch. Could he even wait thirty agonising minutes? *Can't do it, make it twenty-five.*

Manzanoni was now tinkering away on the piano. He looked at Peter. 'Any requests? I don't know how to play "Tie Me Kangaroo Down, Sport".' Manzanoni sniggered. A titter wafted through the remaining crowd.

'How about "My Funny Valentine"? It was my parents' favourite.'

'One of my favourites too,' Manzanoni replied as he played the first haunting chords.

'Have you got a light, honey bunny?' a woman rasped at Peter, throwing a slender arm around his shoulders.

Olivia Michaels, gaunt and glassy-eyed, looked the worse for wear. This was the first time tonight that Peter had spoken to Olivia, thanks to Ruby's efforts to avoid her. Olivia had mastered heroin-wasted chic. Her crumpled gown, panda-eyed mascara and dishevelled hair all added to the look. She had a bent, unlit cigarette hanging out of the corner of her mouth. *Was this really the movie actress, once regarded as Britain's most beautiful and most talented actor of her generation? The next Vivian Leigh?* Now she was just someone famous, who looked better in magazines and on-screen than she did in real life.

'Sorry, Olivia. I don't smoke.'

'Then fuck you. You're no fucking good to me,' she slurred, stumbling and falling against Peter. He righted her, as Olivia Michaels giggled hysterically. 'My come-fuck-me shoes are too high...' she focused on Peter's face. 'I know you.'

Peter sucked in a lungful of air. *She recognises me from the* Gazer *and I'm gone.*

'Where's your Ruby-red girlfriend? Has she deserted you already? She's not much fun. Always been a straight lace. But not me.' She checked out Peter and placed an arm around his waist.

'She's gone inside. Got a headache,' Peter replied awkwardly.

'I'd still want to fuck you, even if I'd just had surgery on my cunt.'

'Language please,' Manzanoni interrupted.

'Sorry, Uncle Richard,' Olivia snapped back. 'Surgery on my vagina. You're such a prude.'

'You know I love you,' Manzanoni said, 'but there's a time and place.' He waved to a statuesque Asian girl nearby with a large Louis Vuitton handbag slung over her shoulder. 'Go inside with Ting, there's a good girl. Have a rest, Olivia.'

Olivia's personal assistant pushed through the small crowd and took her by the arm. 'Come now, Livvie,' Ting said. 'I'll take care of you now.'

'No, not yet.'

'Livvie, please. Time to go.'

Olivia flashed her an angry look. 'Not before I sing you one of my songs,' she announced to the crowd. 'Not only am I the British movie queen, I'm also a talented singer and songwriter; a triple fucking threat, darling.'

'Please, Livvie, not one of your songs,' Manzanoni said. 'Not now.'

Ting attempted to pull Olivia away, but she resisted. She started to sing loudly. Manzanoni sighed and hung his head, waiting for the inevitable. Peter noticed that many of the audience were doing the same. Several started to extricate themselves from the situation. Reggie and his entourage had disappeared.

'It's not the friends you know… It's the people you blow… It's not the lines you know… It's the lines of snow,' Olivia sang, accompanied by a flurry of dramatic hand gestures.

Peter grimaced. She had no discernible talent, just a lot of pitch, a lot of noise. *Great lyrics though.*

'Enough!' Manzanoni shouted and marched towards Olivia. He took hold of one of her arms; Ting took hold of the other.

'Thanks for taking care of me, Uncle Richard. You've always been good to me.'

'Why do you do this to yourself?' Manzanoni growled. The unsteady threesome stumbled through the parting crowd towards the house.

'Looks like Olivia Michaels has left the building,' someone said aloud after the trio had gone.

'More like she's left the planet.'

Peter gazed across to see who had spoken. He recognised the grey-haired man as a movie producer Ruby had introduced him to. 'They don't call her the British Screen Queen anymore. Now it's the Snow Queen.'

'Shame,' Peter stated. 'I've seen her in some great movies.'

'That's showbiz, I'm afraid,' the movie producer replied. 'It eats you if you can't keep up.'

18

Peter stirred from his post-coital, exhausted sleep. *This must be the closest that anyone comes to experiencing heaven. I hate poetry, but being with Ruby is worthy of a poem.* He rolled over to snuggle against Ruby's nakedness. She was making little murmuring noises as she breathed in her sleep. Peter stroked her moist, tangled hair. He checked the bedside clock. It was two o'clock. Should he stay or go?

'Ruby,' Peter whispered.

'Don't go, lover.' She stirred and turned her head to kiss him on the lips. She stuck her tongue in his mouth and their tongues met briefly before he pulled away.

'I don't want to get you in trouble. I don't really want to be chased across the estate with your dad blasting at me with a shotgun.'

'I'd like to see that. My father would likely shoot himself by mistake. He's not a very good marksman.' She yawned. 'Stay just a little longer.'

'You're such a temptress. Okay. You broke me.'

'You're the long-distance runner of sex,' Ruby said, kissing Peter's chest. 'You have staying power.'

'I like that,' Peter smiled. 'I'll put that on the book blurb: Writer, sexual athlete.' He stretched out and laced his hands under his head. He lay silently for a moment, deep in thought. 'I met Olivia Michaels tonight, after you left.'

'Really? And what did you think?'

'Not what I expected. I used to have a big crush on her. Before I met you, of course.'

'Of course.' Ruby propped herself up. 'You didn't think of her when we were fucking?'

'Perhaps.'

She slapped Peter playfully.

'Ow. No. Not now. Definitely not now. I met her tonight, or rather she met me. She tried to sing one of her songs and your father took her inside. It was a little tragic.'

'I'm glad I wasn't there. Her songs are terrible. She's really hit a new low,' Ruby said. 'Ever since the break up from Justin Greene. She should get over it. That was two years ago.'

'A broken heart?'

'Her last three movies have also flopped. She's also taking that hard.'

'How does she know your dad? She kept calling him Uncle Richard.'

'He hates that,' Ruby laughed. 'When Olivia was a child actor, she was in one of my father's musicals. She had a horrible mother. No father in sight. Manz felt sorry for her. Ever since then he's kept an eye on her. Given her advice, helped her stay on her feet. My father is generous that way. He's helped a few young actors get their break.'

'But you don't sound close to Olivia. You did everything to avoid her.'

'We were friends once, but we now move in different circles. I'm a successful fashion designer, she's the Snow Queen.'

'Shame. So much wasted talent.'

'It happens. You need more than talent in showbiz,' Ruby said dryly. 'Anyway…enough of her. Since we're both awake, you want to…' Ruby snuggled into Peter's neck and felt for his penis. 'Well, that's an emphatic yes.'

'About time,' Peter laughed. 'I could do with a nightcap.'

19

I feel like I'm in an Agatha Christie book. Peter skulked along an endless, unlit corridor, seemingly leading nowhere, carrying his shoes in his hand. *Yes, I'm the murderous villain in the manor house. Fuck Agatha, now I'm just bloody lost. This place is too big. It's like trying to find your way around a shopping centre in the dark.*

Having left Ruby at a little after three, he tried to find his room. It must have been down the other hallway. Navigating at night was difficult but navigating through an enormous estate on a moonless night was even worse; it was so dark he could barely see his hand in front of him. *If I run into one of the ghosts, I'll ask for spectral directions.*

If it was possible, the hallway only seemed to get darker. He carefully felt his way along the wall until he touched something large, cold and metallic. He discerned it was probably a suit of armour. He eased himself around it, pleased that he hadn't knocked the pile of scrap metal over, and kept going. Suddenly, the walls receded. He entered an open space, probably the entrance to a sitting room. Once again, he found himself brushing against another large object; this time it was a grandfather clock.

Peter sighed with relief when he saw a faint light coming from the doorway to the sitting room. As his eyes became accustomed to the light, he could make out a sofa, several antique chairs and a large table covered with photographs. On the other wall was a fireplace with a few still-glowing embers, casting a little light on a painting above. Unsurprisingly, it was another painting of Manzanoni. Peter concluded that he must have wandered into the private wing of the Manzanonis.

I know, I'll just wake them up and ask them how to find my bedroom. Or, I'll make out that I'm sleep walking. But how many sleep walkers carry their shoes with them? He was about to make the long journey back to his starting point, when he heard loud voices coming from the lit doorway. He ducked behind the grandfather clock, large enough to conceal him entirely.

He heard Richard's booming voice first, then Olivia's, followed by another male voice. The trio came through the doorway and stopped at the fireplace. He could make out Manzanoni because he was still wearing his loud suit. Manzanoni fumbled around before finally switching on a table lamp. Peter could now see all three in shadowy silhouette. Olivia was also still dressed in her evening apparel. Peter recognised the other man; the movie producer that he had spoken to briefly at the party.

'Olivia, darling,' Manzanoni grabbed her by the shoulders, 'don't just storm off. Listen to Sir Clifford's proposal.'

'I would much prefer the lead,' she said. She had sobered up, or so it sounded to Peter. 'I haven't played a character role for five years. Five years. That's like dying slowly in this business.' She pulled away from Manzanoni.

'Calm down, Livvie,' Manzanoni replied.

'I've had enough of this stinking business anyway.' Olivia leant against the fireplace, took a packet of cigarettes from her handbag and lit one. 'I should just pack it all in,' she said, gesturing wildly with her cigarette. 'I'll go and live on a Greek island and grow vegetables.'

'It might do you good, Olivia,' said Sir Clifford. 'A healthy lifestyle would get you back on track. Can you go without your… necessities?'

'On second thoughts, maybe I'll do that when I'm old. Shit, I need something to sleep. Where's Ting?' Olivia asked anxiously as she stubbed out the cigarette in a nearby ashtray.

'You don't need that right now,' Sir Clifford said.

'You've come to us for help. We're helping,' Manzanoni whispered, as he embraced her. Olivia was becoming agitated, pushing free of him.

'We don't want you to fail,' he continued. 'You're just going through a rough patch at the moment. That's how show business works. We all know it runs in cycles. You just need to clean up your act a little. Cut back on your excesses, go to bed before midnight, stay in and learn your lines.' He kissed Olivia lightly on the cheek.

'Sounds terribly boring,' she replied dismissively. 'I may as well become a fucking nun. I know what I could do...' She lit another cigarette.

Peter leaned around the grandfather clock to stay within earshot. *Agatha Christie dialogue this is not.*

'I don't care anymore,' Olivia continued. 'That's it... I've been thinking about writing a book about my shitty life in show business, or should I call it, show exploitation. *My Fucked Life* by Olivia Michaels; real name Taylor. Then I'll call it quits. I'll go to rehab then I'll go to university.'

'Have you told Lou about your...idea?'

'He went completely bonkers, as usual, and then he mentioned this movie.'

'Like Lou, we only have your best interests at heart,' Sir Clifford said. 'This project will put you back on track. I promise.'

'Don't be so hasty,' Manzanoni jumped in. 'You can't throw away such a beautiful talent as yours like that. A tell-all book will only end in misery, especially for you. Wouldn't you agree, Sir Clifford?'

'It won't end well. It'll tip you over the edge. I've seen it happen before. Actors only write books when their careers are finished.'

'But mine's as good as. I'm dead in the water at the moment, if you haven't noticed. What choice do I have?'

'Believe me, Olivia, this is a good part. You'll be able to steal the focus off the lead. You have the ability to really shine. I can see major awards out of this. Believe me, this movie is going to be huge. Don't forget that I'm the producer.'

She mulled it over. 'I'd probably get bored writing a book anyway,' she conceded. 'I'll consider it on one condition: I want more lines.'

'Okay,' Sir Clifford exhaled with frustration, 'We'll look at that.'

'Then it's all arranged?' Manzanoni said.

'I guess so.' Olivia took a final drag of her cigarette and stubbed it out.

'We'll go over the contracts with Lou in my office on Monday,' Sir Clifford said. 'There's a good girl.'

'Thanks for listening. You've always tried to look after me.'

'There'll be no more silly nonsense,' said Sir Clifford. 'Now then, let's get you off to bed.'

'Not until I see Ting. Go and wake her up for me. I can't sleep without Ting. Where is she sleeping?'

Manzanoni glanced at Sir Clifford, who nodded gently. 'Okay,' he sighed, 'I'll go and wake her.'

Peter pushed himself as far as he could into the narrow space between the clock and the wall. He held his breath, wishing he'd been a whippet with worms. If Manzanoni looked around, he'd see him. Manzanoni passed by and his footsteps echoed down the hallway, as Peter silently swallowed his relief.

Sir Clifford and Olivia remained standing by the fireplace. Sir Clifford picked up a poker and prodded at the dying embers. It seemed to awaken the fire for a moment, but then it quickly died down again. In a moment, it was all but extinguished. Peter used the sudden darkness as his opportunity to retrace his steps back down the hallway, in the opposite direction.

20

Expecting to enjoy a lie in, a late breakfast and a leisurely drive back to London, Peter finally reached his bedroom just before the dawn chorus. His plans were disturbed at eight o'clock by a forceful knock on his door. *Shit, I've only just laid my head on the pillow.* He managed to pull himself out of bed and push himself towards the door. As he shook off his slumber it occurred to him that it was probably Ruby. Maybe she had managed to sneak past the prying eyes? Could he manage a morning glory? Was the Pope Catholic?

Anticipation was quickly dispelled when he opened the door. Seamus, Manzanoni's old retainer, handed him a roll of riding clothes and a pair of riding boots.

'The clothes should fit but the boots may be a little loose and the skullcap may be a little tight. The kit had once belonged to...' Peter knew what was coming next. '...Mr Sebastian,' said Seamus.

What the hell? Him again. I am not Sebastian and I don't want to be.

Seamus finally added that Peter was to meet the others outside in fifteen minutes.

Horse-riding? Haven't done that since I was thirteen. Will my long-unridden arse hold up? He slipped on the jodhpurs (no bushman in his right mind ever wore jodhpurs, that was the purview of the English), eased his head into the cap and then took it off again. The cap fitted like a condom and the boots were so loose that they felt as if they could fall off at any time. Still, fifteen minutes later, he managed to impress Manzanoni, Megan, Ruby and Sir Clifford with his riding skills. Did none of them need sleep?

Peter was matched up to a gelding with peculiar eyes and a short tail. He was toey even before Peter had approached. *Someone's got it in for me. So, you think it's funny to put the new boy on a skittish horse? Don't you know that I was raised by a brood mare?*

He slipped into the saddle with as much grace as his untrained legs could manage. Then he let the horse have its head and took off across the field at a flat gallop, leaning into his ride's neck, his body hardly moving, with the others following. He jumped a fence and brought the horse to a halt, to allow the others to catch up. Peter felt exhilarated. *My arse may not be happy in a few hours, but it feels good to be back in the saddle.* Having lost his father in a horse-riding accident, he knew how dangerous it could be, but horses had never frightened him. They were a large part of his DNA.

Ruby caught up first and her horse milled around his. She looked like she wanted to shag him there and then. When he finally cantered up, Manzanoni nodded at him with begrudging respect.

Fuck Sebastian. I'm king of the saddle.

'Looks like you were taught how to ride by an expert,' Manzanoni puffed.

'My father taught me.'

'Really? He must have been good in the saddle,' said Megan. 'What? What did I say?' she added when Ruby giggled.

'Dad died when I was a kid; a riding accident.'

'Sorry—Manz lost his father when he was a child, too,' Ruby said.

'Mine accident,' Manzanoni said. 'But we move on.'

'We do. I have to,' Peter replied.

Manzanoni nodded at Peter again, kicked his horse and rode away. 'Onwards,' he shouted.

The old coot may never like me but he might grow to respect me.

*

After an hour of riding, Peter was starving and looking forward to a proper meal. His overnight activities had been fuelled by nothing more than champagne and a few canapés, and he'd eaten nothing of substance since yesterday's lunch. Back at the house, a full English breakfast was laid out in the main dining room and he piled his plate high. It was only after his second cup of coffee that he noticed that Olivia and Ting were absent. Manzanoni said they had already gone back to London.

Ruby sipped her tea and rubbed Peter's foot under the table. While he piled his plate high with sausages and eggs, she cut into a slice of tofu bacon. 'We're going to have to head back to London earlier than anticipated. I have to go into the boutique today. We're having some problems with one of the seamstresses.' She smiled at Peter enigmatically.

She's up to no good, Peter thought.

DD

I've been so busy with rehearsals this week, I've hardly had time to eat a proper meal. Mum's not very happy about it, but I love it. I can't wait till we open. Two weeks to go. I can't wait.

You know how I said that I met some-one really lovely? We even have our own made-up names for each other. I call him Tinker, and he calls me Belle. It's our own personal, private code. He's so sweet to me. I wasn't feeling very well yesterday, so you know what Tinker did? He made me a big cup of cocoa and sat with me while I drank it. Then we watched Dolores Wright run through her lines. She's supposed to be the star of the show. He was making funny comments all the way through. He makes me laugh.

Oh well, Mum's at the door.

Bye for now.

21

'Florence Baker and Jeremiah Lord back together again? For the moment. They've had more bust ups than I've done warm shits,' Devrille said. He rocked in his chair and added, 'And Reggie gave a little concert. How endearing. Was his boyfriend swooning?'

'He had a small entourage. No boyfriend,' Peter said.

'Was he misbehaving himself?'

'He was well behaved.'

'Shame. We don't do well-behaved.' Devrille sat forward in his chair to take a mouthful of his coffee. 'Take a seat. You're making me feel bloody uncomfortable.'

'I can't. My arse is sore.' Peter said, wincing.

'What the fuck happened to you, JB? You didn't hook up with Reggie, did you? Should you admit to a case of sodomy in front of me? I thought you were into the sheilas, as you lot say; I didn't think you were a sausage jockey.' Devrille exploded with laughter.

'It was a long overdue episode of horse-riding. I went riding with the Manzanonis on Sunday morning.' Peter tensed as he eased himself into a chair, positioning himself on the edge of it.

'You should ask one of the office girls to give you a rub.' Devrille laughed again. 'Was Lord Richard impressed with your riding skills?'

'I think he was but he doesn't like me much. I'll work on him.'

'And Ruby Manzanoni? Should Richard be alarmed? Did you get to practise your riding skills on that sweet, innocent girl?'

'We get along very well.'

'My God, you're blushing like a schoolboy. Oh fuck, you're enamoured of her.' Devrille sighed. 'This'll make it harder for you. You can't mix work and pleasure.'

'I'm okay. No worries.'

'Good. I don't want you growing a conscience. Is that all you got?'

'Olivia Michaels was there. She was all about misbehaving at the party. I overheard Sir Clifford Duncan offer her a movie part.'

'Sir Clifford? Was she blowing him at the time?' Devrille asked. 'I'm amazed that anyone will touch her now, especially Clifford Duncan. He could pick anyone he wants; he's the top producer in this country.'

'The biggest surprise is that she's still alive. You know she's called the Snow Queen.'

'So I've heard. Looks like you know everything about this. How about I let you loose on the story? You can write it under a fictitious by-line. You can use Joe Borgen; one of my favourites.'

'Won't that expose me?' Peter squirmed into a more comfortable position.

'It'll make it a better story if you do it. Besides you can't just go and have fun at my expense; you have to do some work.'

Devrille appeared to enjoy Peter's physical and emotional discomfort.

'I don't have a choice, do I?'

'Hardly.' Devrille unfolded a piece of paper on his desk. 'Speaking of the Snow Queen, this just came in from one of our sources earlier this morning.'

Devrille pushed it across the desk towards Peter. He pulled himself out of the chair and read it, standing up.

Miss Michaels passed out in my taxi. Had to be helped by me and her companion, an Asian woman, into her house. Poor girl looked off her head. Regards, Barry.

'She gets around, doesn't she?' said Devrille.

'Who's Barry?' Peter asked. 'But she only left Manzanoni's on Sunday.'

'She was coming home from a club. Olivia likes clubbing. We've taken great snaps of her staggering out of them in the early hours, sometimes with some bloke she's picked up. Best snap of all was one of her falling into a cab, dress up over her head. The silly girl wasn't wearing underwear. We sold a lot of papers that day. What was the headline? "Show Us Your Knickers, Livvie".'

'Does she look after her lawn?'

'It's an overgrown bloody jungle. Looks good in a photo though,' Devrille chuckled.

'And Barry?'

'Barry's a local lad, a taxi-driver. Great source of information on celebrities he's driven around. Old Barry has given us some good stuff. The rich and famous occasionally like to shag in Barry's taxi. They occasionally like to pass out in his taxi. This is great fodder for the paper.'

'If I go and talk to her she'll probably recognise me,' said Peter.

'Go and talk to her manager first. His name's Lou Lipmann,' Devrille replied. 'Ask him about her forthcoming movie part and last night. You can take a snapper with you too. His heavies prefer to work the snapper over first, if Lou gets too upset. Lou's a little photophobic.'

'Lou's a tough bastard by all accounts.'

'Not as tough as you. Didn't you tell me once you'd wrestled the odd crocodile?'

'On occasion; Russian mafia versus Lou Lipmann? I'll let you know.'

'Russian mafia? Now, that's impressive. You'll have to tell that story one day.'

'I just hope no-one decides to kick my delicate arse,' Peter joked.

'Just tell them: no-one touches my arse; leave my arse alone,' Devrille laughed.

'What if Olivia Michaels is there?'

'That could be a problem,' Devrille pondered. 'Hopefully she'll be so far off her head she'll never recognise you. Or she could recognise you in a brief moment of sobriety. Fuck. You're ahead of me. Maybe I should put someone else on it?'

'Shit no. I'm taking all the risks, I'll see the story right through. I'll find a way around this.'

'Oh?'

'The cunning kit,' Peter smiled. 'Lucky I brought it from Australia with me. It's served me well many times.'

'What in the fuck is a cunning kit, when it's at home?' Devrille shook his head.

'You'll find out.'

22

'I don't know who gave you such information, my son, but it's all fucking fantasy. Olivia Michaels in an intoxicated state? I am personally affronted by your questioning, Mr Flannery, you miserable Irish peasant. If you did your fucking homework you would know that she suffers from debilitating cluster migraines and has done so for most of her life. Poor girl. Olivia Michaels has been like a daughter to me and I'm tired of the muckraking press trying to drag her down. If you persist with this questioning I will have you removed via the nearest exit and that may not be a fucking door. Get it?' Lipmann ranted as he looked over his shoulder at a window behind him. Peter looked at the window too and shuddered. They were three storeys up.

I've only asked Lou Lipmann one question and already he's threatening to harm me. Help! Please punch the snapper.

'Yes, Mr Lipmann,' said Peter, 'Got it.'

'Are you sure you're not on drugs?' Lipmann asked. 'Or in the IRA?'

'Only addicted to strong coffee and I have no time for the IRA,' Peter replied in his best lilting Irish accent. Thanks to one Desmond Flannery, an Irish flatmate during his university days, Peter could add a creditable Irish accent to his cunning kit arsenal, together with the use of Des's name.

'Why did you let this drug addict in here, Terry?' Lipmann asked quietly without looking at Terry. Terry took a handkerchief from his pocket and dabbed his brow. Lipmann then opened a wooden box on his desk and took out the largest cigar Peter had ever seen. It looked one foot long and thick as a vacuum cleaner hose. Lipmann screwed it into his cavernous mouth and chewed it several times. His mouth reminded Peter of a baboon's arse, red and pouty. In fact, the legendary impresario had strong simian features, except for the eyes. Whereas a monkey had gentle eyes, Lipmann's were like a shark's, except maybe the shark's looked more sympathetic. In fact, the last time he'd seen eyes like those, they were in the skull of a crazy Russian with a meat cleaver.

Lipmann picked up a gold lighter the size of a vase and lit the cigar. He turned slowly in his leather chair to stare down Terry. Terry was one of a large number of attendants. He was human bulldog squeezed into a suit the colour of putty. Or preserved human skin. There was one difference between Terry and a canine: a bulldog was more handsome.

'Irish 'ere showed me his identification, guv. It was all legit. He's from that reputable paper, the *Gazer*. He wanted to know about Miss Michael's next movie.' Terry snuffled. Just like a bulldog, he had trouble breathing through a nose the shape of a cauliflower floret.

'Terry, Terry, Terry. How many times have I got to tell you? *The Times* is reputable. The *Guardian* is reputable. Even the *Daily Mail* is reputable. The *Geezer* is toilet paper. In other words, Tel, my lad, it's excrement.' Lipmann banged the desk with his hand. 'The *Geezer* has as much a decent reputation as a used condom dumped in an East London laneway.'

'Yes, guv'nor,' Terry stammered. 'I won't let it happen again.'

'No. You won't. Besides, the readers of the *Geezer* can't even read. That's why they have big, colour pictures.'

The phone rang. Lipmann didn't pick up. Instead, Terry leaned over, picked up the receiver and handed it to him. Lipmann barked into the phone. 'Look, mate, you better get your bleeding head examined, because that amount is loose change. You should know by now how I work. You must be getting dementia in your declining years, Henry. No, no, no, Henry, it's not the amount you think you can offer me, it's the amount I'm satisfied with what's important. Get it?' Lipmann slammed the receiver onto the desk. With well-practised familiarity, Terry leaned over the desk and replaced the receiver.

Peter took that moment to pat down the false moustache that was slowly lifting off his upper lip. Apart from the peeling moustache, the blond wig was starting to itch like it had a colony of lice breeding in it. He debated whether he should take it to a hairdresser for a perm, as he surreptitiously scratched his forehead. *Or maybe get it debugged with pet shampoo? What in the hell do you do to an itchy wig anyway?*

'I think we've got off on the wrong foot, Mr Lipmann,' he said, trying the softer approach. It was either that or Terry would be showing him to the door, or possibly the window, very quickly.

'I see. So now you're going to ask me a nice question. You're learning, my son. And when you learn, Lou Lipmann is happy, which means everyone is happy.' He removed his cigar from his mouth and flicked a pile of ash on the desk. 'I hate smelly ashtrays,' he casually remarked.

Terry responded by wiping the ash off the desk with one hand into his other one. He then threw the ash into a waste paper bin.

'Can you confirm that Olivia Michaels is going to star in a new Sir Clifford Duncan movie?'

'You surprise me. And nothing ever surprises me. How did the *Geezer* get ahead of the pack? I was going to issue a press release about that later today. How did the *Geezer* get in the know? If I find out someone's been getting intelligence by unorthodox means, I will be very, very unhappy.'

'Mr Lipmann, sir, you know I can't disclose that,' Peter replied coolly.

'I could deny it and cause your toe-rag paper great inconvenience, but I can proudly confirm that Livvie will be in a new adaption of *Wuthering Heights*, starting tomorrow,' Lipmann beamed.

'What role will she be playing?' Peter asked.

'A starring role of course. What else would she play? She is a bleeding star,' Lipmann replied tersely.

'Will that be a challenging role for Olivia? She doesn't usually do costume dramas does she? She's more romantic comedies?'

'Livvie can act in anything. She can sing and write music. She's so talented it makes you want to cry. In *My Hundredth Wedding*, she made Terry bawl like a newborn.'

'I cried like a baby when I saw her in *Love and the Plague*,' said Terry.

'Shut up, Terry. You see, Livvie can even reduce Terry to mush and he was the head man in the Scrubs when he was doing time there.'

Peter wanted to respond that Olivia's singing had also nearly reduced him to tears, but for all the wrong reasons.

'She loves challenges. This movie is going to take her to another level. I can see accolades. Lots of them.'

'She's been having a hiatus. Is she looking forward to returning?'

'Returning?' Lipmann laughed as he flicked more ash on the desk. 'She's already started filming, my son. She started this morning.'

'That was quick. Is it possible to interview her?'

'She's a consummate professional, despite what your rubbish redtop says about her. I've forgotten your name, Paddy.'

'It's Desmond. Desmond Flannery.'

'Of course it is,' Lipmann smirked. 'No interview without going through me, Mr Flannery, and I won't be granting any further access to your paper. Your paper doesn't fit Olivia's image.'

'I'll be sympathetic,' Peter replied. 'I'll talk her up.'

'I like that,' Lipmann sniggered, shaking his head. 'If you were a social worker, I might believe you, but you're a stinking journalist from the *Geezer*.'

The phone rang again. Terry picked up the phone.

'Henry,' Lipmann barked, 'you're finally coming to your senses. Has the missus just given you a blowjob to get the brain cells going? That figure sounds better but it's not quite there... What... I'll send you broke? You've got more readies in your underpants drawer then the Queen has in the Bank of England. Have another think over it. You should really have your dementia checked... It's worrying me.' Lipmann slammed the receiver on the desk. Terry replaced it.

'I'll do a...' Peter started.

'He's still here,' Lipmann interrupted. 'Terry. Why is Paddy still here? Why is he still talking to me? I ask you?'

'I thought that...'

'I don't pay you to think,' Lipmann replied. 'Thought is not your forté, Terry. Your forté is brawn. If I wanted to employ thought, I would have employed Stephen fucking Hawking.'

Terry flexed his arms and moved towards Peter. With that overt signal, Peter leapt out of his chair. He glanced across at Simon the snapper, who had been standing as still as a lampshade in the corner of the office throughout the interview.

'A photo, Mr Lipmann?' Simon asked. He was still sporting a black eye from an altercation with Jeremiah Lord and all indications suggested he might soon have a matched pair. Terry took hold of his arm and pointed him towards the door.

Lipmann removed the cigar from his mouth and stubbed it out on the desk. 'You Paddies really are stupid,' he smiled. 'I don't do snaps. Didn't anyone tell you that? I could have Terry insert the lens into your photographer's arsehole and he can take a snap of his own fucking colon. They'll be the only photos you'll get today, my son. Now, fuck off.'

23

Peter found himself in the Savoy again. He had arranged to meet Ruby at the American Bar, but he couldn't help thinking of Nick Georgiou as he walked through the foyer. Elise wasn't half as tough as she talked, and, along with Devrille's twenty-thousand pounds, she had settled quickly with the *Morning Courier* for an undisclosed sum.

The *Gazer* had led with the story and her revelations had caused an almighty furore, but it was hardly enough to bring down the *Morning Courier*. All it had done was knock it around for a few days and require Morton to answer some embarrassing questions at the Press Council. *The Press Council—what a joke.* Peter realised all too soon that the Press Council was a toothless tiger, and Morton would survive intact. *Well, at least they'll think twice before sending anyone else in undercover. Look out* London Morning Courier, *the* Geezer's *balls are finally descending.*

It had been too long since the visit to Manzanoni's country estate. Too long without Ruby. In many ways, it was convenient for Peter that Ruby had a busy work schedule, in that he didn't have to maintain his thriller-writer persona around the clock.

He hated lying to her. *I've got to go to Berlin for a few days to research the files of the former East German secret police. I'll meet you at the American Bar when I get back.*

The lies sometimes came out so effortlessly, that it scared him. Was he morphing into his alter ego? He wondered if Ian Fleming really had a hankering to be James Bond. Or perhaps he already was. He too might become Peter Clancy, thriller writer, in time. *I hate doing it, really I do. Of all the people I've lied to over my lifetime, it's dear, sweet Ruby I hate lying to the most.*

He thought about coming clean with Ruby, before it blew out of all proportion. Would she still want to date a low-life journalist from the *Star Gazer*? *Okay, I'll forget that for a while.*

Ruby was sitting at a corner table at the back of the room, far enough away from the piano man who was playing 'Piano Man'. Peter smiled the instant he saw her; looking at Ruby was like feeling sunshine on one's skin. He gestured as he approached, but Ruby only gave a cursory wave in return. She wasn't smiling. *She's found out who I am. Already?* A second glance. He realised why she was looking solemn: Olivia Michaels was sitting next to Ruby, knocking back a cocktail as if she had just crossed the Sahara. In summer. On foot. She looked like she hadn't slept for days. If Ruby was sunshine on a beach, Olivia Michaels was a junkie's shooting gallery in the pitch dark.

'Hello, gorgeous. I missed you.' Peter had eyes only for Ruby. She looked up and smiled, her brow crinkled as if she was staring into the sun. Then she rose from her chair and kissed him. Her lips lingered, gripped by her lipstick to his, and he felt a tug as she pulled away. 'I'll have to stay away longer, just so I can come home again.'

'How was Berlin?' she asked. 'God, I missed you.'

'Amazing. I got some great material. We have to go there together next time.'

Ruby's eyes flitted across to the third wheel. 'You remember Olivia?'

Olivia seemed oblivious to everything around her. The only thing that had captured and held her attention was her cocktail. She fiddled with the straw for a moment, tossed it onto the table and drained the coupe.

'Of course. From the launch party.'

By this time, Olivia was collecting the dregs with her tongue as she gazed at Peter. Eyes barely focused, she seemed to think the gesture was provocative. Peter found it embarrassing.

'I don't remember you.' She turned the empty cocktail glass upside down. 'I should remember. I usually remember cute guys.'

'His name is Peter,' said Ruby, 'and he's off-limits.'

'Last time we met, you were singing one of your original compositions.' As agonising as the performance had been, he found the memory amusing.

'Hmm,' she replied nonchalantly. 'I'm so talented, I'm so famous, so why can't I get a fucking cocktail when I want one?' She stood up and waved manically at a nearby waiter.

'Keep it down, Livvie,' Ruby chastised. 'If you're going to put on a performance, we're walking.'

The waiter took Olivia's order, and one for a martini for Ruby, while Peter chose a straight scotch. He was going to need it.

'An honour to see you here again, Miss Michaels.'

'Good for you,' she replied brusquely. 'So while you talk at me, I get thirstier.'

'Sorry, Miss Michaels.' The waiter scurried away.

'How's the movie?' Peter was filling silence.

'I shouldn't ask if I were you,' cautioned Ruby.

'He can ask,' said Olivia. 'You can tell him, if you like. I'm too upset.' She reached into her handbag and retrieved a pack of cigarettes. She pulled out one and lit it. Peter noticed her hands shaking.

'She got dropped from the movie today. It won't be announced until tomorrow.'

'I can see the headline already.' Olivia took a drag. '"Olivia Michaels was suffering from nervous exhaustion and was released from the movie, after concerns were raised about her health." If you were a reporter, you'd be first with the news.'

Peter felt like explaining the difference between a headline and a grab, but he risked blowing his cover. *Is there a phone?* He quickly glanced around the bar. *Tempting. Yes, I'm definitely ringing it through later.* 'That's…that's unfortunate.'

'She rang me for support.' Ruby frowned. 'Manz was busy with the show. She couldn't get hold of him.'

'You don't make many friends in this business, but Ruby and Uncle Richard, well… What can you say? I'd toast you, if I only had something to toast you with.' She threw a gaunt arm around Ruby. 'The worthless pricks said I couldn't remember my lines. They said I had to be fed my lines and I still fucked it up. What an insult. If they had written something worth remembering, I'd...' Olivia lost her train of thought. She was ogling Peter. 'I bet that a man like you'd make me forget everything I ever knew. I can see why you've all over him, Ruby. He's gorgeous. Shagging delicious.'

'Uh-uh. He's not yours,' Ruby replied frostily as she snuggled closer to Peter, throwing a protective arm around him. Peter couldn't remember the last time someone had fought over him. 'You know, Livvie, you're so inappropriate sometimes,' she snapped. 'Tell Peter what you want to do.'

The waiter returned with their drinks. Olivia picked up her cocktail first and took a gulp before Ruby and Peter had even reached over to get theirs.

'Ruby sang your praises. She said you ghost-write books about celebrities.' Olivia took a final drag on her cigarette and stubbed it out.

Peter had a large mouthful of scotch. 'I did in Australia.'

'Now that I'm, as you might say,' Olivia paused, 'between jobs. I'm thinking of embarking on a project. Of my own.'

'Lou will get you a job. You know he's the best manager in the business,' said Ruby.

'I need a break. I've been acting forever. I need a bloody break. All I get now are shitty roles in movies that bomb. He says it's getting harder to get me good roles. I have to change my attitude, he says. Go back to rehab. Lard-arse Lou can fuck himself. He probably thinks I'll be dead soon, anyway. Then he'll really be able to cash in. Being dead is a good career move, I hear.'

'Don't be stupid, stop talking like that. You just need to get healthy,' Ruby replied. 'Get yourself clean, focus. Speaking of getting clean, where's Ting?'

'The silly woman was helping herself rather than helping me, you might say. I had to put her in rehab. She...overindulged the other night. She's meant to be my minder but I could handle myself better.'

'Maybe you should join her.'

'Really. I keep a grip on my habits… Ting's a fucking zombie. She sits around all day with dribble running out of her mouth. I shouldn't have put her in there. I think I'll get her out tomorrow. Besides, I'm all at sea without her.' Olivia shook her head. 'No rehab for me.'

'It's your life, Livvie. I'm only trying to prolong it.'

'Olivia Michaels' life, I hope, will be short and sweet and full of treats. There's a song in that.'

Peter chose to cut in. 'Am I right in thinking you want me to help you write a book?'

'Help me? No,' she replied. 'I want you to write the whole fucking book for me. It's what you do, isn't it?'

Act nonchalant and uncommitted. 'I'm afraid I can't help you, Olivia. Ruby will tell you, the book I'm currently writing is consuming all of my time.'

'I'll make it worth your while.'

'How's that?' he asked.

'I'll share the money with you. How about you get twenty per cent of my royalties?'

Peter nearly choked on his scotch. 'That's…' He was about to say *unbelievably generous of you.*

'All right. Thirty per cent.'

'But any publisher you approach will want to bring their own writers on board.'

'And I'll walk away.'

'But why me? You don't even know me. You couldn't even remember who I was a minute ago.'

'You never met a celebrity with an agenda before? How long have you been at this caper? I don't tell everyone everything all the time—that's for my book.' She softened. 'Besides, I like you. Ruby says you're a good writer. Amongst your other talents. Now, I'll be interviewing publishers as soon as it's written. They'll be falling over themselves, for certain.'

'Is Lou behind all this?' Ruby asked.

'It's my project. I'm doing this myself.'

'You don't do anything by yourself. I can't ever remember you doing anything yourself. Lou does everything.'

'A biography about my life would be a great first step for me, don't you think?'

'Autobiography,' Peter added.

'Whatever. This could be therapeutic. But nothing too filthy, mind. I'm a star. I have an image to maintain.'

'It's going to be a very short book then,' Ruby laughed.

'Be serious. I want it to be tasteful. From a humble beginning to a world star, just like Liz Taylor.' Olivia cradled her face with her hands, as if it were an illuminated globe. She pulled out another cigarette and lit it, her hands still shaking.

'He's going to be really angry, Livvie. You have a contract with him.'

'Currently up for renewal, but I'm not renewing. I'm done. It's time to move on.'

'Lou will go bloody ballistic. And then he'll have a stroke. Are you sure you want to do this?'

'I've been under his thumb all my life. He's always told me what to do, what to say, what to sign. Endless control. What to eat, what not to eat and who to see, even. No wonder I'm a mess. I'm sick of it. I want to be free of him. I want to manage myself.' Olivia stabbed out her cigarette several times in the ashtray.

'Manage yourself?'

'Not really,' Olivia corrected. 'Ting can be my new manager.'

'Ting,' Ruby laughed. 'She's in rehab, remember, for substance addiction. How is she going to manage you from there?'

'That's just a one-off. She has a Master's degree in business. I trust her. She's very savvy. Ting just needs to cut back on her habit.'

'I think it's unwise.'

'I want to stand on my own two feet like you have. I need to be free,' Olivia started to cry.

'I guess I could help you,' Peter ventured. 'I could arrange to have some spare time on my hands. Your royalty split's fair.'

'I'm raring to go,' Olivia said. 'We could start tomorrow.'

'Well, I'll need to finish off some things first. I'm a writer, not a journalist, so I can't take shorthand,' he lied. 'I'll need to tape all of our interviews. For the book.'

'Fine. I'll get Ting to arrange a contract. When can you start?'

'Two days?'

'Right. It's arranged.'

Ruby grabbed her handbag. 'Can we go now?'

'Let's seal it with a celebratory drink. There'll be plenty of time for you two to shag each other stupid after,' Olivia said.

'Just one, then, Livvie.'

'Waiter,' Olivia yelled. 'Moet. Three glasses, quickly. Pronto. Presto. Whatever.'

Ruby frowned at her and put down her handbag.

24

Peter narrowed the flow of the shower head until the water felt like needles against his skin. He needed to flush out the last remnants of sleep; it was going to be a big day. He widened the flow again and turned the pressure up and let the water pound his head. Unlike in Hammersmith, there was no-one to disturb him here, no-one knocking on the door, reminding him that he'd already used up his allocated bath time and that he needed to get out. How he missed having his own, private bathroom, in his own flat.

Warwick Gardens, Kensington, was definitely an address to crow over. Ruby's flat was luxurious in a minimalist, Scandinavian way. It contrasted starkly with her bedroom at the manor and her boho-chic aesthetic: they were two sides of the same coin. Everything here was utilitarian. Everything was scrubbed clean. He doubted that Ruby was responsible for it. He was mulling it over when Ruby slid around the glass partition.

'Mind if we share?' she asked. 'I'm going to be awfully late for work.'

'Be my guest.' He watched the water slide off her shoulders and into the gully between her breasts. Her skin was perfect, unblemished, burnished by summer. He could feel himself getting aroused. He took the soap from Ruby's hand and washed her breasts, paying particular attention to her dark brown nipples. Then he moved down to her groin, soaping the neat triangle of fur until she groaned with pleasure.

'Fuck me,' she sighed, pressing up hard against him.

'Won't you be late…' he breathed. Before he could finish the sentence, she was crouched down. She had him in her mouth, tongue probing him; the pressure from her lips was exhilarating. He stood her up and balanced her on his thighs. In a moment, they were moving in unison, her arms splayed against the tiles, faster and faster.

Later, they sat on adjoining stools in her kitchen, wrapped in matching towelling robes, drinking coffee she had made in her own espresso machine. *Paradise. What a perfect start to a perfect day. Perfect Ruby, perfect sex, perfect coffee.* The white towel made her skin appear even more fragile, beautiful and translucent. 'You're extraordinary,' he said, 'but I need to distract myself.' He took another sip of coffee. 'So, I guess it's an opportunity for you to tell me all you know about Olivia. If you have the time, that is.'

'You'll get me into strife with the boss. Worried that I'll have to give myself a warning for being late?'

Peter laughed. He could spend the rest of his life exactly like this.

'I hope I haven't put you in it,' she said.

'With Olivia? No, it's fine. It'll be fine as long as I can keep her focused.'

'I've sort of thrown you into it, but I thought you'd do a good job. You'd be sympathetic. Olivia lives her life in the open: it's a matter of time before an unauthorised biography comes out and it won't be pretty.'

'It's fine. If I can make a few quid out of it I'll be able to spend more money on you.'

'She always rings Manz first when she's in trouble. Then Lou gets involved. Manz becomes the go-between. I can see why he might be disappointed with her at the moment. He did help get her that part.'

Peter assumed his best poker-face. 'Is that so?'

'He's done so much for her, but he just can't keep bailing her out. When she rang me, I thought, she just needs a shoulder to cry on. The book was news to me too. I'm sorry I dropped you in it. Do you really want to do this?'

'I've agreed.'

'You're so very decent,' she replied. She leaned over and gave him a kiss.

'Is she really your friend?' he asked. 'I get the feeling she annoys the shit out of you.'

'It's complicated,' she began slowly. 'She was a bit like an older sister, I guess. We were close once, but then our paths diverged. We crash into each other occasionally. We have a different attitude about life. I have to admit, I feel a little sorry for her. She hasn't had it easy.'

'Pity is no basis for a friendship.'

'I guess it's more complicated than just friendship. If my father is Uncle Richard then I guess I must be Cousin Ruby.'

'Where are her parents?'

'Father disappeared before she was born. As far as I know, she hasn't talked to her mother since she had to take her to court when she was a child.'

'Why's that?'

'Her mother was apparently spending all of Livvie's money, so she took her to court and won. Lou became her legal guardian and has managed her career ever since.'

'I don't really have to interview Olivia Michaels,' he said, 'when I can get the information from you.'

'I can only give you the background,' she sighed. 'Livvie never talks about her personal life. Maybe she'll open up to you. She'll have to if she wants you to do this book.'

'So, how did she know your father again?'

'I feel like I'm the one being interrogated. Okay,' Ruby said, 'this is my last answer. Lou was Manz's manager when he was in his band. That's it. No more questions. I'm hungry. I'm making lentil burgers for breakfast.'

'For breakfast? The only vegetables I eat are potato chips.'

'Then I'm widening your horizons. No animals were harmed, bothered or touched in any way whatsoever in producing my food, and that makes me happy.'

Ruby crossed to the refrigerator. A photograph in a silver frame on the far wall caught Peter's eye. 'Is that your mother and you?'

'It is. I thought you weren't asking any more questions,' she called out.

'Sorry.'

She slid the patties into an oiled pan and started frying. The scent that wafted across was unlike anything he had smelled before. He told himself that he had better get used to it. *What I wouldn't do for sausages and eggs right about now.* He drank in the aroma once more.

Dear God, I hope that's not the smell of Paradise Lost.

25

'From now on, I'm either calling you glycerin suppository or KY gel,' Devrille laughed as he spun in his chair.

'Why's that?' Peter grimaced. 'I'm a pain the arse?'

'No. You appear to have inserted yourself into the celebrity world with incredible ease.'

'I have the knack I guess,' he replied, working himself back into his chair.

'I've never seen it happen in my journalistic career.' Devrille shook his head. 'One minute you're shagging Ruby Manzanoni, next you've been asked by Olivia Michaels to write her biography. I can't keep up. You're not doing her as well?'

'Not my type. But you know I won't be able to get away with this forever.'

'The time being suits me just fine. We're not here to make friends. In the end, the story is all that counts.' Devrille paused to take a sip of coffee. 'I don't want you to get ahead of yourself, but your recent activity has coincided with an increase in our circulation. Just imagine what it could do for your career. You'll be able to write a book about it one day.'

'Talking of books, should I actually write this book on Olivia Michaels?'

'Of course you bloody should. Are you crazy? Olivia Michaels has taken every drug that's known to humanity and slept with more men than Liberace. It'll be a knock-out!'

'It's going to be complicated.'

'How did you tee it up with Lou Lipmann? I didn't think he'd agree to it.'

'I didn't. She's not renewing her contract with Lou. She wants to do this book on her own.'

'Lou's not going to like that. He'll try to bully her into re-signing.'

Peter frowned. 'That thought's occurred to me too.'

'Does she have a publisher yet?'

'She's looking. She has a new manager called Ting. Promoted from personal assistant. I've heard that Ting's doing a stint in rehab at the moment.'

Devrille laughed until tears rolled down his cheeks. 'A drug-fucked manager could really work for us. What I wouldn't give to be a fly on Lipmann's wall! You know, JB, this could all work to our benefit.'

'Of course, if she manages to get a publisher we'd have to negotiate a deal to get the serial rights.'

'I shouldn't worry about that. When Lou finds out, we can count on him to do the ring around and scare the shit out of them. That's how the bastard operates.'

'So no publisher. That'll definitely work in our favour.'

'This is how it will play out,' Devrille began. 'You keep the tapes of the interviews with you. You must stipulate that the tapes remain in your possession.'

'Unorthodox but all right.'

'You'll write the manuscript as you go.'

'For sure. I want to get this out of the way as quickly as possible.'

'Just stroke her fucking ego all the time. Stroke her pussy too, if you have to. And the other thing…' Devrille leaned forward. 'Lou Lipmann… Try to stay away from that old bastard. He likes to hang people out of windows for fun.'

'I won't be doing any interviews at her house then, since he knows where she lives.'

'Good. Take her to a hotel room or somewhere.'

'I'm going to need Snoddy to do some background work for me.'

'That's what she's good at. What would you like her to do?'

'I'd like to know a bit more about Richard Manzanoni. All I know is that Lou managed his old band and that Olivia was in his musical. She doesn't appear to have any connection with her family but she still calls Uncle Richard for advice.'

'I remember there was a court case ages ago. Olivia versus her mother. Something about mum stealing all her money.'

'So I heard. Lou became her legal guardian as a result,' Peter added. 'I reckon it would be great for the *Gazer* if we could find Olivia's mother. The public would love that.'

'Olivia might not want you to find her mother. That's if she's still alive.'

'What? Have you heard something?' He paused to search Devrille's face. 'I was hoping the book might be more human interest than star anecdotes.'

'Fact is, JB, star anecdotes sell more papers.'

Peter caught Devrille smiling under his moustache and thought of Nick's nickname for him. The Dark Lord. It seemed appropriate. *Lack of horns aside, he looks like the fucking devil.* Then he thought of Ruby. *She's my redemption. She's all sweetness and light. I'll do everything I can to protect her.* Olivia Michaels, on the other hand, was fair game. He was providing a legitimate service while exposing her to some much-needed publicity. *That's all. No need for any conscience-pangs.* And then he thought of the bargain he had just made.

26

Peter stepped into the red phone box in front of the office, armed with a piece of paper and a bag of loose change. He checked his wrist watch; it was two o'clock in the afternoon, London time. By his calculations, that meant it was nine o'clock in the morning in Washington DC. He unfolded the scrappy piece of paper on which he had listed all of the major American newspapers. There was a full page of them. Over the last few months, most had been ticked off. There was only one left: *The Washington Post*.

He had left the illustrious paper until last because Stella had told him once that she would rather work for the Biloxi *Sun Herald* because she had once clashed with the *Post's* editor. *Well, Stella, I've already contacted Biloxi and you're not working there. I've rung them all. From north to south, east to west, and wasted a pile of change in between.*

Could Stella have left the industry altogether? Bob's death might have been too much for her. *She could be running a cattle ranch in Montana? Very much doubt it. She hated the country. Doubt if she's ever seen it. She was too New York. Running a coffee shop in Greenwich Village? Doubt that too. She'd argue with the customers. Writing a best-seller in Martha's Vineyard? Possibly, but she'd probably get bored to death pounding away every day on the typewriter.* Just like Peter, she wasn't wired to do anything else. No, he and Stella had so much newsprint running through their veins that it was probably causing them arteriosclerosis. What else would they do? Who else would employ them, to be more accurate?

Peter dialled the number for *The Washington Post* and waited. It was the direct number to the newsroom. The phone rang for an eternity. *Typical news desk. No-one wants to pick up a bloody phone.*

'Bob Woodward. What do you want?'

Peter nearly dropped the phone.

Should I be starstruck? Carl Bernstein. Bob Woodward. The Water-gate scandal. I'm talking to one of my all-time heroes. At least, sort of.

'Err...' Peter fumbled for words. 'Stella Reimers? Is Stella Reimers there?'

'Who are you?' Woodward asked.

'Peter Clancy. Sorry to trouble you. I'm an old colleague from Australia, Mr Woodward.' Peter was a hopeless schoolboy.

'Stella...' Woodward said vaguely. 'I'm not sure...'

Peter dejectedly slipped a pile of coins into the phone slot. *Another waste of time.* He was about to hang up.

'Yeah, Stella. She's only just started here. She's at her desk. I'll transfer you.'

'Thank you, Mist...' The call went on hold. Peter was giddy. *I've spoken to Bob Woodward. I've spoken to Bob Woodward.*

'Stella Reimers here. Who's this?'

Again, he nearly dropped the phone. 'Long time, no hear. It's Peter. Peter Clancy. From Melbourne. I've been looking for you in every bloody paper in America. I'd just about given up.'

'I've been looking for you too, you sonofabitch,' Stella laughed. 'It's so good to hear from you. I rang *The Truth* one day and they said you were in London, but they didn't know where you were working. Bill Symes told me you cracked open that story in Melbourne. Congratulations. You nearly got yourself killed, I heard. Are you in London at the moment?'

'I'm in London working for a tabloid. Yeah, that story nearly killed me in lots of ways... But I couldn't have cracked it without your help, Stella. I wish you could have been there to share the glory.'

'Well, you know why I left,' she said sadly, 'but we have to keep going, don't we? Bob wouldn't have wanted it any other way. Now I'm at *The Washington Post*. That makes me a little happier.'

'Who would have thought you'd be working there after all you've said about it?'

'We all change, especially when they throw a lot of cash at you. I really love you now, Katherine. Love, love, love her.'

'Any jobs there for a hack like me?'

'I could ask if you like.'

'It's okay, I'll let you know when and if I need a change.'

'So, where are you working?'

'The *Star Gazer*.' Peter cringed.

'Sounds classy,' Stella chuckled. 'London's version of *The Melbourne Truth*?'

'You guessed it.'

'Call me psychic, but I get the feeling you didn't call me to chew the fat. You want something, don't you?'

'Sadly, you've pegged me right. I wanted to know if you were okay.'

'Really? That's all? I'm not only okay but I'm happy.' There was lightness in her voice. 'I'm glad you found me.'

'That's not exactly the only reason I rang. I also need a reference. That prick Bill Symes wouldn't give me one.'

'I can write you a reference. Now, is that all?'

'Not really.' The phone meter started to flash that it was running low. He scooped a handful of coins and topped it up. 'I don't know what to do, Stella. I don't know if I should keep working for this paper.'

'What's going on there?'

'The eternal dilemma. What are you prepared to do to get a story? How far is too far? At what point do you wake up and find the Devrille's got your soul?'

'How far will you go for a story? We've all been there; don't ask me. Would my opinion make any difference? It's your decision in the end. How good is this story you're working on, this story that's compromising your eternal peace?'

'I don't know yet. It's not really a story. Just gossip stuff. I'm kind of undercover in the celebrity world. If I dig deeper, I'm hoping I may find something. Listening in on gossip is a drag, but I'm hoping there could be more.'

'Just don't get into something you can't get out of. You're a world-class troublemaker.'

'I know. I just want something big to happen. I'm going crazy thinking about it.'

'You'll work it out. And your love life?'

'I've met someone, but it's complicated.'

'Of course it is.' Stella sighed loudly. 'If I was there, I would slap you. I'm not, so all I can do is tell you to be careful.'

He noticed the warning light on the phone and the coin bag was empty. 'I'm running out of change, Stella. Sorry. I'm going to have to go. What's your home number? I'll ring you again.'

'Now that's convenient, Mr Clancy, just when I was going to get mad at you.'

Peter scrawled her number down on the piece of paper as she spoke.

'Feel free to call me anytime, Peter,' she began, 'especially when…'

The phone went dead.

27

Peter arrived at Olivia's apartment in Bloomsbury at eight in the morning. When the door was finally opened, it was Olivia who opened it. She stood unsteadily in the doorway, dressed in a stained t-shirt and sweat pants, a cigarette hanging from her mouth. She looked like shit. Her hair looked like it had been sucked by a vacuum cleaner.

'Shit, is that the time?' she slurred, rubbing her eyes.

'Big party last night?' he asked as he stepped through the front door.

'Follow me.'

He tagged along behind her to a sitting room. All of the furniture looked like it had been tossed about, and a large mirror hanging over the mantelpiece was smashed.

'Where are all the empties?' Peter righted a chair to sit on.

'It wasn't a fucking party.'

Olivia fell into the chair that Peter had allocated for himself. He pushed the sofa over, replaced the cushions and sat down. A moment later, he felt something cold touch his throat. From behind him he heard, 'If you're from Lou's, you can get out. She doesn't want him anymore. I'm her manager now, you tell him that.' Ting pushed the blade closer and the tape recorder slipped from his grasp.

'Stop it, Ting,' garbled Olivia. 'He's not from Lou. He's just my writer.'

'Don't you fucking believe it.'

I'm going to be diced up by a crazy Ninja bitch.

'He's all right,' Olivia cried. 'He's the man writing my book.'

The blade fell from Ting's hand. Peter picked it up. 'I see. I apologise. I thought you…'

'No, I'm not,' he said. 'What's this about Lou Lipmann?'

'His boys came around last night, when I was away,' Ting began. She reached down and handed Peter his tape recorder.

'Is this about the contract?' Peter asked as he checked to see if the recorder was still working. Thankfully it was. 'Or the book?'

'This is why no-one leaves Lou,' Ting said. 'He doesn't know about any book. Nobody is brave enough to leave him. He gets rid of you, not the other way around. Prick.' She took her knife from Peter and tucked the blade back into the handle. 'Do you want smoke, blow or drink?'

'Just a bottle of scotch and a glass will be fine.' *Sobriety is the first casualty of creativity. That, and near death experiences.*

'Okay.' Ting scurried from the room.

'One of his singers was going to leave him a few years ago,' Olivia related, 'but he soon changed his mind after Terry got hold of him. Broke his leg. Had to record his next album seated in a wheelchair.'

'Has all this persuaded you to re-sign?'

Olivia pouted. 'No. I'm not giving in.'

'I admire your bravery.'

'It's not bravery.' She swept back her tousled hair. 'It's about not wanting to live in this fucking zoo any more.'

'You didn't happen to mention your plans about the book to him?'

'Fuck no. He'd have gotten really angry if he found out about the book.' A hint of a smile crossed her lips.

Just then, Ting returned with a tray containing a bottle of Black Label Johnny Walker whisky and three glasses. Peter turned the coffee table over so she could place the tray on it. Peter filled his glass to the brim, then half-filled the other two before he thought to ask them. He took a big gulp of scotch.

'You're not an alcoholic?' said Ting, scrutinising him. 'No good to us if you're drunk all the time.'

'I'm only an alcoholic when I'm stressed.'

'That's funny,' Olivia said dryly. 'No wonder Ruby loves you.'

'Loves me?'

'She's mad about you. Lucky girl.'

Peter felt himself blush. 'Shall we start?'

'I'm here, I guess.'

'As long as you're sure.'

'Switch on the tape recorder and let's go.'

'You're a real trouper,' Peter said. 'I have one suggestion though.'

'What's that?'

'We go to a hotel and do the rest of the interviews there. In case they come back here. We can't take any risks. I suggest you find a safe house.'

'I'm a trouper, all right.' Olivia started to sing in her pitchy, girly voice. 'Things you do to escape the hungry zoo… But there's nothing those poor little animals can do… The zoo is where the hungry get their fill… If the tiger doesn't get you the snake-eye will…' She chuckled and lit a cigarette.

*

Ting drove Olivia's Jag around Kensington like the unlicensed, maniacal, substance-affected driver she actually was. Peter felt it necessary to close his eyes and hang on. Just after she had nearly cleaned up an old lady negotiating a pedestrian crossing, she found a cheap hotel on the Old Brompton Road. Things didn't improve from there.

'Shit,' Olivia cried out in horror as she entered the hotel room first. 'Do people really stay in these places?'

It was just another sparse, ugly, budget hotel room to Peter, not unlike the many that he had crashed in over the years. It was certainly better appointed than his flat in Hammersmith. 'They come here to stay and then they die,' he joked as he set up his tape recorder on the bed. He then sat down beside it.

'Smells like someone died here.' Olivia sniffed. 'Fucking reeks.'

'Don't complain, Livvie. It's cheap,' Ting said, drawing the curtains. 'We have to be careful. Have to stay away from where you usually hang out.'

Olivia took a towel from the bathroom. 'At least this looks clean.' She laid it out on the bed. 'I'll sit on this.'

'That's good.' Peter fiddled with the tape recorder settings, unaware that she was sprawled out beside him.

'Bet you never thought you'd have Olivia Michaels in bed with you?'

Peter looked across and chuckled.

'You behave,' Ting chastised. 'This is business. No sex. And no drugs until you finish.'

'Isn't she cruel?' Olivia purred, sitting up. 'Get me a decent cup of coffee, Ting. And I'd like cigarettes. There's a dear.'

'Okay.' Ting pulled a packet of cigarettes out of her handbag, lit one and handed it to Olivia. 'I'll go get coffee. Don't go anywhere. Don't do anything naughty, okay?'

'Try not to. I promise.'

'Don't!' Ting snapped back as she shook her finger at Olivia.

Peter switched on the tape recorder and began the interview. 'So, Olivia Michaels, shall we begin at the beginning? And spare none of the gory details.'

'Why not?' She blew a perfect circle of smoke and punctured it with her finger. 'I was born in Haggerston in 1962 to Caroline Taylor and some bloke I never met. Is that honest enough for you?'

She leaned back on the towel, relaxing as she went. What she said was nothing new to Peter and it probably wasn't going to be for her audience. Olivia could have been reciting a biography sheet handed out by her agent to the press corps. It continued until Ting had returned with coffee. She rattled it off like she probably had many times before: the sanitised, Hollywood version of her life. After an hour, Peter was starting to get worried. *If there's no dirt, no filth, who's going to want to read her biography? The public want dirt not sugar-coated, Shirley Temple soda. I know them, they want filth.*

He decided to change tack and throw in a shock question. 'Tell me about your mum. The truth. Why did it have to end up in court?'

There was silence: a long painful one. Olivia's eyes flicked around the room and her face turned crimson. He braced for an eruption. 'Who in the fuck told you to ask me about my mother?' She jumped off the bed.

'You've upset her!' Ting weighed in. 'You stupid, stupid man.'

'If it was Ruby,' Olivia continued as she stormed around the room, 'I'll punch her fucking lights out.'

'It wasn't her,' Peter lied. 'I looked up old press clippings. That's all.'

'You've overstepped it, mate,' she growled. She snatched a lit cigarette from Ting and inhaled deeply.

'If you want this book to sell anything more than five hundred copies, you're going to have to get away from the script and tell me the full story. The full story.'

'Five hundred? You sure?' Ting looked anxious. 'But Olivia Michaels is a big star.'

'As sure as the stench from a blocked toilet.' Peter switched off the tape player.

'I won't do it. I can't do it.' Olivia started to hyperventilate. She began to stagger, grabbing Ting by the arm. 'I need help,' she whined. 'I can't breathe. Give me some blow. Now! I need blow.'

Ting took hold of Olivia with one hand, her handbag with the other one and steered her towards the bathroom. Then she slammed the door after them.

'You'll have to face it eventually,' Peter called out.

'Why do I have to tell everyone my secrets? Don't I deserve to have them like everyone else?' she yelled from inside the bathroom.

'Your choice. You wanted to spill the beans, remember?'

'But it has to be done my way.'

'I can't do this. This is a waste of my time. I'm out of here.' Peter slid off the bed and walked out of the room.

He wandered along Old Brompton Road and had just passed Freddie Mercury's favourite drinking hole, when he noticed what he had been looking for: the West Brompton tube sign. *Relief for the moment. At least I don't have to deal with Olivia anymore. But how am I going to break it to Devrille? There'll be another volcanic eruption.* He was so engrossed in thought that he didn't notice a Rolls Royce Silver Spirit pull up at the kerb next to him. The front passenger door flew open and a bald-headed West Indian man the size of Annapurna leapt out, blocking out the light.

28

'The guv wants to talk to you,' he said, the words resonating as if they had been delivered in a cavern. He deliberately folded his arms across his barrel chest. For a moment, Peter thought the man was Lennox Lewis. Except bigger.

'No thanks. I think you may have the wrong person. I don't need a lift. Nice car though,' Peter replied. Before he could move around the man, he was grabbed by his coat lapels and flung through the open rear door onto the floor of the Roller. The West Indian man hopped in after him and slammed the door. Then he gave a signal to the driver and the Rolls Royce slowly pulled away from the kerb.

Peter was enveloped by a cloud of cigar smoke, making it impossible to see. He knew exactly who it was. He was flung onto a leather seat and found himself squeezed in tightly between the muscle man and Lou Lipmann.

Please don't dangle me from a bridge, Mr Lipmann.

'You may not yet be knowledgeable enough to have made my acquaintance, my friend,' Lou said quietly and deliberately. He sucked on the cigar and blew the smoke in Peter's face. Peter coughed. Through the haze, he could see that Terry was driving the Roller.

'Sorry? I don't seem to be able to place you,' Peter lied.

'Lou Lipmann, manager for the most glittering stars in Britain's firmament. Including Olivia Michaels. Word is that you know her.'

'We've been introduced.'

Lipmann stopped talking to Peter and reached forward. 'Step on it, Terry, we're not in a bloody funeral procession.'

'Yes guv'nor,' Terry replied as he pushed down the accelerator.

'I was just walking along the street...'

'Did I ask you to talk?' Lipmann slapped Peter's face with an open hand. His only reaction was to grimace. He wasn't going to give Lipmann any pleasure by crying out.

'Do you want me to do that for you, Mr Lipmann?'

If I'm going to be slapped, let Lou do it. If toughie does it, I won't have a head, let alone a face.

'No thank you, Malcolm.' Lipmann smiled. 'We're only having a friendly chat at the moment.'

'I'd love to stay and chat, as you say, but I'm not a big talker. If it's all right with you, I'll go now.'

'You look strangely familiar,' Lipmann said as he stared at Peter between puffs on his cigar.

'No, nup. I've never seen you before in my life.'

'I don't usually forget a face, a debt or an insult,' said Lipmann, continuing to stare. 'It'll come to me... I have heard from my sources that you're the writer what has conned my Livvie into writing a book about her life. I don't yet know the basis of your influence on my girl, but I would be most unhappy if I were ever to learn that you had something to do with her dumping me as her manager. I'm deeply hurt by your actions, Mr Clancy.'

'How do you know who I am?'

'I know everything about my stars. That's my fucking job.'

'I never conned her into anything. She asked me.'

'Don't you be telling me porky pies, now.' Lipmann slapped Peter's face again. 'I need you to be forthcoming with the truth.'

'I've told you. She asked me.' Peter winced. His face felt as if it had been stung by a swarm of wasps.

'How much did she tell you?' Lipmann asked, looking at the tape recorder that Peter was resting on his lap.

'I've only done one interview. She just talked about her career. Movies she'd been in. Nothing too interesting.'

'Give me the tape recorder.' Lipmann held out his hand.

'I can't do that.'

'If you ever want to walk again you will.'

Peter slowly handed it over. Lipmann ejected the cassette, pulled out the tape and then snapped it. Lowering his window, he flung the broken cassette out into the street.

'Doesn't look like there'll be any more interviews, will there?' Lipmann smiled.

'Doesn't look like it.'

'I would suggest you return to Australia where you belong. Go fuck some sheep and don't ever bother trying to write another book on my Livvie. Get it?'

'I'll try writing poetry. No-one will get upset then.'

'That's the way, my son,' Lipmann replied as he patted Peter's face. 'Not so dumb after all, are we?'

'Is that all?' asked Peter. *Please God, let that be all he wants.* His bladder was rapidly weakening, but he wasn't about to let Lipmann know it.

'One more question. My Livvie's at that hotel you came out of, isn't she?'

'Possibly.'

'Got Alzheimer's have we? It seems you need some help remembering.' Lipmann nodded at Malcolm, who wrapped a beefy hand around Peter's throat and squeezed. Hard.

Peter soon felt his throat being crushed and all air being removed from his lungs. *I'll be unconscious and dead within minutes. Shit no. I'm not going to die to protect Olivia Michaels.* 'Probably,' Peter gurgled with his last breath.

Lipmann nodded again and Malcolm released his grip. 'See, now that wasn't very hard, was it? Very easy when you don't lie.'

Peter gasped and coughed. He raised his hand to check if he still had a larynx. 'Can I go now?' he asked hoarsely. 'I'm only the writer.'

'I think we're finished chatting for the moment.' Lipmann sniggered. 'We'll let you out at the next corner… Terry give it some gas.'

'Would you mind slowing down?' The Rolls was rapidly approaching the corner.

'You having Alzheimer's and all, in time, you may forget our little chat and that wouldn't be good. This is just a little reminder,

in case you decide to change your mind at some future date...
Cheerio.'

The Rolls Royce accelerated again as it took the turn. Malcolm flung open the door, grabbed Peter by the coat lapels again, and tossed him like a piece of broken luggage out of the door. Peter felt his body hitting the footpath and then rolling. Excruciating pain and then silence.

29

At first, Peter thought he heard a motor bike or possibly a car whizzing past. He tried to open his eyes, but he couldn't manage it. Was he lying on a street? He discerned the sound of beeping and incessant chattering—lots of chattering. He was surrounded by a crowd of men and women. They all sounded foreign.

'Shut the fuck up,' he whispered. 'Can't you see that I'm trying to sleep?' Was he in India? He'd never been to India. *How the fuck did I get here? Have I died and gone to India?*

Then a pinpoint light shone in his eyes. He tried to block it out by squeezing his eyelids together tightly. The babble grew louder and more urgent. A familiar voice rose above the others. He prised his eyes open. He only just made out a vaporous outline standing over him. It was Ruby. She seemed to be floating in the clouds.

'You're finally awake,' she said happily. She descended from on high to kiss him. He forced his eyes wider. She was standing next to an Indian woman with a stethoscope around her neck, and a turbaned man with a stethoscope around his. All three were looking at him. It was then that he realised he was lying on a hospital bed. He tried to grab hold of the rails and sit up, but he had no strength in his hands. His grip slipped from the rails and he fell back.

'Just relax,' Ruby said reassuringly. 'You're in good hands. The doctors here will make you better.'

'Can you tell me your name please?' asked the woman.

Peter searched his brain for a moment. 'Peter Clancy.' His response sounded more like a question than a statement.

'Do you know what day it is today, Mr Clancy?'

'I'm not too sure. Is it my birthday?'

Ruby giggled.

'No, Mr Clancy,' the man replied dryly. 'It's Thursday. You're in the Royal Brompton Hospital. You were brought here after your accident.'

'Hospital?' Peter repeated softly. His throat hurt. Then his back, head and ribcage joined the party. 'Everything aches,' he groaned.

'We will give you something for that shortly.' The woman was scribbling on a clipboard.

'Do you know how you had your accident?' the man asked.

'Accident?'

'You were seen falling out of a Rolls Royce on the Old Brompton Road,' Ruby interrupted.

'Me?' Peter thought as hard as his aching head would allow. Gradually it was coming back, but this time he was watching the action, rather than participating in it. 'I remember being in a car talking to someone. Then a door opened and I was falling. That's it.'

'You're not intoxicated. We checked that. Might you have been thrown out, perhaps?'

'I don't know. I don't think so,' Peter replied. 'Maybe I didn't understand that they weren't going to slow down when I got out.'

'Well, the police will want to interview you after you've had your CT scan.'

'CT scan?'

'We have to rule out a head injury.'

'Do you remember who you were in the car with?' the woman asked.

'Not at the moment.'

'Can you excuse me, I need to make a phone call,' Ruby interrupted. 'Be back soon, darling.' She opened the curtains surrounding the trolley and was gone. Peter listened to her high heels clatter along the tiled floor.

'Well. Here is the plan, Mr Clancy,' the male doctor began. 'You have been very lucky. You have no fractures, mainly soft tissue injury only. You will be in some pain for which we will give you pain relief. After the CT scan, we will keep you in overnight just for observation.'

'In hospital?'

'As a precaution.'

'I'm not big on hospitals.'

'Well, you could have been somewhere else if you had fallen directly on your head. You're a lucky man,' he added.

'So you keep telling me.' He grimaced as the pain in his ribs increased. 'I don't bloody feel like I am.'

As soon as Peter was settled into a hospital private room, the police interviewed him. He reiterated that he couldn't remember who he was in the car with. Never mind, they said, it might come back to him later. Ruby remained by his side, plumping up his pillows and looking concerned whenever he moaned as he tried to find a position that didn't hurt.

'I wanted to tell you something,' he said, sipping from the glass of water she was holding for him.

'You need to rest,' she replied. 'We can talk later.'

'No. I have to tell you now.'

'All right.' Ruby replaced the glass on the bedside table.

'Firstly, I'm really grateful for your concern. I can't thank you enough.'

'Hasn't anyone ever been concerned for you before?'

'No, not really...but that's possibly my fault,' he replied. 'Just never wanted to attach myself to anyone.'

'And?'

'I love you, Ruby Red Lips.' He held out his hand and stroked her face. 'I really do... If you want to run away, I'd understand. I'm complex and I don't lead a quiet life. I might cause you trouble.'

She smiled. 'But I've already told you that I love you.'

'So, I'm not the first to say it?'

'I told you when you were lying unconscious in the emergency room.'

'If I haven't heard it, does it count?'

She laughed. 'Well, since you missed it, I'm going to have to repeat myself. I love you.' She kissed him. 'Even if you are a heap of trouble.'

'I know who threw me out of the car, by the way.'

'I do too,' she sighed.

'What I can't work out is how Lipmann found out about the book and, more particularly, about me.'

'Olivia's a very leaky ship. Apparently, she did a star turn on the set just before she stormed off. No names were mentioned then, but I think she may have told Sir Clifford.'

'I'm not going to tell the police anything. I don't want Lou's goon squad coming back and doing anything worse to me.'

'I don't know how he's still in business.'

'Everyone's too frightened to cross him. Did you speak to your father?'

'Just before, when I left the room. He said I should stay out of it. It's between Lou and Olivia. He said that she can sort out her own mess. He's done with her. Also…' She paused to clear her throat.

'Also?'

'He said I should stay away from you.'

'I can understand why. I don't want to cause a rift between your father and you.'

'I care about my father but I care more about you. I respect my father but I love you.'

'Well, there won't be any Olivia Michaels biography. So I don't have to worry about Lou or Olivia causing me any more trouble.'

'Good. We can get on with our lives. You concentrate on your book. Olivia can go to hell.' She kissed Peter again. He tried to hide the pain her kisses were causing him. 'You rest.' She grabbed her handbag. 'I'm going to get a cup of coffee.'

'I'll wait anxiously for your return.' He had just closed his eyes when the phone on the bedside table rang. With a lot of discomfort, he managed to reach the receiver. He knew who it was going to be even before a single word was exchanged. 'Hello, John. I thought you'd ring.' Peter grimaced as he shifted himself into a more comfortable position.

'I heard you were in a coma,' Devrille said matter-of-factly.

'Coma? Only when my head hit the footpath,' Peter replied, pinching himself to check. 'Would I be talking to you if I was?'

'Good. We need you back on this story straight way. Lipmann did this?'

'Sure did.'

'This is going to make an explosive story.'

'There isn't going to be a story.' Peter held the phone away from his ear.

'What do you mean, there isn't going to be a story? There has to be a story.'

From a distance, distorted by the telephone, Devrille's voice sounded like a demented chipmunk's. Peter waited for him to stop. 'Olivia walked out of the interview when I pressed her too hard. She wasn't giving me anything.'

'Well, you bloody well have to get her back,' he said. 'We need her to spill her guts.'

'I tried.'

'Not hard enough, evidently.'

'Nearly ending up in a coma isn't enough for you? Fuck you, fuck the job. I'm not dying to get a story. I'll become a fucking war correspondent if I want to do that,' he snapped.

'You better listen to me, Clancy.' Devrille lowered his voice to a threatening growl. 'Lipmann knows people and so do I. I'll deal with him. I've invested a lot of money in you maintaining your disguise. That means you owe me a huge story on Olivia Michaels. You're thinking right now you can walk away from this and get another job, become a writer, keep your pretty girlfriend but guess again. I'll make some calls. Do you think Ruby will still want to shag you when she finds out you're just another low-life tabloid journo? Think about it. Oh yes, and I'll also sue your arse off.'

The phone went dead. He dropped the receiver over the side of the bed and lay his head back on the pillows, staring up at the ceiling. He thought about the mess he had created. *I've been dropped in the vat of shit again and this time I'm drowning in it.* He closed his eyes again, trying to work out a solution to this massive dilemma.

'Can we come in? If you want us to leave we'd understand,' a timid female voice asked from the doorway. Peter's eyes snapped open. It was Olivia and Ting. They both looked messed up. Ting's head was wrapped in a bandage.

Remind me not to mention that I gave away their location. I was under duress.

'Sure, as long as you haven't brought Lipmann and his heavies with you.'

'No. We left them back at the hotel,' said Olivia. 'We were here having Ting attended to, when we bumped into Ruby. She was furious.'

'What happened to you?' Peter asked.

'I was just about to ask the same thing.'

'Malcolm threw me out of Lou's Roller. Nothing serious. They're just keeping me in for observation.'

Ting pulled out a chair and sat down. Olivia perched on the edge of the bed near Peter's feet. 'We would have brought flowers,' she said, 'but it looks like someone's already brought you some.'

'Ruby.'

'Of course. Isn't she sweet?'

He looked closely at Ting, who had the beginnings of two black eyes. 'So, what happened to you?'

'Lou came to the hotel and tried to get me to renew my contract. It quickly went downhill from there,' Olivia replied.

'They blame me for everything and tried to hurt me, but they don't know that I know martial arts. Kung fu. I was a stunt woman in Hong Kong. So, one hits me but I break his arm. Stupid fucker. Then I kick the black guy in the head. I wanted to do him lots of harm but Livvie stopped me. So I just hold his head out the window sill and close the window on it. He cried like a girl. Then we run. Lou just watched. He is too fat to even walk.'

'This could get much worse, you know,' Peter said. 'Is all this worth it?'

'The price of freedom.'

'Freedom could become very expensive.'

'Don't you worry. I'll look after her,' said Ting.

'I want to keep going with the book.' Olivia fidgeted. 'I need you.'

'Why would I want to help you after what's happened?'

'I'm sorry I didn't want to talk to you. I've had lots of pain in my life and you pushed the wrong fucking button. We could start again.'

143

He took a short time to answer. 'Even if I was interested, I really don't like being beaten up. Also I don't want to write a lightweight, bullshit, vanity version of your life.'

'I'm ready to do it now. I want you to write it. Your way.'

Peter shook his head. He didn't trust himself to answer. The drugs the doctors had given him might cloud his judgment. 'I don't know. Let me think about it.'

'I can go to thirty-five percent, but no more. Peter?'

'Go home. No. Go somewhere safe. I'll ring you tomorrow on your mobile and let you know what I've decided.'

30

'Right,' said Peter the moment he entered Devrille's office. 'We need to talk.' He settled himself gently into a chair without invitation. His body was still bruised and he probably should have called in sick, but he was determined to get things sorted.

'The only words I want to hear from you begin with the following: I'm incredibly, profusely and obsequiously sorry for causing you angst, Mr Devrille. I have the true, unabridged story of Olivia Bleeding Michaels' life in my hand, ready for typesetting.'

'Not exactly.'

'Well then, you already know where the door is. Mind it doesn't slap you as you leave.'

'I came to tell you that the Olivia Michaels interview is back on. You said you know people. I need you to keep Lipmann off our backs and to arrange a safe house for Olivia. I don't care what you do, or how you do it.'

'Is it worth my trouble? Or are you going to ring me again next week and bleat about being roughed up by some lag and left for dead on the side of the road, and that you're not doing the story again?'

'She's one hundred per cent committed this time. Oh, and I'm also asking for a raise in pay.'

'You must be fucking joking, Clancy! Are you wanking off in my presence?'

'No joke, John. This,' he said waving a hand over his body, 'is more than I signed on for. You pay copy boys more than you pay me. I'm not desperate enough to put up with this shit for two hundred and fifty quid a week. It's fifty quid a week more or I go, and my story goes with me. You know I've got the goods.'

Devrille watched Peter like a hawk watches a hare—confident of the kill but uncertain whether the hare would prove to be too big a prey. It was a stare-down. Devrille clicked his pen repeatedly but said nothing. Peter never blinked.

'Right,' said Devrille. 'I'll set up in a safe house for Olivia and give you the details. You should get her in there as soon as possible, but keep quiet about the *Gazer's* involvement. Don't worry about Lipmann. Keep a lid on the arrangements and don't tell anyone, not even your precious Ruby. As for your raise...' He stumbled. 'Twenty quid a week.'

Peter stopped himself from saying yes straight away. 'No deal,' he heard himself say. 'My arse is on the line here. Fifty quid. Not negotiable.'

'That's a lot of money...'

'And loose change to your Saudi investor.'

'How? How did you know...about him?'

Peter could see that Devrille was rattled. 'It's my job to know everything. Do the research and dish the dirt. Isn't that's what you're going to be paying me three hundred quid a week for?'

'Right, fine, okay. Three hundred pounds. You've just upped the stakes as well as your shares, JB. You'd better bloody deliver.'

JB? Joh's Boy? Please stop! That joke's a bit stale, Devrille, isn't it? It was on the tip of his tongue, but he'd already had his victory for the day. Peter smiled. Instead he said, 'Don't you worry about that.'

31

The following day, Peter made time to pop into Hoboh to catch up with Ruby for lunch. He told her he'd be in the vicinity, visiting his literary agent. He hoped she wouldn't ask him any questions. She didn't.

Playing the dutiful boyfriend, he picked up a hamper from Harrods which cost him most of the week's salary (less his rent and alcohol allowance). It wasn't too hard to get one that was vegan. He'd added in a piece of cold roast beef for himself.

Ruby was perched on a stool behind the counter, chin cradled in one hand and with the other, she was doodling. He loved catching her unaware. She looked up when he rang the doorbell. As soon as she saw who it was, her nose crinkled up. *I love her smile.* The lock released with a click, and he went in.

'Hey, baby,' she said. 'I thought you would be coming in earlier.'

'I decided to bring lunch with me,' Peter replied, giving Ruby a kiss. 'I thought we could have a picnic.'

'What a charming idea.'

There was just enough space on the floor behind the counter to spread out the blanket Peter had ripped off his sad, single bed and brought in with him.

'This is cosy,' she said. She looked at the blanket with a tinge of distaste. 'I'm not going to catch anything from this, I hope.'

Peter blushed. He regretted not having noticed some of the more dubious stains—probably from former occupants of his flat—earlier. 'No. It looks worse than it is. We can ditch it if you're worried.' *That's the thing about being raised on a cattle station: I'm used to grime and not much repulses me. How could I forget that Ruby is a princess?*

'I think I'd rather.'

He folded the blanket up again. Ruby brought out another stool from the workroom and they sat next to one another. She cleared the desk and opened up the hamper.

'This is extraordinary!' She opened one of the two piccolos of champagne. 'You're such a romantic; it's one of the many, many things I love about you.' She leaned over and kissed him. They clung to each other for a while.

It makes the pain so much better. I wonder if she has an office in the back? Somewhere private we could go? His thoughts were interrupted by the doorbell.

'Blast!' said Ruby, peering towards the window. 'What's Olivia Michaels doing here?'

Peter was wondering the same thing. 'Are you going to let her in?' Olivia was thumping on the door and waving.

'That's why I had the lock installed,' Ruby replied, 'so I could decide who comes into the shop and who doesn't.' She sighed. 'I suppose I'd better.'

The door swung open the moment Ruby released the lock. Behind Olivia was Ting. Olivia crossed the floor, pulling at a dress that had caught her attention as she approached.

'Well, from the looks of things, you two need to take a cold shower.' She leaned over the counter, picked up one of the mugs Ruby had filled with champagne, and downed it in one. 'What was that?' she asked. 'Piper Heidsieck? Humph. Tastes different out of a cup.'

'What are you doing here, Livvie?' Ruby snapped. 'You've got a hide coming here.'

'I needed something to wear at Ascot. Finding Peter here was a bonus, since he hasn't been answering his mobile, the naughty boy.' She waggled her finger at him.

'I was going to call you later this afternoon.'

Ruby tossed him an angry look. He hadn't yet mentioned to her that he would still be writing the book, despite everything that had happened. *That's what lunch was for. Please don't ask me any details, Ruby, I don't want to have to lie to you.*

'Ting and I have been staying in the car. Too scared to go home yet.' Olivia focused in on Peter's bruises. 'I didn't know Lou was going to do this to you.'

'You could simply go back to Lou and leave us alone.'

'That would seem to be the solution, Ruby, but I can't,' Olivia replied.

'You've never been decisive about anything in your life. Why change now? Uncle Richard's over helping you. I'm over helping you.'

'Please listen, Ruby,' she continued. 'I wish it were that easy.'

'We're tired. You put Peter in hospital. Stop being a selfish bitch.'

'I'm not.' Olivia looked at Ting.

Ting was about to pull out a cigarette when Ruby shook her head. 'Not in my shop you don't. Light up and I'll shove it down your throat.'

'In rehab they said I should forgive the past. I realise now that that's precisely what's fucking me up. I need to write this book.'

'A stupid book isn't going to help you bury the past, Olivia. This is utter madness,' said Ruby.

'Peter was right, I can't do it in half measures. I have to tell the full story.'

'Has it completely escaped you that he hasn't phoned you like he said he would? It's clear he's not interested.' Peter and Ruby exchanged glances. Her face turned from steely to quizzical. 'Well you're not, are you? Peter?'

'I haven't decided yet,' he lied. 'I'm still thinking it over. I'm interested to hear what Olivia has to say. Before I commit.'

'I want to get Lou for what he's done,' Olivia continued, flicking away a tear with her thumb.

'For beating up Peter?'

'Not just that. There are a lot of other evil things that Lou has done.'

'Yes, I've heard about that too. He's a bit heavy-handed, a bit too quick to seek retribution. As far as I know, he's never hurt Manz, though.'

Olivia lowered her eyes and sniffed.

'That's not it, is it?' Ruby added. 'What are you talking about, then? Livvie?'

Olivia took a deep breath. 'Remember when we were children, and that time when you came to play at my place?'

Ruby's brow puckered. 'Only vaguely. I was probably only about five.'

'And I think I was about nine or ten. We were playing with a doll's house, and then we made cakes out of flour and water, and tried to feed them to my mother?'

'Oh, that's right. I remember her running away from us.' Ruby smiled. 'We had fun that day. That was a great day.'

'Not for all of us,' said Olivia. 'Do you remember how we'd just finished afternoon tea? And then two men came to visit?'

Ruby looked at Peter. 'Has she told you any of this?'

'No. This is the first time I've heard it.'

'One of the men asked my mother if it would be all right if they took me to a children's party. Somewhere where there would be a clown and lots of other children to play with.'

'I remember you left suddenly with someone. I assumed he was your dad.'

'Remember, I was crying,' Olivia sobbed, 'because I wanted my mother to go with me? I didn't want to go to the party without her.'

'Oh that's right. Some of it's coming back to me. And I got upset because he wouldn't take me too. I couldn't understand why I couldn't go to the party too.'

'Do you know why?'

'Not really. I haven't thought about it in years.'

'You weren't allowed to come because you were Richard Manzanoni's daughter.'

Ruby hesitated. 'That man...wasn't your dad, was he?'

'No, he wasn't. He didn't want you to be involved. It wasn't going to be that kind of party.'

The colour drained out of Ruby's face. 'Please tell me it's not what I'm thinking.' She fell onto the stool. 'Tell me it's not what I think it is.'

Olivia wiped her eyes and whispered, 'It's what you think it is, Ruby.'

Ruby stood up and wrapped her arms around Olivia. 'Oh, God.'

Olivia dropped her head onto Ruby's shoulder and sang the words slowly and deliberately: *I thought the party was for girls and boys, when it was really for the fat goblins of the underworld.*

'I remember who the man was. The one I thought was your dad,' said Ruby. 'I can't believe I'd forgotten until now.'

Olivia nodded. 'You remember?' she said.

'I remember.'

'You remember it was Lumpy Lou? That's what we called him. Lumpy Lou, with the spotty flu.'

'It was Lou Lipmann.'

'That's right, Ruby. It was Lou Lipmann.'

32

'My father wasn't involved. Please tell me he wasn't,' Ruby searched Olivia's face. She was shaking with tears.

'No. No, he wasn't. That's why I trust him. He's one of the few decent men in the world.'

'Thank God. I couldn't bear it if he was a…' Ruby couldn't finish the sentence. 'You have to go to the police, Livvie. These men need to be punished. Don't worry about the book.'

Olivia stiffened. 'I can't. It won't help.'

'Of course it will. They'll investigate it even if it happened a long time ago.'

'No they won't.'

'Why not?'

'Because some of them are the police,' Olivia whispered.

Peter shifted on his stool.

'And not just police. There are others.'

'Others?' he repeated.

'I don't want to go into it here.'

This is far bigger than I thought. No wonder Lipmann wants it all hushed up. Peter grimaced. 'Is all this true?'

'Of course, it's fucking true,' Olivia snapped. 'I haven't made it up, if that's what you think. They call themselves lovers of children? That's what the word means, you know. What a joke. They destroy children. Killers of children—paedocide—that's what it should be called. The drink and drugs help me live with the memory of what they did to me. There's your truth. Ugly enough for you?'

Peter stared at his hands for a moment. *The lawyers are not going to like this. Not one little bit.* 'I absolutely believe you, but it's a legal minefield out there. If you're thinking of naming names…'

'They deserve to be named. Every single one of them.'

'If you're thinking of naming names, then, well… Do you have anything to back up what you're saying Olivia?'

'Like what?'

'Oh, I don't know. Some evidence. Witnesses, tapes, photos?'

'No…'

'Someone who can back up your story?'

Olivia slumped against the wall. 'Why do I need evidence? I'm a star. Isn't my word enough?'

'The blow helps with the pain,' Ting said as she grabbed Olivia's handbag. 'It's her medication.'

'Not now.' Olivia pushed the bag away.

'The thing is, they'll deny everything and then they'll sue you for defamation.'

She remained silent for a while. 'My mother might have been able to…'

'Your mother?' Peter repeated with disbelief. 'But you walked out of the interview when I mentioned her last time.'

'She's dead. My mother's dead. That's why I walked out.'

Peter felt foolish. 'I'm sorry. I didn't know.'

'No, not many people do. She died not long after the court case. I never saw her again after that final day in court. I don't know what I feel anymore. I feel numb, most of the time. I don't know who else to turn to.'

'None of this will be easy,' said Peter. 'Even if you can prove what you're saying, you'll be opening a Pandora's box of unholy hell.'

'They can't destroy me any more,' Olivia replied. 'Enough. Maybe this will encourage others to do something too.'

Ruby bit her lip. 'We've had our moments, Livvie, but I'll help you any way I can.'

'I don't want you involved,' Olivia replied. 'You have nothing to do with this.'

'But I want to help you. I'll do everything I can. As will Manz.'

'You can both help me by staying away for the moment. And please don't tell Uncle Richard what I've told you. He'd want to protect me and that would be bad for both your careers.' She turned to Peter. 'I'm going to spill the beans: a whole fucking truckload of them. It will make for an interesting read.'

'I'll do it as long as we can find others to back you up. I'll find a safe house for you and Ting, but, once I do, you can't leave it or contact anyone. Not for drugs or any reason. Nobody will know where it is. I won't even tell Ruby.' He turned to her. 'For your own safety, you understand. The less you know, the better.'

Ruby nodded. 'I understand.'

'There's just one more thing…' Olivia began.

'I won't be acting as your drug mule, Olivia. You can forget that.'

'But what if Lou follows you?'

'I'm not worried about that. I've learned the art of invisibility.'

Ruby smiled.

I'm not joking, Ravishing Ruby. Sam Saturday's lessons in bushcraft when I was a kid, and my cunning kit. Lou won't even see me coming. 'I have a research assistant helping me with my book. She used to work for the government. She might be able to help us find others to back you up.'

'I haven't seen any of the other children for fifteen years. It wasn't like we were going to church every Sunday or to a clubhouse, you know.'

'Not much to go on,' he remarked.

'It's all I know.' Olivia picked up her handbag.

'I'll ring the researcher as soon as you leave.'

Peter rang Devrille the moment he left Ruby's shop. 'I'll be out for the rest of the afternoon and most of tomorrow. But I haven't taken Snoddy's number with me.'

Devrille read her number out to him. 'What do you need Snoddy for?'

'I have to find others who might have been affected.'

'Others? What's this about?'

'I can't say yet. All I can tell you is this: imagine for a moment you have both the greatest and the worst story of your career in your grasp.'

'Please don't tell me you're bringing down the government.'

Not yet, Devrille. Not yet.

33

Peter had no sooner hung up from Devrille than he glimpsed a familiar face standing behind a lamp post. *I can see you Yuppie. You might be as thin as a rake but you still can't hide behind something with only a twelve-inch diameter, you fool.* Instead of turning and walking away, Peter strode directly up to him.

Yuppie laughed. 'What happened to you?' he asked.

'What are you doing here?' Peter returned.

'I long suspected you'd be the type to wear dresses, Clancy, but Hoboh's a bit out of your price range, isn't it?'

'None of your business.' From the bulge of Yuppie's suit pocket, there was something hidden there. From the shape and the look of the strap hanging out of the corner, Peter suspected a camera. He scanned Yuppie for any other lumps that might be rolls of film. He didn't detect any.

'You and Miss Ruby seem very cosy. Make a good story now, that would. The Socialite and the Gazer Scum. Or is it a *ménage à trois?* You doing Livvie the Loser at the same time?'

'You don't know shit,' replied Peter. 'You saw nothing.'

'No? Well you can tell that to my editor.'

'You try printing that crap and Morton will find himself defending yet another lawsuit.'

'The photographs will make the crap appear very convincing. You know the camera never lies.' He patted the bulge in his pocket and then crossed his arms.

How stupid can you be? Peter chuckled and shrugged his shoulders. 'It's a good thing I'm not a violent man,' he said. A look of

156

satisfaction flashed across Yuppie's face. *He thinks he's won.* Then, ignoring the scream in his shoulder, Peter raised his right fist and drew it back as if preparing for a punch, while Yuppie raised his hands to protect his face. Quick as a flash, Peter simultaneously reached out with his left hand, grasped the strap and flicked the camera towards him. In the same, fluid movement, he smashed it against the lamp post. The film canister popped out. Peter caught it and exposed the entire length to the sunlight.

Yuppie dropped to his knees. 'No!' he cried. 'You bastard!'

'I told you, you've got the wrong end of the stick. Now go back to Liverpool, and find something else to occupy your time. I suggest you pick something other than spying and journalism. You just don't have the necessary skills for either.'

'One day I'll catch you with your dick up Red Ruby's clacker. You won't be able to deny it then, will you? You and your slag.'

'Bugger it!' said Peter. 'I've tried to be diplomatic, but there's a limit.' He caught Yuppie's chin with a left uppercut and dropped him with the right hook that followed. 'Now please go away.' And then he limped off, leaving Yuppie to whimper alone.

34

Peter spent his last few nights of freedom at Ruby's. *Once we start the book, I'll be constantly looking over my shoulder. Long hours with Olivia. I have to start working on finding other sources. Starting yesterday.*

He took a long shower, massaging the ache in his shoulder, partly a legacy of his encounter with Lou and partly of that with Yuppie. Then he joined Ruby in the kitchen.

Ruby pushed a mug of coffee across the bench. 'Good morning, lover.'

'Thanks,' He wrapped his arms around her waist, lifted up her blouse and lightly kissed her belly button. She shivered.

'Stop it!' She pulled away from Peter. 'I'm trying to be furious with you. You're going to burn yourself out.'

'As I say: when you burn out, replace the gear box and keep going.'

'You're talking shit. You really think Olivia will be able hold herself together for very long?' she asked.

'Possibly not, but that's probably the least of my problems. In my experience the more controversial the issue, the sooner the opposition gathers to stop it from getting out. And they're usually big bastards with deep pockets.'

'Is that happened when you wrote books in Australia?'

'Writing unauthorised biographies can be interesting to say the least. I'll tell you about it one day.'

'Olivia's book can go to hell if you're going to be in danger.'

'I'm pretty good at taking trouble on headfirst. I just won't accept lifts off strangers again. Promise. The best thing you can do is carry on as normal. Don't tell anyone about this. No-one.'

'I won't.' She smiled. 'I didn't want to mention it sooner while everything else was going on, but I have to go away for a week or two.'

'Oh?' said Peter. 'Where?'

'New York. It's business. I don't really want to go.' She kissed Peter and snuggled into his chest. 'I kept hoping I wouldn't have to, but everyone tells me that it'll be good for my career. Stay here while I'm gone. There's plenty of food in the refrigerator. Ring me when you get a chance. I've left the number of the hotel I'm staying in by the bed.'

'We probably wouldn't have seen all that much of each other anyway.'

'Hmm, I'm sure you're right.' She went into the bedroom to pack and returned a few minutes later with a small leather suitcase. 'I've telephoned for a cab.'

He held her until the taxi arrived. 'I'll miss you.'

She smiled and her kiss lingered. Then she grabbed her handbag and luggage, and spun hurriedly on her high heels.

'I'll keep you up-to-date with any developments. I'll stay well clear of Lou. Don't worry.'

'You know you make me mad,' Ruby said, 'but I still love you.'

'Love and insanity are nearly the same things.'

After she left, Peter limped to the front steps of Ruby's flat to wait for Snoddy. He still felt the odd twinge from time to time. The first thing that came into his head as he waited was the conversation he'd had with Devrille a few nights earlier. There were no whoops of impending success once Peter had explained Olivia's allegations, only Devrille saying over and over again, 'We must be careful. We must be careful. And you, especially, JB.'

Snoddy drove Peter to the safe house that Devrille had rented for Olivia and Ting. The safe house was still located in the West End. Olivia had demanded Belgravia: Olivia didn't do down-market safe houses. After days of haggling, they'd settled on Notting Hill. He could have walked to it in a few minutes, but Snoddy deemed that too unsafe. Instead, she followed a convoluted route, so that the journey took the best part of thirty minutes.

Once he and Olivia had settled into the snug off the tiny hallway, Ting disappeared. He could hear her in the kitchen, muttering and clanging pots. He hoped that, whatever it was she was cooking up, it wouldn't give the police a reason to organise a clandestine raid, unconnected with the book.

He clicked the recorder on. 'Peter Clancy interview with Olivia Michaels. Thursday, Fifteenth September, 1990. Tell me a bit about your early career. How did you get into acting?'

'Well,' she said, tucking her legs under her. 'My mother first took me to a modelling agency when I was a baby. She said I was a little poser from the day I was born. I was a natural.' She took out a cigarette, placed it between her lips and kept talking. 'They signed me up there and then. I got my first job before I could walk. Coincidentally, it was also my first nude scene.' She watched Peter turn pale. 'No, not like that. It was a commercial for nappies.'

Olivia was unexpectedly lucid and the rest of the morning was unspectacular. Peter was astounded at her meticulous memory, particularly when it came to her work. *Drug-induced psychoses aside, maybe she will prove to be a reliable source after all. Although, how she remembers anything is a total mystery.*

By lunchtime, she was fading. Her hands were shaking so much that she couldn't light her own cigarette. Despite feeling as if he'd already smoked a packet with her, Peter lit her up.

'That's enough for today,' she said, taking a puff. 'You can go away now. I'll call you later and let you know about tomorrow.'

Peter called Snoddy on her mobile and waited with Ting in the sitting room.

'You're getting what you need?' she asked.

'Yes,' he replied, unsure what she meant.

'Good. Olivia is a good girl.' Ting continued, 'I was in the movies, too, you know.'

'Oh really?'

'That's how we became friends. I was in a Bond movie, once. Kung fu expert.'

'That's nice.' He was glad when he saw the Vauxhall Cavalier pull up. 'I'll see you tomorrow, Ting.'

'Maybe,' she replied.

35

Ruby's scent lingered in her flat, even though she'd already been gone hours by the time he returned. He asked Snoddy if she wanted to come in for a drink.

'No thank you,' she replied, tossing her cerise pashmina over the shoulder of her turquoise jumper. 'There's something I'm working on and I think I've almost cracked it.' He was about to ask her what it was when she added, 'You'll have to be patient to find out what I mean by that.'

He didn't have to be patient for very long. The next day, Olivia called in sick and tired. He began to worry that she was losing momentum. *Seen it before. They think they're the next great British author, but they only have two thousand words in them. They're the hundred yard sprinters of literature. A great start, but no stamina.* Instead, he used the spare time to transcribe the tapes meticulously. *I might even get Olivia to sign up to the transcript.* Just in case.

Snoddy called him just after he'd hung up from Ruby in New York.

'Hello gorgeous,' he answered, anticipating Ruby's voice again. 'You miss me already?'

'Oh, thank you,' said Snoddy. 'But not really. Only saw you last, when was it, thirty hours ago?'

'It's you, Snoddy! Sorry, I thought it was...'

'I know, I know, someone else. Story of my life.'

He put down the bottle of Corona he had been sipping. 'So what's new?'

'I've been doing some delving into Olivia's mum's death. You know me, never believe anything till you see it for yourself and never leave anything alone. Got me into so much trouble back in the Met, I can't tell you.'

'Yes, and?'

'Well, you know what she said about her dying soon after the court case? Well, I got to thinking, maybe I should check what she died of, if she was close to anyone and if she said anything to anybody before she died.'

'And did you find anybody?'

'I'll say I did.'

'Well, Snoddy, I'm aging by the minute. How about you just tell me what you found?'

'Hold onto your hat. You're going to love this. I've found Carol-Lee Evans.'

Peter was silent. 'Who the hell is Carol-Lee Evans?'

'Who's Carol-Lee Evans? Good thing you've got old Snoddy on the case. If you'd done your homework, you'd know Carol-Lee Evans is Olivia Michaels' mum.'

'I thought Olivia's mum's name was Caroline Taylor.'

'It was, between 1955 and 1975. After that she became Carol-Lee Evans.'

'So what do you mean by you've found her? You've found what exactly? Her grave?'

'I've found her. Alive.'

Peter's head reeled. He took another sip. Obviously Snoddy had good sources. He should have felt elated, but he actually only felt queasy.

'Once the money ran out she went to live in Wales. I've made contact and she's expecting a visit. She doesn't know what for, thinks she's won a holiday to London. I'll pick you up in the morning.'

'Right, fine.'

36

In anticipation of the three-hour trip, Peter had armed himself with a flask of coffee, a box of paracetamol and a small whisky decanter. Snoddy had mentioned the place they were going to over the phone: somewhere in Wales with a tongue-twisting name. It sounded like gibberish.

Why couldn't Carol-Lee still be living in Spain? I need some bloody sunlight.

He didn't have to wait long before Snoddy pulled up at the kerb in a yellow Rover SD1 V8. *Thank God it isn't the shit-box Vauxhall Cavalier.* He would be travelling in comfort. He shuffled to the car and was about to open the passenger door when Snoddy stepped out of the Rover and rushed to assist him. She was, as always, her own psychedelic fashion statement, wearing a lime trouser suit, tangerine shirt and beige scarf this time. If he looked at Snoddy's ensemble too long, he would probably vomit.

'What happened to the other car?'

'The Vauxhall? That's my husband's. I borrowed it while mine was in the shop.'

Husband? He took another look at Snoddy. *Who'd have thought it? The man must be colour-blind.*

'I brought supplies to help me.' He opened his suit jacket to reveal the decanter tucked in his inner coat pocket. Then he lowered himself carefully into the expansive leather seat. 'So how did you find her?'

'I checked the death records. Then I rang someone in Inland Revenue and someone at Police Records. It's isn't hard when you know the right people.'

'Where are we going again? I didn't quite catch it on the phone.' Peter buckled up his seat belt.

'Methyr Tydfil. Wales.'

'Martha's Titties? Are you serious?'

'Ha ha. Very funny. Don't worry about trying to say it. We're not going there for a holiday.'

'Nice place?'

'You'll see.' Snoddy sniggered as she closed the passenger door.

Thankfully, Peter was able to lie back in his seat and sleep most of the way to Methyr Tydfil in comfort, only having to stop once to take painkillers which he washed down with strong coffee. He didn't care that Snoddy smoked in the car and continually played Bob Marley on the cassette player, he was just glad that they had tracked down Carol-Lee Evans.

He was making progress. The sooner all of this was over, the sooner he could kill off his author alter ego and give the *Geezer* the big flick. Unfortunately, it would also bring him closer to having to tell Ruby the truth. He chose to think of something else. He closed his eyes and rehearsed in his mind what he was going to say to Carol-Lee.

'Wake up,' said Snoddy, 'we're here.'

Peter felt Snoddy shaking him gently and the car slowing down. *We're at Martha's Titties already?* He kept his eyes shut. He'd seen travelogues of Brecon Beacons and Snowdonia. Expecting a scenic Welsh village in the valley, he opened his eyes instead to a row of colourless council estate buildings. They were glued to each other along a dead-end street full of litter. The day may have been sunny but the houses still looked bleak. A battered sign, *Gurnos Estate,* stood alongside a wrecked car with missing tyres. *Says it all.*

'Welcome to Methryr Tydfil. One of Britain's ugliest towns,' Snoddy chortled.

'I'm thinking of a word to describe what I can see.'

'Hideous? Sad? Both apply ever since Maggie shut down the coal mines,' Snoddy remarked as she crept along the street looking at the house numbers. 'This has become the unhappy face of Britain. Unemployment, drinking, drugs. No future. You name it. It's all here.'

'Is it safe to stop?' A group of teenagers sat on the footpath passing a bottle of wine between them. They were wasted, broken and pale. At this rate, they would be lucky to make it to forty.

Snoddy stopped the Rover in front of one of the houses. 'Here we are.' It looked like all of the others they'd passed, except that it had curtains in the window.

'We'll be fine, but I'll stay with the car just in case.'

'That's not very comforting,' Peter said as he unbuckled his seatbelt.

'She lives by herself but if you get into any trouble give me a yell.'

'Trouble?'

'She has form: assault, drunk and disorderly. Nothing too serious. She doesn't like coppers too much, or strangers for that matter. Likes to keep to herself.'

'I can't wait to meet her,' Peter replied flippantly as he opened his door.

'And be sure to give the old bird this.' Snoddy handed Peter a bottle of Bell's whisky decorated with ribbons and a card with *Congratulations!* emblazoned on it.

'It'll break the ice. She doesn't mind the odd tipple.'

He hurried to the front door, checking the street as he went. He rapped on the door, and repeated the action every thirty seconds. After about three minutes the door opened slightly. The odour of damp and cigarette smoke hit him moments later.

'What do you want?'

'Carol-Lee Evans?'

'Who wants to know?'

'I'm Peter Clancy.' He leaned forward and the smell of alcohol hit him like bleach.

'Don't know you. Piss off.' Carol-Lee began to close the door. Peter slipped his foot between the gap and pushed the door open.

The old door stop tactic. This time it's going to hurt. No other choice.

'What the f...' Carol-Lee began as she attempted to shut the door. 'I'll ring the five-oh.'

'I'm from the West End Theatre Trust. You were expecting me? I'm here to give you your prize.' He thrust the card into her hand. 'Open the door. I've got another gift for you.' He held up the bottle of whisky.

'Who are you? And how do you know my name?' She opened the door slowly and stuck out her head.

Great idea, Snoddy.

'You received a call from my assistant. She's organised a car to whisk us off to London, where you'll be staying in the West End and visiting with the greatest lights of stage and screen.'

'Oh, that's right,' Carol-Lee replied. 'My bag's almost packed. I forget things, you know.'

Not a promising start. Hopefully, she's only blown her short-term memory.

'I live in this shithole and I'm drunk most of the time. I've forgotten more things than I can remember. I can't even remember entering the competition. Never mind, never look at the gift horse, isn't that what they say? Come in while I finish packing.'

Carol-Lee opened up the door and Peter stepped straight into the dark front room. It stank. She snapped on the light and he saw Carol-Lee Evans in all her jaundiced, decrepit glory. She'd definitely lost the battle with the bottle. Peter jiggled the bottle of whisky. She snatched it from him and swept back her hair, admiring the bottle.

'Used to drink single malt,' she reminisced. She lowered the bottle to her side. 'Now, who are you again and who sent you?'

'Peter Clancy.' He paused. 'West End Theatre Trust.'

'This is such a coincidence, me winning this prize.'

'Oh, really?'

'I used to be involved in the theatre, you know.'

'Is that so?' said Peter. 'What did you do there?'

'Oh, not me personally. I'm Olivia Michaels' mother. You must have heard of her.'

She put the bottle down on the sideboard and disappeared. Peter sat down on a chair uninvited. The coffee table was stacked with empty scotch bottles, an overflowing ashtray and a television. On the nicotine-stained wall, there was a photograph of a pretty blonde woman in her twenties holding a little girl, hair tied up in ringlets. Carol-Lee returned, her bag in hand.

'Yes, Livvie's my daughter,' Carol-Lee muttered sadly as she lit up a cigarette. 'She's probably dead.' She flicked the ash on the floor. 'I need a drink.'

Peter opened the Bell's and filled one of the dirty glasses next to her to the brim. Carol-Lee put down her bag and threw down the whisky in one gulp. 'If she's not dead yet, she probably soon will be. Like mother like daughter. The doctor says I'll die if I keep drinking. I said to him, I'll bloody drink to that.' She smiled faintly and then looked Peter directly in the eyes. 'Do you see that photograph on the wall?'

'You and Olivia?'

'Yes. Beautiful, isn't she?'

'You both are,' Peter replied.

'It was taken soon after Livvie got her role in *Please Marry My Dad*.'

'It was a romantic comedy, wasn't it?'

'Yes. It was a sad title, considering that she never knew her dad. She was so, so good in it. She stole all of her scenes off the adult actors.' Carol-Lee looked lovingly at the picture.

'She was a great actor. You can be proud of her.'

'I'd give anything to have that time back. Anything. We were so happy. She was such a beautiful child. Then something horrible happened. It was like been swallowed up in a black cloud. I should never have allowed her to be an actor.' She picked up an enormous book and handed it to Peter. 'That's Livvie's scrapbook. Do you mind if I take it with me?'

'Of course not.'

'It's my only memory of her. I take it with me everywhere I go. That way, we're always together. Shall we go?'

Carol-Lee passed out in the back seat of the Rover two hours into the trip. Her head was resting on the album she'd taken with her, balanced on top of a kit bag. Peter was worried that taking Carol-Lee to London was going to be a waste of time. Was she going to remember anything or had she totally pickled her brain? Would she even remember her own daughter after all these years?

It was Devrille's idea that they reunite mother and daughter and record the moment on film. That way, if all else failed, he still had a scoop. Of sorts. It was also his idea to move Carol-Lee to the safe house, in case someone else discovered she wasn't dead and sought to remedy that deficit.

Carol-Lee's snores resembled a honking pig. He tried to rouse her every now and again, but Snoddy advised him to let her sleep it off; better that than listen to her crying and moaning about her shitty life. *Was that any better than having to listen to Bob Marley again on the return trip?* He might get some information out of Carol-Lee. *I'll be glad when this day is over.*

Carol-Lee woke up not far from the safe house.

'I need a bloody drink. My nerves have gone crazy,' Carol-Lee uttered as soon as she sat herself upright.

'I thought you might say that.' Snoddy turned down Bob, just as 'Rastaman Live Up' was about to start for the fourth time.

'Who are you? Where did you come from?' she said vaguely.

'I'm Winifred Snodgrass,' she replied. 'We met back in Merthyr. I'm…the…research assistant. And the driver.'

'I've never seen you before.'

This is going to be good. Peter shook his head. 'Do you happen to remember me, Carol-Lee?'

'Of course I do. You're the theatre bloke. I'm not totally brain dead. I'm just a bit stressed. You would be too if you hadn't left your village in over a decade. Something to settle my nerves might help.'

'Okay.' Peter pulled out the flask from his inner coat pocket and handed it back to Carol-Lee.

Carol-Lee took a long guzzle from the flask. 'Thanks, love. See, I'm better already.'

'Try not to drink too much,' said Peter, 'You'll want to remember this occasion.'

169

'I'm feeling poorly.'

'Hang in there. I'll be with you every inch of the way. Take another sip.' He turned to Snoddy. 'How much longer? She's going nuts.'

'Nearly there, thank God. If she vomits or pisses herself, I'll throw her out of the car myself.' Moments later, the Rover screeched to a stop. 'There,' said Snoddy. 'We'd have been here sooner, if it wasn't for the market.'

'This isn't the Dorchester.'

'I never said anything about the Dorchester,' Peter retorted.

'You didn't but she,' she pointed at Snoddy, 'did.'

That, she remembers. 'It's better than the Dorchester. It's your own, private townhouse. Right here in London.'

'Around the corner from Portobello Road? You must be joking. I shouldn't have agreed. I wish I could go back to Merthyr. I feel like I've been forced here.'

'You'll love it. Wined and dined. Meet old faces and some new ones.'

'I won't.'

Peter's budget didn't stretch to a night at the Dorchester. 'How about a posh flat in Kensington for the night and we'll start over tomorrow? It's my place. That way, you won't feel lonely.'

'Kensington's all right, I suppose. Strange kind of competition this is, but then again, I've never won anything before. If we're both staying in your flat, I'll be locking my door, just so you know.'

'You do that. We'll sort things out first thing in the morning.' *I'm so sorry, Ruby. Really I am.*

37

Carol-Lee was up remarkably early the next day. She had washed and dried her hair and looked sober. Peter checked the bottles in the cellaret. *Shit!* A bottle of Courvoisier was missing. Evidently, the old bird had expensive tastes. Ruby would be sure to notice. He'd have to replace it before she returned. *That's going to hurt.*

Snoddy arrived punctually at ten. Peter had read Olivia the riot act the night before. 'You have to be reliable, or this thing can't work. No more days off for you.' He'd neglected to mention that her mother had been found, that she was indeed alive and relatively well, and he'd be bringing her around at ten-thirty. Instead, he told her his assistant would be coming over first and that she'd be taking some snaps. For the book.

He bundled Carol-Lee into the back seat. 'We're going on a bit of a tour first,' he said.

'Before the Dorchester?'

'Ah… Yes.'

'Now, you remember what we discussed?' he asked Snoddy as she pulled up in front of the safe house.

'I remember. Get Ting away. The first person to see Ca…'

'Shh.'

Snoddy went off to set up the scene.

Carol-Lee looked around. 'We're back in Notting Hill. Why?'

'There's an old thespian, I'd like you to meet. Extraordinary actor but very reclusive. I had to pull a lot of strings to arrange it. But if you're not interested…'

'Really? And this actor wants to meet me?'

'The actor has an amazing cognac collection. I won't mention names, that way it'll be a surprise.'

'Should I take my scrapbook with me? I mean, it might be of interest…to her.' She scrutinised Peter's face. 'I knew straight up you were never a theatrical type. What do you take me for?'

'So why did you come with me?'

'Why not? What have I got to be scared of? I always knew Livvie would come calling one day. I never thought it'd be in the guise of a man with a bad wig and a woman who dresses like something out of Barnum and sodding Bailey.'

Peter pulled off his cunning kit toupée. 'I've underestimated you.'

'Don't worry, you're not the first. So what does Livvie want with me?'

'Nothing. She just wants to see you.' He couldn't see the point of telling her that she was believed dead all these years. 'I just helped her find you. She's inside that house.'

'That's funny,' she chuckled. 'I last saw her fifteen years ago. Her last words to me were "I hope I never see you again. I hope you kill yourself."'

'I know about the court case.'

Carol-Lee looked at him and laughed so hard that she broke into a spasm of coughing.

'What's so funny about that?'

'You don't know nothing. You only know what they wanted you to know. The court case was a scam.'

'The past is the past. Time heals. Let's go in together, shall we? She's waiting.'

'I don't know…' Carol-Lee's eyes flitted around the car, like a bird searching for a way out.

He got out and opened the rear passenger door. 'Come on, love. Take hold of my hand. I'll help you. You're going to see your daughter. How many years have you dreamed about this?'

'A very long time.' She took hold of Peter's hand. 'Even if she never wants to see me again after this, at least I can go to my grave knowing that I saw her one last time.'

'That's the spirit. You can do this.' He helped her out of the car. They stumbled arm in arm the short distance to the house. There were two steps to the front door and a railing on either side. Peter held onto Carol-Lee as she hauled herself up. Above them, Snoddy held the door open with one hand, clicking off photographs with the other. She followed them to the snug, where Olivia was waiting. Carol-Lee stepped through the door. *Mother and child reunion...*

'Who the fuck is this?' Olivia shouted as soon as she caught sight of her. Snoddy's camera was whirring. 'What the fuck is this?'

'Livvie! Livvie darling! It's Mum.' Carol-Lee was trying to catch Olivia in a hug.

Olivia sidestepped her and was down the hallway like a shot. 'You had no fucking right! No fucking right! I don't know who this woman is. My mum's dead. I went to the fucking funeral. Who is she? This is a fucking circus. Fuck you, Peter Clancy!'

Ting appeared from the kitchen with a knife. 'What's wrong?'

Olivia ran to the door and fiddled with it. It flew open and she darted through. Behind Peter, Carol-Lee was weeping.

'You stay here,' cried Snoddy, camera still hanging around her neck. 'I'll get her back.' She darted through the front door after Olivia.

Ting followed. 'I don't know what you did, but I'll fix you later.'

38

Peter and Carol-Lee were left behind. Carol-Lee had dissolved into tears and was wiping them away with the hem of her coat. Peter handed her a handkerchief.

'I'm sorry,' he said.

Carol-Lee blew her nose. 'Can you tell me what's going on? What just happened? And who are you exactly?'

'I'm Peter Clancy, that much is true. I'm a writer. Olivia has engaged me to write her autobiography for her. She wants it to be a tell-all book about her life. She's made some—how do I put this— allegations, about some of the people she met along the road to stardom. The dilemma we face is that she has no-one to back up her side of the story. That's where you fit in.'

'You want me to tell you what happened.'

'Precisely.'

'But she still hates me. You can see that, can't you? She obviously wasn't expecting me…'

'She thought you were dead. And then I found out you were alive. We tracked you down and brought you here. I thought it would be okay, after all these years.'

'You never heard the one about sleeping dogs, have you?'

'These allegations are serious. If they're true, she could get some justice for herself and others.'

Carol-Lee wiped her eyes. 'Can I have a drink, please?'

He poured her a scotch. 'Will you tell me what you know?'

'Only if it'll help Livvie.'

Peter pulled out his recorder. 'Would you mind if I tape you?'

'Well...' A moment later, she nodded.

He clicked on the recorder. 'Interview with Carol-Lee Evans...'

'I'm saying this from my own free will, right? It's time I stopped hiding and set the record straight.'

'Go ahead.'

'First I want to make it clear that I love my daughter. Always have, always will.'

'I understand.'

Carol-Lee took a deep breath. 'Everything was fine until Livvie decided she wanted to be a movie star. The press has always painted me like I was a monster, always pushing her, when it was her decision. Lou Lipmann wasn't just a theatrical agent. He was a pimp. He sold children to his acquaintances and he used them for his own enjoyment, may he rot in hell. He stole Livvie off me. She still blames me for it.' She downed the first glass of scotch. 'He poisoned her mind and stole her off me. I'm surprised Lou hasn't tried to kill me.'

Peter shook his head. 'He doesn't need to. You're dead for all intents and purposes.'

'He'll try to, once he knows I've returned from the dead. That man is beyond evil.'

'So I've experienced. Olivia's determined to tell her side of the story and that's where I come in. She wants to expose everything.'

'Everything?' Carol-Lee wrung her hands. 'Do you know how far this goes?'

'You tell me. How far does it go?'

'Well, I only found out about Lou Lipmann and some of the others a few months before Livvie took me to court. I didn't know what was going on before that, I swear. Livvie never told me. Maybe I was silly, maybe I was too gullible, but I thought they were good, upright citizens. Most of them had their own families. You'd think that type wears raincoats and hangs around schools giving out sweets to kids, but they don't.'

Carol-Lee waggled the glass. Peter refilled it and poured another for himself. It was past twelve, and there was no sign yet of Snoddy.

'I didn't handle things right, back then,' she continued. 'Don't you think I wanted to protect my daughter? If she'd told me about it earlier, I'd have done something, but by then it was too late. The damage was done.'

'Can you give me any names?'

'There were a few of them, in their club. All very posh. When I read the papers, I see their faces. When I look at the television, I see their faces. I saw one of those entertainers getting a knighthood once on the telly. I got so mad that I threw a bottle of whisky at it and smashed it. Didn't do me much good, did it? Some of them are household names. Some of them even help run this country. Fancy that; a mob of filthy paedophiles making us laugh or telling us what we can and can't do. They should be rotting in jail or better yet, dead.'

'Give me names.'

'Not yet. I have Livvie's best interests to think of. Her career will be finished if she writes this book. Doesn't she get it? I know she's always in the paper for partying and taking drugs, but this is different. This is dangerous.'

Peter sighed. Without Carol-Lee he had nothing. Chances were that even with Carol-Lee he still had nothing. 'The way she sees it is that she just can't take any more of the bullshit. She can't take being the nation's darling when, behind the scenes, people have destroyed her childhood and told her to stay quiet about it. She's just realised that there is a heavy price for fame. She knows that if she keeps living like she does, she'll probably end up dead in a year or two.'

'And it all started with Lou Lipmann. You know many times I wanted to kill that man? Every time I take a drink I think about killing him. I even hired a hit man once but the bastard nicked off with my money.'

'Just tell the truth. Name names. The truth always wins, Carol-Lee. That's what I've always found.'

'Do you really think so? If you believe that, then you're a fool.' She took another gulp.

Peter heard the front doorbell sound. Someone was holding the button down. He looked through the spyhole and unlocked the door. Ting was standing in the doorway, alone, eyes wild. Peter couldn't tell if she'd seen something terrible or if she was just missing her medications.

'Where's Olivia?' he said.

'Let me get inside quick.' Ting looked up and down the street and dived inside. She slammed the door shut and bolted the locks.

'Where's Olivia?' Peter repeated.

'She's gone,' said Ting.

'Gone? Gone where?'

'They've taken her.'

Carol-Lee had slumped in the hallway.

'Who took her?' asked Peter.

'The doctors and the police. I followed her to Portobello market. She started screaming and breaking things and throwing things from the stalls and someone called the police. She was out of control. They tell her she needs help. Then Lou Lipmann turns up—just like that—and she attacks him. He wants to take her away, but she screams that he wants to murder her. She begs the police not to let him take her, so the police say, okay, they are going to get a doctor. The doctor comes and he says she has to go to hospital. When she doesn't go, they force her to go. I try to stop them, but they ask me who am I, and they say they will throw me in jail. Then they take Livvie. I nearly go crazy. They said they've taken her to a hospital for treatment.'

'Calm down. Do you know where they took her?'

'I don't know. They wouldn't tell me anything.'

Peter picked up his telephone and searched for Snoddy's number. It rang twice before she answered.

'She's been sectioned,' said Snoddy, 'under the *Mental Health Act*. When you get sectioned you can be forcibly taken to a mental health facility for treatment. Good chance she's been taken to a clinic that caters for celebrities.'

'Can you make enquiries?' he asked.

'I'll do it now. I'll call in some favours.'

'Could you come back here as soon as you can?'

'I've got something I must do for John first. In the meantime, stay indoors and I'll be there by five. When you have power, you can do what you want. Lou has very powerful friends.'

'All right. I'll see you later.' He hung up. 'Did anyone say where they were taking her?' he asked Ting.

'Didn't say. To a hospital. That's it. Are they going to kill her?'

'No, they won't do that. They'll probably put her away for a while. Give her a heavy dose of counselling and medication. Lou Lipmann might try to win her back.'

'I don't know about that,' said Ting. 'She was pretty angry with him. You should have seen what she did with the sword from the antique stall. If I didn't turn up I don't know what would happen. She was waving the sword at Lou. She wanted to take off his nuts.'

'Did she get close?'

'Not really, but I was scared she might hurt herself.'

What a shame. Now that would have made some story. 'Any press there?'

'They came later. After they take Livvie away.'

'You stay here, Ting, and keep an eye on her.' Peter pointed at Carol-Lee who was coming to her senses. 'Keep the alcohol up to her, okay?'

'Okay.'

'I'll be back in a few minutes.'

Peter left them and locked himself in the back bathroom. First, he rang the newsdesk, to call in the story about Olivia Michaels. If only there'd been a snapper there. Still, there was mileage in the report.

'Mr Devrille wants to talk to you,' said Willy Prager.

'Okay.'

The newsdesk put him through.

'JB? Is that you?' said Devrille.

If he's still calling me JB, he can't hate me.

'Good work on getting the story,' he said. 'The newsdesk editor just told me. Are you sure you don't want a by-line?'

'What?' said Peter. 'No.'

'Snoddy took some snaps down at Portobello market. We've just finished developing them. The ones of Olivia Michaels brandishing the samurai sword are delicious. With the story you just called in, it's brilliant.'

Peter was incredulous. 'What?' he repeated.

'We'll scoop everyone. Prager already has some ideas for the headline, but they're a bit tame. Any thoughts?'

Peter contemplated for a few moments. 'How about "Not Again! Livvie's Banzai at the Bazaar!"?'

'That's it! Another splash. Keep up the good work.'

Devrille hung up before Peter could tell him that he'd lost Olivia in the melee. *Why spoil an otherwise joyous moment?* That would have to be a story for another day.

39

Peter dragged himself into the office the next morning. *Thank God Ruby's been delayed in New York for a while longer.* A quick nightly call was about all he could manage for the time being.

Devrille scarcely raised an eyebrow when Peter told him that Olivia had been committed to a sanitorium as a consequence of her performance at the market. He was unimpressed to learn that she'd been denied any visitors.

'So what's the brilliant plan, Clancy?' Devrille tapped his pen repeatedly on the desk. 'Time for you to go undercover again, perhaps? Maybe this time you could disguise yourself as Sigmund Bloody Freud?'

Peter shifted uneasily in his chair. 'I'll work something out. She's in the Chelsea Care Clinic. It's hardly Fort Knox.'

Snoddy also shifted uneasily. 'It's a favourite of celebrities, so they're very security conscious. They can spot the press at one hundred yards.'

'I can't believe this!' Devrille yelled as he took hold of the pen, snapped it and fired it at Peter. The broken pen landed at Peter's feet. 'You're bloody useless, Clancy. You find the mother but lose the daughter? This is shit. Utter shit. We're going to lose this story if we can't get Olivia Michaels out of there. If the others catch on…'

'I know. I know.'

'Where is Mum by the way?' Devrille asked as he grabbed another pen out of the pen holder. 'Not wandering the streets or selling her story to another paper, I hope?'

'Mum and Ting were moved to a hotel late last night,' Snoddy replied. 'Not safe for them to stay in Notting Hill any longer. Not with Lipmann snooping about. One of my boys is taking care of security.'

'Thank heavens you're on the case, Snoddy.'

'I have an idea how we might get her out of the clinic,' said Peter after a short silence, keeping his head down in case Devrille decided to shoot it off.

'I should think so. Isn't that why I pay you? No more muck ups.' Devrille snapped the pen and dropped it on the desk. 'I'll end up having a heart attack.'

We can only hope you have several in a row, Johnny boy.

40

Snoddy had a connection at the Summit Nurses Agency, whom she used on occasion to obtain information about which celebrity was in what hospital. One of Summit's clients just happened to be Chelsea Care. Old Betty, the shift manager, supplemented her gambling habit helping out the *Geezer; for the right price*.

'I'm sure she'll fix you up with false ID and a shift at the Chelsea Care, if the *Gazer* throws enough of the folding stuff at her,' Snoddy told Peter.

Devrille wasn't happy about the flow of money; *like a sodding gushing pipe*. He reluctantly agreed to the ruse. 'Just don't make it our version of *The Great Escape*, Clancy. You're not Steve McQueen, you know.'

'I dated a nurse for a while. I know a bit about it. This could work,' he said.

'What other options have we got?' Devrille picked yet another pen from the holder. 'Employ the SAS to get the stupid bitch out?'

Later, Peter found himself sitting opposite Betty Flannery while she scrutinised him. Her eyes reminded him of those of a crow looking down on a dying sheep. Old Betty had been a psychiatric nurse for many years. She seemed the type who might inject a complete stranger with a heavy anti-psychotic sedative, just for the sheer enjoyment of it. He couldn't imagine Betty having a strong compulsion to the horses. *Goes to show, you can't judge a person by their addictions.*

'I'm not mad enough to let you do a shift in the hospital. A bit of extra money for a bit of gossip's one thing, but putting patients in harm's way, well, that's potentially murder, isn't it?' She unwrapped a mint and slipped it between her cracked lips, like she was posting a letter. 'So,' she continued, 'I've got you a job as Miss Michaels' private nurse. That way, you shouldn't be asked to do any real work. If you are asked to do anything, for heaven's sake, say no.'

'Right.'

'The nurses don't wear uniforms there, but they don't overdress. No jeans allowed. If you wear a suit, they'll be straight onto you.' She fumbled in a drawer. 'Here's your identification.' She pushed a card attached to a lanyard across the desk.

'Thank you.'

She then opened another drawer and took out a piece of paper. 'This is the handover sheet and patient list from last night. No-one particularly famous there at the moment. Mostly rich and depressed. Occasionally schizophrenic.'

'I'm only breaking out one patient.'

'Just in case you're asked any questions. Do you know what ECT is?' Betty asked.

'Shock therapy? Only what I've seen in movies and what friends have told me. Anything else I should know?'

'I can't very well teach you nursing in an hour, can I? Remember it's a seven o'clock shift, tomorrow morning. As you know, if you get caught, the agency has no knowledge of you. The ID was forged and you're an imposter. You're on your own.'

'You're a betting person, Betty,' he said with a grin. 'What odds do you give me getting in there and bringing Olivia Michaels out?'

'An outside chance at the most,' she said, her face cracking into a grin. 'Twenty-five to one.'

'Doesn't sound hopeful. But taking the big risks is where you make the big money, isn't that so?'

Betty's smile disappeared. She rummaged through her drawer again. 'Here's a map of the clinic. Some names to remember. Oh,' she added, 'and you won't forget to call Snoddy Doctor Snowdon tomorrow, will you?'

41

Except for a discreet sign at the gate, the Chelsea Care Centre might have been just another understated Georgian mansion on the King's Road. Even the security guard was inconspicuous, dressed like a concierge and standing just inside the front door. He was checking the identification of each person who entered with the thoroughness of a prison guard. When his turn came, Peter took a deep breath and stepped forward.

'You're the private nurse?' He looked at the ID Peter was holding out. The guard checked his list, then closely scrutinised the photo and the details.

'Nurse Howson.' The security guard poised his pen against the name. 'We don't get many male nurses here.'

'Really? I'm a qualified psych nurse, as you can see,' Peter muttered.

'The last one turned out to be a member of the gutter press.'

'What cheek!' he said. 'Doctor Snowdon can vouch for me.'

'Who's Doctor Snowdon when he's at home?'

'Who's Doctor Snowdon? She's the pre-eminent authority on the effect of psychotropic medication on immature and semi-adult paranoid psychotic behaviours. She also happens to be Olivia Michaels' attending psychiatrist.'

'Never heard of her.'

'Your loss I'm sure.'

'What's in your backpack there?' the guard asked. 'I'll have to check it.'

'Nothing much; just a book, my lunch and a coat.' *If he looks too hard…I'm gone.*

'Hurry up or we're going to miss handover,' said someone behind Peter to the guard. 'And you can explain it to the charge nurse.'

'Okay,' the guard replied, scanning Peter. 'Go, before I get strung up by Nurse Ratched.' Then he ticked off Peter's name.

Peter climbed the stairs to an office on the first floor. By what he had seen so far, Chelsea Care looked like a comfortable place to go mad; it was far closer to the Ritz than it was to Bedlam. Through the office window, he spied the conservatory, landscaped to look like an English country garden. There, patients could sit 'outside', without being spotted. There was no vantage point from which to focus a zoom lens. If he ever had a nervous breakdown—and Lord knows, he'd come close to it—this was the clinic he wanted to be taken to.

He scoured the office looking for keys. He knew roughly where Olivia's suite was located from the map, but the rooms would be locked. *Surely, they were locked. They were, weren't they?* Why hadn't he given Betty his undivided attention when she'd briefed him? He checked every desk, every wall and every surface. No keys. As he was rifling through the final drawer, the door creaked open.

'Who are you and what do you want here?'

'Nurse Hanson,' he said, tugging at his lanyard.

She looked at the identification card jangling at the end of a swivel. 'Hanson or Howson?' said the nurse. 'Either way, never heard of you.'

'Yes, it's my accent. I'm Nurse Howson, Olivia Michaels' temporary nurse. I'm filling in. Until her real one starts.'

'What are you doing here?'

'I just told you… Oh, you mean in the office?' *She probably thinks I'm a thief.* 'I'm looking for keys.'

'Her room's not locked. Surely you knew that.'

'The drugs cabinet? I have to administer chlorpromazine hydro-chloride. Twenty-five micrograms BD.'

'Except that Miss Michaels isn't taking chlorpromazine.'

'Well,' he retorted, 'she is according to Doctor Snowdon.'

'Doctor Snowdon? I've never heard of him either. This is all very irregular...'

'Doctor Snowdon has written her up for chlorpromazine twice daily. You can ask the doctor yourself, if you like. She's Miss Michaels' private psychiatrist. She'll be in shortly.' The nurse sniffed. Peter sensed weakness. 'You know, I wish hospitals were all run uniformly. In all my twelve years as a psych nurse, this is the first hospital I've worked in that's had such lax security.'

She ran an eye over him. Peter remained ice-cold. *Charge nurses can smell fear. They taste it in the air, like lizards.* 'Well, Nurse Howson,' she said finally, 'we like to think of this as a clinic, rather than a hospital. If it's been prescribed for Miss Michaels, you'll find it in her room. I suppose you'd better get to it.'

Olivia's room was located on the second floor, in the 'detoxification' wing. The night staff had reported that, unlike the previous day, she had been settled during the night. How was he going to sneak her out?

'Thank you,' said Peter. 'I'll take over from here. She's to have her own nurse and her own medicos from now on.'

The night nurse had already been informed about Peter's arrival and had waited for him. She was bleary-eyed and itching to leave. 'Right,' she said. 'One less is fine by me.'

After she left, Peter looked up and down the corridor. The only movement on the floor was a cleaning woman vacuuming at the other end. Olivia's suite was number fifteen. But where was the nurse who was supposed to be in charge of Olivia and the select few on the second floor? He guessed that she might be in the dining room, setting up for the medication round at breakfast. He couldn't bet his life on it. There was only one way to find out.

That's it. A flashing light. He left the security of the doorway, crossed the corridor in two steps and entered number ten. *Please be asleep or escaped.* The bed was empty but through a glass door he could see a man on the balcony beyond. He was middle-aged, his long hair tied back in a ponytail, looking at the ground as he smoked a cigarette.

Peter went to the bed and pressed the alarm, and hoped the nurse would be diligent enough to answer the call button immediately. Then he checked outside the room. Nurse Diligent was rushing up the corridor. He ducked back into the room.

His plan was either ingenious or imbecilic. *Time will tell.* He waited behind the entrance door. The man was staring vacantly; he hadn't noticed Peter.

'Mr Garland?' said the nurse as she entered the room. She cancelled the call bell. 'Oh, there you are.' She opened the glass door and stepped onto the balcony. Mr Garland still hadn't noticed her. 'Did you call me?' Mr Garland looked up and blew smoke in her face.

Peter took a closer look at Mr Garland. *That's Jack Garland? He looks so old. Bit different from when he was the lead singer of one of the greatest rock bands in history. I should have brought a camera.*

While she checked Garland over, Peter slipped from behind the door, darted across the room and quietly closed the glass door. The nurse looked around when she heard the lock to the balcony door click, but she didn't turn around. He ran through the room and out the door, jamming an intravenous pole through the handle and locking the nurse into the room. He ran down the corridor and ducked into room fifteen. Olivia was still asleep.

'Wake up, Olivia!' He shook her vigorously. She didn't stir. He heard the toilet in the adjoining bathroom flush. He looked behind him.

Snoddy came out of the bathroom, wiping her hands on a paper towel. 'Good,' she said. 'You're here.'

'I've locked the nurse on the balcony of number ten.'

'What?' Snoddy looked at him calmly. Peter was wild-eyed. 'What did you do that for?'

'So we could get Olivia out without being seen.'

Snoddy sighed. 'I'm here as her doctor. We can do as we want, within reason, as long as we don't draw attention to ourselves.'

'Umm. It might be too late for that.' Peter wiped his brow with his forearm. 'I locked the nurse on the balcony and then I jammed the door shut with an IV pole.'

'Did anyone see you?'

'I don't know.'

'Then you'd better un-jam it, hadn't you?'

Peter opened the door and peered down the corridor. The cleaner had moved away and it was silent. The pole was still in position. He strode across to the door of room ten, calling aloud, 'Hello, is anybody in there?' And then, with a flourish, he unwedged the pole. He heard the thumping as soon as he opened the door. Nurse Diligent was rosy cheeked and red fisted from pounding the door. Jack Garland had finished his cigarette. He still had a thousand-yard stare.

Peter scooted to the balcony door and unlocked it. 'What happened to you?' he blurted, trying to sound like he'd stumbled upon the situation.

'I don't know. I was locked out somehow. Thank you for getting me out. I'm awfully glad you happened past.' She blustered. 'By the way, I'm Sandy Gray.'

'Please don't thank me, Sandy.' He was a modest hero of the moment. 'I was just about to take Ms Michaels on her morning stroll. I'm her nurse, you know. Pete Howson.'

'Really?'

Really?' Why, what does she know? 'Yes. But Ms Michaels is lethargic this morning and a bit unsteady on her feet.'

'She was rather unsettled yesterday, so her meds were changed. If you need a hand with her, just call out.'

There are going to be problems if they've knocked her out. 'Thanks.'

'Don't mention it.' Nurse Gray followed Peter out of the room, as Jack Garland swivelled to watch. As they moved into the corridor, she spotted the IV pole and moved it along. 'That shouldn't be there,' she said.

Peter sucked in a lungful of relief.

42

'For fuck's sake, wake the fuck up, Olivia,' Peter growled as he tapped on her forehead with his knuckles. She squirmed and her eyes snapped open. Just as quickly, they shut again.

'Piss off, Nurse Bitch,' Olivia slurred, flailing her arms around in an attempt to hit him. She opened her eyes again, wider this time, in an effort to focus. She looked groggy.

'It's Peter. We haven't got much time.'

'Good to see you,' she garbled as she held out her arms to embrace him. 'Thanks for visiting.' She caught sight of Snoddy in a white coat. 'Oh, hello, Doctor. I didn't see you there. This is my boy-friend.' She gestured towards Peter. 'I've forgotten his name.'

'I'm Peter, remember? I'm not your boyfriend. And I'm not here to visit,' he returned, brushing her hands aside. 'I'm here to bust you out.'

'Oh, you're the director. You're very good looking for a director. Am I sleeping with you too? Is this a movie? Only, I seem to have forgotten my lines.'

'That's right, pretend you're in a movie if you have to. Ad lib. You can do that, can't you, dear?' said Snoddy.

'I don't like you,' replied Olivia. 'I've seen you somewhere before.'

Peter opened the knapsack, took out a bag and emptied it on the bed. A grey wig, a set of enormous cat's eye glasses, slippers and a floral dress fell on the bed.

'Presents?' Olivia said happily.

'It's your disguise. You're impersonating that former star of stage and screen, Mavis Cockle. Get dressed.'

'What are you doing?' said Snoddy. 'She doesn't need those.'

'But what if we're seen trying to sneak her out?'

'Blimey, Charlie,' Snoddy retorted. 'Don't you get it? We're here officially. We don't need to sneak her anywhere.'

'This disguise is our insurance. Official or not, Olivia Michaels may arouse suspicion. A pensioner, on the other hand, definitely won't.'

Olivia sat up. 'Ssh. Can you two take your artistic differences elsewhere?' she blathered. 'People are sleeping here.'

'Be a sweetheart and put them on,' Peter insisted, glaring Snoddy down.

'It's what an old lady would wear. I'm not wearing that.'

'Yes, you are. I'm the director and here's the direction: *I'm ready for my escape, Mr De Mille.* So fucking hurry up and put the costume on.'

'Hurrying.' Olivia flicked back the bedcover and raised herself into a sitting position. She picked up the wig and screwed it onto her head.

'I'm going to get a wheelchair. Anyone asks you, you're Mavis, the charlady, remember?'

'I can do charlady,' she said, shaking away the cobwebs. 'Cheeky monkey,' she added in a cockney accent. 'I am Mavis.'

Peter slipped out the door, scanning the corridor for staff. He spotted a couple of wheelchairs parked three doors away. As he ran towards them, Jack Garland came out of his room. They nearly collided.

'So sorry,' Peter apologised. 'Slight emergency.'

'Yes it is,' said Garland. 'You'd best hurry out of here.'

Peter was aghast at his sudden lucidity. 'What? What do you mean?'

'I just overheard Nurse Gray chatting over the telephone. She's in the nurse's station down there.' He gestured towards the far end of the floor with his thumb. 'She's put a call through to Lou Lipmann. Fortunately for you, he's put her on hold. If you're going to get Olivia Michaels out of here you'd best hurry.'

'How...' began Peter.

'Don't ask how I know,' replied Garland. 'I hear things.'

By the time Peter returned with the wheelchair, Olivia was dressed. She had even whitened her face, rouged her cheeks and slapped on red lipstick. Her brows were two brown ticks, halfway up her forehead. She looked enough like Mavis Cockle, an East-Ender, retired thespian and fellow inmate of the Chelsea Centre, to fool a guard from a distance. 'Have I got time for a cigarette?' she asked.

'No. Just get in the bloody wheelchair.'

Peter hushed down Snoddy's protests and pushed Olivia into the wheelchair.

'I feel quite relaxed, now,' she said.

'Well, you have a shitload of psych drugs on board.' He wheeled Olivia out into the corridor, Snoddy following close behind.

A little further along, Jack Garland had seated himself in another wheelchair. As they moved towards him, he turned and implored, 'Can you take me too?'

'No, of course we can't, dear,' said Snoddy. 'You have to stay here. There's a good lad.'

'I can make things very difficult for you if you don't,' Jack added.

'Give the man a break,' Olivia chipped in. She glared at Snoddy. 'I still don't like you, but I like him. He's coming with us.'

Snoddy rolled her eyes. 'This is fast turning into a French farce,' she muttered. 'We'll be lucky if any of us get out of here. Well, all right.'

She took up Jack Garland's wheelchair and pushed him towards the lift door, pulling up alongside Olivia's. Peter frantically pressed the down button. It felt like an eternity before the doors opened. He wheeled Olivia into the back corner, and Snoddy pushed Garland's wheelchair in with such force that he nearly came out of it. Peter pressed the ground floor button and they waited. *Hurry up! I hate hydraulic lifts.*

'Careful, love,' Olivia said in her Mavis accent, 'You'll do him an injury.' She put out her hand. 'Mavis Cockle,' she said.

Jack Garland took her hand and shook it. 'Arthur C Beeson,' he replied. 'Pleased to meet you, Miss Cockle.'

Peter frowned. *Is that who he thinks he is? Or is he being funny?* 'We still have to get past security. Behave.'

'Don't get yourself all hot and bothered.' Olivia winked, as she made an adjustment to the wig.

The lift door opened onto the foyer. A security guard was sitting at the reception desk. *Not the same one. We're in luck.*

The guard eyed the approaching foursome. 'Sorry,' he said raising his hand. 'No-one's to go in or out for the moment.'

'What do you mean?' began Peter. 'Mavis is going for an outing today. It's been approved. She'll be leaving us for good in a week.'

'I just got a call,' he repeated. 'No-one's to go in or out.'

'You got a call about Mavis Cockle and Arthur C Beeson?' Peter remarked as he pushed the wheelchair to the counter.

'No, but someone's trying to get Olivia Michaels out,' he confided. 'I can't let anyone pass until further notice.'

Olivia smiled cheekily at the security guard. 'No-one could mistake me for Olivia Michaels now, could they, luvvie,' she croaked.

'You're looking well, Mavis,' the guard smiled back as he checked his clipboard.

'You make a woman blush, you do. Cheeky,' she replied.

'I can't see your name on the list. Or his.' He pointed at Garland.

We're fucked. Well and truly. It will have to be The Great Wheelchair Escape.

'But the doctor said I've been so well behaved that I can escape for the day. Be a pet.'

'All right, Mavis.' The guard relented. 'I'll let you go. Who's picking you up?'

'The Queen Mum, of course. We're going to the races today at Epsom. One of her horses is running.'

Peter breathed a sigh of relief. *The Award for Best Charlady Impersonator goes to...* He was about to push the wheelchair past the first of two sets of automatic doors leading to the street, when the guard took a call. *Just keep on going. He who hesitates is caught. Come on, Snoddy.*

'Stop!' yelled the guard.

The first set of automatic doors opened. Peter was charging towards them, Garland and Snoddy alongside.

'Stop!' the guard repeated.

The second set of doors opened. Olivia's wheelchair was half-way through.

'Miss Michaels!' cried the guard.

To Peter's horror, Olivia turned her head. 'Yes?' she said.

Fuck! Never break character!

The guard was stabbing at the emergency door lock. Peter threw Olivia through the external door, but he, Snoddy and Garland were about to be caught in the airlock. The guard had activated the alarm and the set of external doors were slowly closing. Olivia was outside, watching in horror, wig skewed, glasses at an angle.

Just then, Garland wedged his wheelchair alongside Olivia's, creating a gap between the doors just wide enough for them to climb through. The guard had left the counter and was grabbing at them, and two others were just behind him. One grasped Snoddy's arm and was twisting it back as she cried in pain.

'No!' shouted Garland. 'Arthur C Beeson forbids it!' He swung around and punched the guard in the face. 'Run free, homo sapiens,' he roared, 'save yourselves. No more alien abductions, no more anal probing!'

Snoddy and Peter clambered over the tangle of chairs and through the doors. Behind them Garland was thrashing about, bellowing about extra terrestrials and the injustice of human vivisection. He had caught up the guards, who were trying to pacify him as he jerked and twitched.

A moment later, Snoddy's yellow Rover drove up and all three of them fell into the back seat. Peter glimpsed the driver's coffee skin. *Malcolm?* 'We're in trouble. Lipmann's heavy's just picked us up,' he whispered to Snoddy.

'What are you talking about?' she replied. 'That's my son Clyde.'

The Rover pulled away before Peter could drag the door shut. As they drove off, he could just make out, through the glass door, Jack Garland lying on the floor between the sets of doors, arms outstretched like a man crucified. He was catatonic again.

Steve McQueen couldn't have done it any better.

43

Peter had never expected any tearful, falling-into-each-other's-arms, mother and daughter reunion but this was awkward. Silent, tense, awkward.

Olivia sat next to Ting, chain smoking as she stared blankly at the ceiling. They had all moved into a suite at the Athaneum. Carol-Lee sat on the other side of the room. She was throwing down whiskies, the only sign of her stress being her shaking hands. Peter had taken up a no-man's-land position on a chair in the middle of the room. Someone had to open the proceedings and it might as well be him. *Sometimes editors should issue helmets to journalists.*

'So what's going through your head right now?' Peter's eyes darted from Olivia to Carol-Lee. He braced for a reaction.

'What do you think? That's a stupid question,' Olivia snapped as she stabbed out her cigarette in an ashtray. 'Until a couple of days ago, my mother was dead. Lou even organised a funeral to prove it, God knows whose that was. Now I find out she's not some miserable ghost come back to life, but she's been living these fifteen years in a hole in Wales. I'm so happy that you've brought my mother back.'

'Really?' said Carol-Lee.

'No, not really, you ugly old slag,' Olivia replied. 'You're a bloody festering carbuncle that won't go away.'

At least it's all coming out now. Time to heal. Hopefully no trips to hospital.

'It's good to know that you look like you're nearly dead. For real, this time. It's comforting in a way.'

'Very good, Olivia. Get it off your chest,' said Peter, feeling as if he'd morphed into a psychologist. 'What about you, Carol-Lee?'

Olivia stood up before Carol-Lee could answer. 'I really want to throw her back in the gutter right now. If you don't throw her out, I will.' Ting took hold of Olivia's arm and gently pushed her down onto the seat. 'You want to know the ugly truth? You want to know what this bitch did to me? My so-called mother sold me to child molesters so she could get rich. She used my fame. Is that enough of a best-seller for you? That should catch the readers' attention.'

Carol-Lee's reaction to the outburst was to have another mouthful of whisky. She swirled what was left around the sides of the glass. 'There's always another side to the story.'

'Bullshit! There's no other side. Another side doesn't exist. If there is another side, it will just be another pack of lies.'

'I need to say something.' Carol-Lee put down her now empty glass on the small table next to her. She missed and it fell on the carpet, scattering the ice across the floor.

'Are you always drunk?' Olivia ranted as she glanced at her mother.

'Only since he stole you off me. Since then, I've been drunk every day. I've been trying to forget it. But how could I forget you?' Carol-Lee sobbed. 'A mother never forgets her child.'

'You call yourself a mother? There's a laugh. Say it quickly then get out,' Olivia replied coldly as she folded her arms.

'Granted, I'm not much of a mother, but I'm your mother all the same. Ever since you were a little girl you wanted to be on the stage. You were the little actress since the day you were born. A natural talent. Well, you were picking up some modelling jobs here and there. Then I got a call from him. Lou Lipmann. He said he could take your career to the next level. If I was star struck, well, so were you.'

'Don't you dare suggest I was to blame for what happened.'

'Oh no, love. Of course not. At first, he was nice, you see, taking us to posh hotels, organising holidays by the seaside. After you started making hit movies, Lipmann wanted total control of you.'

'And you let him have it, you stupid cow.'

'I didn't, my love,' Carol-Lee cried. 'Honest to God. He used his powerful friends to have me declared an unfit mother and made himself your guardian.'

'But you stole all the money I'd earned.' Olivia jumped out of the chair before Ting could restrain her, and rushed at Carol-Lee. Peter placed himself between the two women. He wound his arm around Olivia while Ting held her back.

'It was a lie. I didn't steal any money. I didn't leave you in his care and go and live it up in Spain. That's all lies. I was putting it away for you.'

'So where is it then?'

'I... I...'

'Spent it. Why don't you admit it? You stole from a child—your own child. That's bad enough, but what I really want to know is why you let them... Why did you...let them...let them touch...' Olivia tried to push Peter and Ting aside. '...me.'

Carol-Lee rose slowly and unsteadily from her chair and came towards her daughter. 'Let her go. If Olivia wants to hit me, let her. I can understand why she is so angry with me.'

Olivia slumped to the floor, holding her face. Peter and Ting crouched down beside her in an effort to comfort her. She pushed them away. 'Why don't you all leave me alone?'

'No, baby, don't cry,' said Ting. 'Here, let me help you. You want something for your nerves?'

Olivia shook her head. She looked up and wiped her eyes on her sleeve. One of her false eyelashes peeled off and attached itself to the cuff of her shirt. 'Why?' she cried. 'Why?'

'I thought he was trustworthy. He seemed nice. He had connections with an acting academy for children. That's where you started, remember?'

'Sort of,' she whimpered.

'Lou seemed to have a big heart when it came to the kids. "I never knew my parents," he'd say, "so I don't want these kids to have to be brought up like I was. I want to give them a chance." I remember many of the kids were from broken homes. A lot were living in foster homes. Come to think of it, not many of the kids actually had parents. I think it was you and one other who was living with family.' Carol-Lee frowned. 'Lou used to take the kids to a toyshop or to the zoo. "This is what Livvie needs," I thought. "She needs a father figure in her life."'

'So, why didn't you come with us? Why did you let me go alone?'

'He said I'd be a distraction for the kids. "Don't you worry your pretty head," he'd say whenever I mentioned it, "I'll take care of her." He let me go to the office to sign papers, let me onto the movie sets, but that was it. After a while you started coming home...' Carol-Lee eased herself to the floor beside Olivia. 'When you came home crying... When you didn't want to go with Lou by yourself,' she continued, 'that's when I got suspicious.'

'I didn't want to go. I never wanted to go,' she wailed. 'Why didn't you do something?'

'I said to him one day that you didn't want to go out any more. He changed his mood totally, from nice to sinister in seconds.'

'And then?' asked Peter.

'Lou shouted at me. "No-one tells Lou Lipmann what to do." He said Livvie had to go with him to meet important people. I said, I was her mother and she didn't want to go. If she had to go, I was going with her.'

'You should have stopped him!' Olivia screeched as she looked at her. 'You should have saved me.'

'I tried, Livvie, really I did.'

'You should have tried harder. You should have tried harder,' she repeated in a whisper.

'You really think I didn't try? "I'm her mother," I kept saying as he dragged you away from me. I tried to stop him but one of his thugs was there and pushed me away like I was pond scum. "You're not a mother," Lou said.' Carol-Lee reached out to touch Olivia's hair. '"You're a fucking filthy whore. Whores shouldn't have children. No wonder her father left you. You're a whore. I'll make sure you never see Olivia again," he yelled. And then he took you.'

Olivia shook her head. 'I thought it was all different. In my head, I remember it differently.'

'It's what Lou put in there. He brainwashed you against me, don't you see?' Carol-Lee said as she gently stroked her daughter's hair. 'That was the last time I saw you, except in the movies and in the newspapers...until now.' Carol-Lee laid her head on the floor and started to cry. 'I wanted to die, I really did. I went to the police. Nobody listened. I took him to court and that's where your money went. I went to the newspapers. I couldn't get anywhere. The papers portrayed me as the mother who stole your money and physically abused you. "The Evil Witch-Mother" they called me. You see, Lou even has the papers doing his bidding. I thought of killing myself many times but I told myself the day would come. I always hoped a day like this might happen. The booze was a way to make the wait bearable.'

Olivia looked at her mother and reached out to her. She was twelve again. Carol-Lee took Olivia in her arms and rocked her. 'I even went to his house to kidnap you. I got caught climbing a fence. Lipmann said to me that if I kept trying to get you back, he'd have the both of us murdered. Just like that. No troubles.'

'Is this true?' she asked as Carol-Lee wiped away her tears.

'I have nothing to gain from lying to you. If you don't believe me then I'll go back to Wales with the knowledge that at least I was able to tell you my side of the story. And to see you one last time. For a long time, that's all I prayed for. And then I got angry at God as well.' She paused. 'It is so good to see you again. To see what a beautiful and strong woman you are.'

Olivia's expression softened. 'Mum,' she said, 'don't ever leave me again.'

'Never, my darling, never. I'll never let those animals come near you again.'

Peter looked across and saw that Ting was crying. It was then that he realised he had tears gathering in the corners of his eyes.

'Help your old mother up, will you?' Carol-Lee struggled to her knees.

Olivia smiled as she supported her weight. 'For a long time I used to imagine you hugging me in bed. I really thought I could feel your arms around me.'

'I imagined it too.'

'At first I could hear your voice, and then after a while I couldn't. But deep down in my heart part of me knew you hadn't done what they said,' Olivia continued.

'I always believed that I'd see you again before I died.' Carol-Lee shut her eyes, savouring the moment. 'But with everything I read about you, I wasn't sure that I'd see you again before you died.' She sniffed. 'I'm so sorry, Livvie. For everything you went through.'

'Me too,' said Olivia.

44

Peter took away the tape recorder, snapping it off only once he'd left the room. They knew that the mother–daughter exchange was being recorded, but he thought that, in all the emotion, they might have forgotten and the click would have sounded clinical and detached. He hung around longer, hoping that Olivia might want to continue with the interview, but all she wanted to do was spend time with Carol-Lee. That was understandable. Olivia didn't go to the bathroom with Ting to *freshen up* and Carol-Lee didn't drink until she passed out. They just talked. He felt glad to have reconnected them.

He wanted to believe that they would never again need their respective addictions to get by, but giving up was going to take time and dedication. He knew how hard it had been for him. They could detox later. *What was my addiction? Alcohol. Oh, and footy, women, greasy food, a headline with my by-line. Easy. Right at this moment, it's just the headline.*

At the end of the day, after everyone had finally drifted off to bed, he made a transatlantic call to New York. Ruby's voice on the other end of the phone felt like an embrace. He told her how much he missed her, and yes, how much he loved her. Then he told her of the events that had transpired. She said she would be home in a week. He said he wished it was today, but he was secretly happy that she'd be away for another seven days, as he would be able to concentrate all his efforts on unravelling the story. Then he would tell her who he really was. *If you really love someone, tell them the truth.*

Of all the women who had walked into his messed up, shambles of a life, Ruby Manzanoni was by far the sweetest. He may have mentioned the L-word in passing to others, but he'd always felt nauseated after saying it, like he'd eaten a bad meal. *Ruby has got me all giddy. But she loves me as the other Peter Clancy. Maybe, I'm a better person as the other one. Maybe.*

He didn't have the energy to go back to Ruby's flat; instead he found a spare couch and crashed fully-clothed and face down into it. *I'm totally spent. I need a long holiday. Yes, I'll take Ruby to the Algarve for a holiday. Sun, sex and sangria. That's right, I have to tell her before she finds out. Maybe, after a holiday?* He had been so busy that he didn't even know how Collingwood was going in the finals back in Melbourne. *What was the last game I saw? Was it at the Outback Hotel in Earls Court? Shit, that was over a month ago.* He was still thinking of the last live game he'd seen them play when he fell into a deep, deep sleep.

They lost to fucking Essendon.

He was still playing kick-to-kick with Peter Daicos, when he felt himself being prodded in the chest. *Hey Peter, not so hard!* The Sherrin was stinging into his chest wall. At first, he tried to ignore it. Then it got too painful. He tried to shake himself awake. It wasn't Daicos's drop punt that had been causing the pain.

They're back.

He threw a wild punch with his right arm even before he'd opened his eyes. The punch didn't connect.

'You bloody nearly hit me,' Olivia protested.

Only then did he open his eyes. 'What? Olivia?' he garbled.

'I need you.'

He was now fully awake and sitting up. 'I'm sorry, Olivia. I'm spoken for. Ruby, remember?'

'No. Not that,' she shot back. 'I don't want to have sex with you. I want to talk.'

'Now?' He wiped sleep from his eyes. 'I'm bloody exhausted.'

She turned on a lamp. He could now see her more clearly. She was wearing flannelette pyjamas with fluffy rabbits stamped all over them. She wasn't a sex symbol or a celebrity now, she was a lost little girl wearing fluffy rabbit pyjamas. Maybe she never was a celebrity.

'I want to talk,' she demanded.

Peter sat up and checked his wristwatch. 'It's two in the morning. Can't it wait?'

'I can't sleep. Seeing Mum has brought back all these horrible thoughts. If I don't talk about it now, I'll go crazy.'

'Okay,' he relented. He reached across to the coffee table and grabbed the tape recorder. 'Before we start, I have to make myself a strong coffee. No. I'll make two strong coffees.'

'None for me, thanks.'

'No. They're both for me.'

After two strong espressos, restored to a semblance of alertness, Peter jotted down a few questions. He was considering how far he could probe without provoking a meltdown, and whether or not he should have a third coffee, or something stronger. He gazed across at Olivia who had settled back on the couch with her legs crossed, cuddling a pillow. For the first time ever, she almost appeared relaxed.

'Do you need anything?'

'No. I'm fine for the moment.'

'Should I start?'

'Certainly.'

Peter switched on the tape recorder. 'If you want me to stop at any time.'

'I'll let you know.'

'You said earlier, that Lou had a children's acting academy. Was it a proper acting academy?'

'On the surface it was. We had acting and dance lessons. We had proper teachers.'

'What do you mean by, "on the surface"?'

'On so-called special occasions, we'd have parties.'

'Parties?'

'They called them parties.'

'You mean balloons, clowns, games?'

'Superficially, I suppose they were.'

'It wasn't a children's party?'

'It was really a party for them...the guests. They were also called benefactors.'

'Guests? Benefactors?'

'They went by a few different titles. But I wouldn't call them nice.' Olivia fished into her pyjama pocket, pulled out a pack of cigarettes and a lighter and lit one.

'They were male?'

'All of them. Some were younger, some really old. They were always well-dressed, like they were someone important. They weren't the man in the street, you might say.'

'Did you recognise any of them?'

'I recognised some from the television.'

'Did you know their names?'

'You really want me to name names, don't you? Do I have to name them?'

'Well, I could make up the names but that won't make your book very credible, will it?'

Olivia took a long drag of her cigarette before stubbing it out. She frowned at Peter before reaching for another cigarette.

'Are you okay?'

'Yes. You're right. It isn't easy but it has to be done.'

'Was he someone everyone knows?'

'I used to like his show when I was a kid...until I met him,' she said softly. 'It was Allan Edgar.' She lit the cigarette shakily.

'Allan Edgar?' Peter repeated. 'He was in that show...'

'Doctor Fixit.'

'I didn't think he'd be...'

'Don't sound surprised. There's more where he came from.'

'I just never suspected that Allan Edgar would be... He seems—I mean, seemed—like a nice guy. Hasn't he raised a lot of money for children's charities?'

'It goes to show, you can't pick them by their good deeds, can you?' She feigned a smile. 'They're like actors. They have a role for the public and another, private one and never the two shall meet.' She took a last drag on her cigarette and stubbed it out as well. She hugged the pillow closer to her body.

'Do you want to keep going?'

'It's all out in the open now. It's too hard now to try and put the paedo back in the bottle.'

'Any other names?'

'I can't remember their names. Honestly, I can't. I know some are celebrities and others are establishment types. I'm having trouble remembering their names right now. But their ugly faces are always there in my head.' She sighed deeply and pushed her face into the pillow.

'Give it time.'

She raised her head again. 'I hate clowns. Really hate clowns.'

'Clowns? Why them?'

'They used to entertain us, give us lots to eat and drink before the men arrived. They were drugged.'

'Drugged?' He took a deep breath. 'The food and drinks were drugged?'

'So we couldn't put up a fight.'

'You were unconscious?'

'Not quite. I wish. Then I wouldn't have to see those faces or feel...'

He wiped his face with his hands, took another breath and continued. 'I'm so sorry for you.'

Olivia sniffed. 'The guests would molest us while we were drunk, drugged, whatever you want to call it.'

'That is totally depraved.' Peter shook his head.

'Depraved? That's an understatement.'

'Could you avoid being drugged?'

'If you were like me and had been at the Academy for a while, you caught on. If you didn't eat or drink, they would force you. Sometimes it was better if you were drugged. Unfortunately, you can still remember, but you can't resist. I can't get rid of the memories.' Olivia lit another cigarette.

'It was the clowns?'

'Yes, the clowns and others. They were just dressed up.'

Peter felt the nausea rising in his throat. He'd seen and heard a lot more than the average man of his age, but this was evil beyond comprehension. 'Excuse me.' The nausea rose in his throat. He wiped his mouth with a handkerchief he had found in his trouser pocket. He turned off the tape recorder.

'You okay?'

'I have to go the toilet.' He rushed to the bathroom, threw open the door, dropped to his knees in front of the toilet bowl and vomited. After he had finished, he sat on the floor. *I was concerned that Olivia wouldn't be able to bear reliving the horrors of her childhood, now I'm worried that I might not be able to bear her recalling them.* He looked at himself in the mirror and washed his face. His eyes felt and looked like paperweights. *You have to. You have a duty. Keep it together or this story may not be told and the bastards will never be punished.*

He returned to the sitting room feeling as restored to normality as a good spew could achieve. Olivia was hunched over the coffee table snorting three lines of cocaine through a fifty pound note. She jumped when she noticed Peter.

'I needed something,' she said sheepishly as she wiped her nose with her thumb. 'I know you're not into it.'

'I can understand,' he replied as he sat down on the couch. He then noticed the full glass of whisky.

'I poured you a straight scotch.' She smiled faintly as she handed Peter the glass.

'Thanks.' He took a long drink.

'Shall I keep going?'

'If you're up to it.' He returned the glass to the coffee table and switched on the tape recorder.

'Where were we?' Her eyes were unnaturally luminous. She lit a cigarette.

'The clowns drugged you.'

'I don't want to talk about that anymore.'

'That's fine. Do you remember any of the children at the academy?'

'There was another boy whose mum was a single mother, like mine.'

'Do you know where the children came from?'

'Lou Lipmann mainly went to foster homes to get the children.'

'How do you know?'

'I heard the kids saying it.'

'How did you and this boy become part of this? You'd think Lou wouldn't want any parents becoming suspicious.'

'I think Lou thought that two single mothers living in council flats wouldn't be a threat. The other boy's mother took drugs, or at least that's what I believe. I don't think she had a clue. Mum seemed more aware, later on at least. I think we were chosen because we were very beautiful. I looked very innocent back then.'

'Do you know what happened to him?'

'His name was Andy,' Olivia recalled. 'We eventually did a musical together at Her Majesty's. Then Andy disappeared. I haven't seen him for years.' She chuckled. 'I used to have such a crush on him.'

'What happened to the foster kids?'

'Don't know. They just came and went.'

'And no-one said anything.' He finished the glass of whisky.

'The kids were too scared to speak out. Out there, no-one can hear you scream.'

'Is Lou Lipmann a paedophile himself?'

'I heard he liked young boys. That's what I heard. I never...' Her voice trailed off.

'That's all right. So Lou got custody of you, basically, so he could have total control of you?'

'I lived with him until I was sixteen. Then I got my own place. Of course, he still controlled everything. He still does.'

'When did they stop abusing you?'

'When I was about twelve or thirteen. That's when I was no longer of interest to them, and I guess it's when I became famous. I would have probably attracted too much attention.'

'Did Andy stay with his mother?'

'She died from an overdose, I heard.'

'Were Andy and you in the musical, *Children of the Dark*?'

'Yes, we were. I almost forgot.'

'That's how Richard Manzanoni knows you?'

'He'd seen our work. He was impressed and he cast us as the leads.'

'He didn't come to the academy?'

Olivia stiffened and cast the pillow aside. 'Richard wasn't one of them. Andy and I went on an audition. Stop trying to fucking insinuate anything else.'

'Sorry.'

'I'm done.' She hopped off the couch. 'Please don't ask me about Uncle Richard again. He's not part of this.'

'Promise,' he replied as he switched off the tape recorder.

'This is what you wanted for the book?'

'They'll be flying off the shelf if what you've told me is true.'

'Of course it's fucking true,' she snapped. 'It's not lines from a script.'

'Why didn't you ever tell anyone?'

'How? I was a child. Who would have believed me then when you don't even believe me now?'

'It's not about what I believe. We're going to need witnesses to come forward to substantiate your story.'

'You've heard what Mum's had to say. Isn't my story enough?'

'Personally, I don't care if we're sued, I'm indemnified by you. No-one will sue me for correcting your grammar or putting your words into proper sentences. They'll sue the fuck out of you, however. The more witnesses, the less chance of you getting sued.'

'I want them to pay, not me. They have to be punished.'

'And we need some more proof to make sure of that. How about we start with Andy, wherever Andy may be?'

'I'll see what I can find out.'

45

Olivia went back to bed, scowling and sullen. Peter doubted she was in the mood for sleep, but that wasn't his concern. He had just settled back on the couch when the lamp snapped on again.

'What the fuck? Can't a man get any sleep? Go away, Olivia.'

'It's not Olivia, it's Carol-Lee.'

Peter squinted at her. He checked his watch. A little after three.

'We need to talk.'

'Can't it wait?'

'No. I don't want Olivia to hear what I have to say.'

'She's high as a kite, her hearing's probably super-sensitive at the moment.'

'She's listening to music and dancing. She's got her earpieces in.'

He hauled himself into a sitting position. 'Shall I put on the recorder?'

'Yes.'

'Everything Livvie's told you is true,' she said. 'I can prove it.'

He had forgotten all about sleep. He was wide awake. 'Go on.'

'One of the benefactors Livvie was telling you about committed suicide, oh, I don't know, a few months before she started the court case against me. Or it might have even been a year.'

Too vague. Not a good start. 'And?'

She poured herself a scotch and downed it. 'He must have found his conscience. Before he topped himself, he wrote Olivia a letter and sent it to her. Recorded delivery. To our private address, not the agency and not her fan club. I collected the mail and I opened it.' Carol-Lee rummaged around the pocket of her dressing gown and pulled out an envelope. 'Here. See for yourself.'

Of handmade paper, the envelope was embossed with a name Peter instantly recognised. The author had been rich and titled. He took the letter out of the envelope and read it.

> *My dearest, loveliest Olivia,*
>
> *I have been reflecting on my life of late, and realise that I have done many things I profoundly regret. One of those things was falling in love with you. You were my Lolita and I an unlikely Humbert. My crime of passion wasn't the sentiment, however (for who could not but be smitten by you), but the deed. You were the most precious of flowers and I plucked you from the bush too early and without thought. It was inconsiderate and cruel. I ought to have waited.*
>
> *Guilt hangs around my neck like a noose. I was wrong. I cannot return to you what I took from you, but I can make amends a little. This letter is my confession to you, in expiation of my many, many sins. Would the others do as much? I do not think so. Therefore, I beseech you to look beyond this letter, keep it safe and forgive a dying man, a fool, a lover, a sinner, who never meant to hurt you—if you can.*

It was signed with his name.

'Then he hanged himself,' said Carol-Lee. 'I call him the Suicide Lord. I can't bear to say his name. I would have preferred he'd lived and then I could have cut him into small pieces and fed him to the swine.'

The letter sickened Peter, as much for the act itself, as for the spin the Suicide Lord had tried to place on the act. 'So what did you do with the letter?'

'First I went to the police. They were interested at the beginning. They promised me an investigation. If there were others, they were going to find them and bring them to justice. Then, all of a

209

sudden, the inspector I'd been talking to was taken off the case. I was told I was mad and that the Suicide Lord hadn't admitted to anything really, and besides, he was dead, so what was I complaining about? I said, "What about the others, like he's written in the letter?" They said it proved nothing.' Hands trembling, she poured herself another glass. 'So then I went to Lipmann.'

'And?'

'I told him about the letter and he denied I even had it at first. Then I showed him a copy I had made of it. Lipmann was furious. He put his hands around my neck and tried to throttle me. He said if I ever said anything about it to anyone ever again, I was dead and Olivia was dead. I'd be signing my own death warrant, he said.'

Peter looked at the letter again. The mention of Lolita left little doubt that the Suicide Lord had abused Olivia. It didn't implicate anyone else directly. He shook his head doubtfully.

Carol-Lee stood up and turned off the tape recorder. 'I know what you're about to say, but there was more. This is strictly between us. He didn't just send me a letter, he sent me a whole package. I think he wanted the others to go down with him.' She paused. 'You see, these animals didn't just enjoy doing things to innocent children, they enjoyed filming themselves doing things. And watching others doing things. They shared the films around. Can you believe it?' Carol-Lee wiped her eyes and her nose. 'In the package, were some of the films. The Suicide Lord sent them to Olivia. He must have known I'd be the one collecting it from the post office.'

Peter sat forward. 'What happened to the films?'

'I thought about giving them to the police, but something in the back of my mind told me not to. I never mentioned them to a living soul, not even Lipmann, because I was afraid that if he knew I had them he'd kill us to get them. I never said a thing, until now. Except...'

'Except?'

Carol-Lee finished her drink and put down the glass. 'Livvie's dad isn't some anonymous git I met in a pub once. Ever heard of Walter Evans?'

Peter searched the recesses of his brain and came up with a blank. 'Not that I can recall.'

'Ever heard of *Yorkside Terrace*?'

'Vaguely. It was a TV series, wasn't it? It was popular in Australia in the sixties. I never watched it, though.'

'It's still running every Wednesday night. Well, Walter Evans was one of the actors on *Yorkside Terrace* back in 1962. I was a make-up artist, and that's how we met. We were head over heels in love with one another. We were together for a year.'

'But you never married?'

'Couldn't do, he was already married and he already had a family. I was seventeen when I found out I was pregnant. He wanted me to get rid of the baby, but I wouldn't and that was the end of that.'

'You took his name?'

'Not at first. Only after I disappeared. Only after Lou Lipmann said he'd kill Livvie if he ever saw or heard from me again.'

'So why are you telling me this?'

'After I saw Lipmann about the letter, I got to thinking. If he ever found out about the films it would be the end for us. The only way to get back at Lipmann and the others was to keep the films safe, so I gave them to Walter. Justice delayed is still justice. I told him to put them somewhere very safe and to keep schtum. If anything ever happened to either one of us, he was to go straight to the papers with them. Not to the police, mind, I told him. To the papers.'

'Any idea what he did with them?'

'He wrote me a few weeks later to say he'd put them in a bank safe deposit. I didn't want to know the details in case I was ever tortured. He said that if I ever needed them, he'd get them for me.'

Peter's brow furrowed.

'Oh, believe me, Lipmann's capable of it. That man's capable of murder. I doubt he'd break a sweat. I knew the films were safe with Walter. I never ever mentioned who Livvie's father was then or now, and I'm very glad I didn't. No way to get to him, you see.'

'Did you ever watch the films?'

'I saw about a minute of one. I thought I was going to go crazy. These men are beyond sick.'

'And where's Walter now?'

'I don't know. I wrote him one last time back in 1976 and the letter was returned. I never heard from him again.'

'Give me everything you know about him and I'll put out some feelers.'

'All right.' She bit her lip. 'Lipmann's beyond evil. I suppose it's the reckoning now.'

'Well, it will be if we can find Walter Evans and get those films. That's all the proof we'd need to put them away for a very long time.'

Peter added Walter Evans to the list of missing persons he needed to locate.

DD

I think I'm in love. In fact, I know I'm in love and Tinker says he loves me too. He tells me everything. He says I'm the only person he can really talk to.

Tinker wants to be with me all the time. We're like Romeo and Juliet, I suppose. I'll love him forever.

He's not like anyone I've ever met before. I told him everything about me and I know everything about him. There are no secrets between us. I don't want anything from him and I would never ever hurt him. One day, the whole entire universe will know how much we love each other.

xoxoxo
Belle.

46

Despite only having three hours' sleep on an uncomfortable couch, Peter woke up early. A strong coffee would have probably fixed the lack of sleep and the sore back, but there was no time for that. He had to get to the office. Get hold of Snoddy. If he could prove Olivia's and Carol-Lee's claims, this story was going to be history-making. *This is the story every investigative journalist has fantasies and nightmares about.*

He grabbed his coat and the tape recorder and headed for the door. He noticed Carol-Lee sitting at the dining table in a dressing gown, having a glass of whisky. She looked as if she hadn't gone back to bed. The bottle was almost empty. She was flicking through what looked like a small photo album.

'I'm trying,' she said sadly when she noticed Peter's gaze. She placed the glass back on the table. 'It's really hard to stop.'

'I know.' *I've been there myself.* He sat beside her on a spare chair.

'Did you want a glass?'

'No thanks. I would kill for an espresso right now, but I'm late for an appointment.'

'Livvie and I will give up our addictions once things settle down.' Carol-Lee smiled. 'She's like her mother, isn't she? She's got my personality.'

'Now you have a good reason to give up the grog.'

She looked away. 'I want to show you something.' She opened the album to a page and pushed it towards Peter.

'That's Olivia and you, isn't it? Looks like it was taken the same time as the one I saw at your home.'

'We were so happy.'

There was a boy of similar age to Olivia, perhaps a little older, sitting at Carol-Lee's feet. The boy had an angelic face but something was wrong: blond hair, and dead, blue eyes. 'Who's the boy?' he asked.

'That's Andrew. Poor little Andy. What a sweet boy. His mother was supposed to be in the photo but she was in hospital that day. She eventually died from the drugs. After that, we lost contact with him for a long time.'

'Yes, Olivia told me. What do you know about him? It would be useful to find him. In case we can't locate Walter.'

'Andy Smith was in the academy with Olivia... They...were...'

Peter interrupted. 'Do you know where he is? If he is still alive?'

'Well, he was a few years ago.'

'How do you know?'

'I bumped into him in Cardiff, oh, a dozen or so years ago. He said he'd moved to America but he was applying to study medicine all over the UK and America, including Cardiff University. Seems he'd turned his life around.'

'Do you know where he is now?'

'I gave him my address, in case he got into the university, and wanted to keep in contact. He wrote a card to me not that long ago.' She slipped it out of the album. 'Here.'

Peter picked up the card. It was decorated with a Turner landscape.

> *Dear Caroline,*
>
> *Just a note to let you know that I just completed my residency in pediatrics at Georgetown University Hospital. From a child actor to pediatrician, who would have believed it?*
>
> *Andy Smith.*

'He's in America?'

'Well, that card came from Washington DC.'

'Did you receive any others?'

'No.'

'Shit.'

'It's a start, isn't it?'

'It's a start.' Peter pushed back his chair. 'I wonder how many paediatricians there are in the United States called Andy Smith.'

'One more thing I should have mentioned last night. Please don't tell Livvie about her father.' She grasped Peter's arm. 'Please. You won't, will you?'

'I won't.'

'And one final thing I want you to know, but please don't tell anyone.' She cast her eyes downwards. 'I only have a couple of months to live. My liver is packing it in. The doctor calls it end-stage cirrhosis of the liver. Even if I stopped drinking now I'd still only have a short time left.'

'I'm sorry.' He placed his arm around her.

'Don't feel sorry for me. Help me get those bastards that molested those poor little kids. Get them all, while I'm still alive. That's all I want now.'

'I promise, Carol-Lee. I'll do everything I can. If I have to walk through hell and break laws, arms and hearts along the way, I promise I will.' And he knew he meant it.

47

Another meeting in Devrille's office. *I'm going to be late. I have an excuse: I couldn't really hurry Carol-Lee up now, could I?*

A private meeting. There would be no sub-editors, no journalists, no-one except Peter, Devrille and Snoddy. Only they were party to what was going on.

Snoddy was resplendent in clashing jewel colours. She was already settled with a drink and a cigarette when Peter arrived. Without speaking to Devrille or Snoddy, he placed the tape recorder on Devrille's desk.

'What the f...' Devrille began as Peter hushed him down.

'I want you both to listen.'

He played the tape of Olivia's interview. Played back, her testimony sounded even more harrowing than when she had told him face to face. He watched their reactions as the tape played. Devrille was tapping the desk with the pads of his fingers, while Snoddy sat silent. Then Peter played Carol-Lee's. By the end, Snoddy had tears in her eyes.

As the tape began to hiss, Devrille wiped his mouth with his hand. 'What do you make of it?'

'I believe they're telling the truth. The letter's no forgery.'

'I'd like to cut their balls off with a blunt knife. Hanging would be too good for these bastards.' Devrille turned off the tape recorder.

'I can vouch for what she's saying,' said Snoddy.

Peter and Devrille glanced over at her.

'What do you mean? You know something?' said Devrille.

'I do. I was a Detective Sergeant when Carol-Lee made her report. The investigation went nowhere fast. There was a name for those men. They were the Untouchables. I always suspected the investigation was shut down, but I never had any solid proof.'

'Anyone else come forward?' Devrille asked.

'Not then,' said Snoddy. 'You see, I believe there were persons within the Met who were sympathetic to the cause.'

'The only other name I have is an Andrew Smith,' said Peter. 'His mum and Carol-Lee were friends. Andy and Olivia were in the academy together. His mum died later from an overdose.'

'A druggie? Hardly a credible witness there. It doesn't get any better,' Devrille complained.

'Andy was in the first Richard Manzanoni musical with Olivia then he left show business for good. I got that out of Carol-Lee this morning.'

'*Children of the Dark*, wasn't it?'

'That's the one.'

'Where's this Andy now?' Devrille asked.

'Living in America. A paediatrician, possibly in Washington DC. There's your credible witness.'

'If you can track him down,' said Devrille, looking at Snoddy.

'I don't have any contacts in America,' she replied.

Stella? 'I know someone who might be able to help,' said Peter. 'I used to work with her at *The Truth*. Her name's Stella Reimers. She's an American. We worked on a big story together and then she went back to the States. One of the best journos I've come across.'

'Where's she working?' Devrille asked.

Peter laughed. 'As it happens, she works at *The Washington Post*. In Washington DC. How lucky are we?'

Devrille sighed. 'Either she'll want a piece of the action or *The Post* will. I don't want them taking the story from us. We've done all the heavy lifting.'

'She owes me a favour,' Peter added. 'I think she'll be fine tracking down Andy. If she can't find him, no-one can.'

Devrille rocked back on his chair. 'Agreed,' he said after a long while. 'But tell her we're just trying to find this former child actor.

Don't mention he was molested. It's for a what-happened-to piece we're doing, okay?'

'I'll run that by her.' *Good chance she won't want to put herself out, if she can't even have a share of the by-line.* He pencilled himself a note and looked up again.

'Do you think Manzanoni is also a...?' Devrille asked.

'I've never heard that said. But then again, I'd never heard that Doctor Fixit was,' Snoddy replied. 'Is she covering up for him? That happens you know.'

'I'm pretty good at working people out. Olivia was adamant that Manzanoni had nothing to do with the academy,' Peter replied. 'And I believe her.'

'Snoddy, you're a prog rocker...' Devrille laughed.

'Not likely. You have to be on drugs to listen to that shit, don't you?'

'I wonder if there are any former members of his band who would be prepared to talk to us? I heard on the grapevine that there was no love lost between Manzanoni and his old band.'

'I'll ask around some of the clubs in Soho. I have a few contacts there,' Snoddy ventured. 'Isn't that where these old bands always seem to end up?'

'No idea, but it seems an excellent suggestion.'

'Oh, and one other thing.' Peter interrupted. 'I'm trying to locate a Walter Evans, actor, aged about sixty, acted in *Yorkside Terrace.*'

'Who's he?' asked Devrille.

'Not sure yet. He might be a relative of Carol-Lee's. He may know something, seen something.'

'I'll see what I can find,' said Snoddy. 'Shouldn't be too hard to locate.'

'If we can pull this together,' Peter said, 'this will be explosive.'

'Not in our face I hope, JB. Not in our fucking face,' Devrille remarked.

Peter decided he'd call America as soon as he got back to his desk. It would be five in the morning there. Willy Prager scowled as he watched him walk past. *Poor Willy.* Cramming last night's chip buttie into his mouth, washed down by a cup of indifferent tea as he typed. *Upset that you've been left out of the team once again, Willy? Memories of your old schooldays?*

Peter sat down at his desk and couldn't believe how tidy it was. Probably because he hadn't used it in weeks. He dialled the number and waited. He was impressed when Stella picked up the phone after only three rings.

'Peter,' Stella said in a groggy voice, 'what's happened?'

'How did you know it was me?' he asked.

'Who else rings at this time of day? Either you think I'm an insomniac or you're in trouble and you need my help.'

'I need your help. I need you to find someone.'

'Big story by the sound of it. Your voice sounds different.'

'He's crucial to authenticating the story.'

'Major investigation?'

'How did you guess?'

'Because you're asking me. What's the backstory?'

'Okay… I'm not supposed to tell you this but there's a paedophile ring here involving some famous and powerful men. I need to find a man who…'

'Your editor thinks I'll steal the story, doesn't he?'

'Correct.'

'I'm much bigger than that,' Stella said.

'Of course you are.'

'I don't know why I would want to help you… You know, I'm going to have to do this on the quiet. If my editor finds out… I'll just have to say I'm a freelancer. Why do you do this to me, Clancy?'

'I don't want to put your job in jeopardy.'

'You'll owe me big time for this.'

'I'm only too willing to return the favour. Anytime.'

'Can you call back in five minutes with the details?' she said.

'Is there someone there?'

'No, Clancy. I need to take a piss. Bye.'

48

The interior of the Blind Lemon Jazz Club on Frith Street was far more sumptuous than Peter had expected. He was expecting a Paul Raymond strip club: smoky, tacky, with darkened corners for the trench-coated patrons to 'enjoy' the show. Instead, it was more sixties supper club.

It could have been Shirley Bassey up there on the small stage, doing a rehearsal for tonight's show, rather than two grey-haired, soberly dressed men. One was tuning a six-stringed guitar and the other an upright bass.

'That's them,' commented Snoddy.

'Gabriel Bailey and Tim Howe? Ex members of Marquis Fission?'

'The same. They're members of the house band now.'

'Looks like they've changed a bit since the seventies.' He narrowed his eyes in an attempt to recognise them from his old posters. Without the long hair, outlandish costumes and make-up, it was nearly impossible. They stopped tuning their instruments when they noticed Peter and Snoddy standing at the stage.

'You want to talk to us?' asked Howe, putting down his guitar.

'I'm Peter Clancy,' Peter said. 'I presume you're Tim Howe?'

Tim Howe now looked like a staid, middle-aged bank clerk who should have been at home watching the television and having a cup of tea. Bailey, on the other hand, was bloated and overweight. He would have looked more comfortable drinking to excess at the local pub.

'You know me? A fan, I presume?' Howe asked.

'Used to be,' Peter replied.

'That's what everyone says,' Bailey sniggered. 'That's why we play here. Now, about the money…'

'Money?' Peter turned to Snoddy.

'They want fifty quid each.'

'That's…'

'You probably think we're rich former rock stars who are now jazz enthusiasts. Not the case,' Howe said bitterly as he unplugged his guitar. 'We wouldn't be playing in this shithole unless we had to.'

'But you're not here to ask about our tale of misery in the entertainment industry, are you?' said Bailey as he laid his double bass down on the stage. 'You want to know about Manzanoni? Hundred quid for us will get you a lot of story.'

'Okay. Pay them,' he directed Snoddy.

Charged with pints of beer, the four found a table near the stage. Peter took a sip before turning on his tape recorder.

'As Snoddy would have told you, I'm writing a book and I need some information on Manzanoni.'

'Is the book about him?' Howe asked.

'No. Someone else. I can't say who.'

'You want something unflattering about our old friend, dear Ricky?' Bailey queried.

'I have certain suspicions that you may be able to clarify.'

'We should be able to help.'

'I remember Marquis Fission were a big band for the time,' Peter began, 'but you seemed to break up at the height of your popularity.'

'Playing at Madison Square Garden is about as big as you can get,' Bailey boasted. 'It was like a dream come true.'

'We thought we had conquered the world,' Howe added. 'Ricky thought that all of the band's success was due to him. Success didn't take long to go to Ricky's head.'

'His keyboards were the band and we were the accompaniment.'

'The band broke up after Madison Square?'

'No. We took time off so Royal Ricky could do his fucking musical thing, Kids in the Dark or whatever.'

'Then we were supposed to tour the States. A massive tour was planned.'

'It didn't happen?'

'Lou Lipmann was our manager,' Bailey recalled. 'One day he gets the band together minus Manzanoni...'

'He tells us the band is breaking up. Manzanoni is going to be pursuing a solo career,' Howe cut in.

'Manzanoni didn't even have the fucking guts to face us.'

'We couldn't even use the band name. Lipmann and Manzanoni made sure they got the rights to the name and most of the royalties.'

'We tried to carry on with a new name and a new keyboard player. But no-one wanted to know us. It was hopeless.'

'I've heard rumours that Lipmann liked young boys?'

'We heard that too,' Bailey replied. 'We didn't see it ourselves because we never mixed in those circles.'

'Lipmann is an evil cunt,' Howe spat.

'So I've heard,' responded Peter.

'There were rumours of other people that associated with Lipmann who were molesting children,' said Bailey.

'Heard that too. We didn't want to ask questions or snoop around.' Howe added, 'We just wanted to be famous. We were selfish young pricks I guess.'

'Is Manzanoni a paedophile?'

'He's a lot of things but... Look, truth is, when you're a member of a big rock band, you do things you shouldn't. You stay up late. You take drugs. You sleep with women. They're always flashing their twats under your nose. You don't usually stop to ask them for their birth certificate,' Bailey replied. 'He likes girly-girls, rather than womanly-girls. Seen his missus? Skinny as a rake and hardly a tit in sight. But I don't think he's one of those.'

'And we lived in each other's pockets for five years. He fucked groupies like all of us did. Just normal fucking, mind you. Nothing too kinky. Maybe the odd threesome but that's normal for a rock star.'

'He was married?' Peter queried.

'Only at home,' Bailey laughed. 'Not when he was on tour.'

'Old press clippings reckon his first wife committed suicide.'

'You've done your homework, I see,' Howe replied.

'Bullshit. Manzanoni murdered her,' Bailey said quietly as he leaned forward.

'Murdered?' Peter was stunned.

'She was having an affair. Ricky got jealous.'

'How do you know this?'

'Jewel died from a heroin overdose, didn't she? But the thing is, she didn't do heroin. She never touched it.'

'How do you know this?'

'Jewel and I were close, in a friendly way,' Howe recalled. 'She told me that Ricky had tried to strangle her a few times. The man was insanely jealous. I told her to leave the prick but they had Ruby. She didn't want to mess Ruby up.'

'So you think he pumped her full of heroin?' Peter asked.

'You could say that,' Bailey replied.

'When did she die?'

'Was it about six months before he put on his musical?' Howe looked to Bailey.

'More seven. Ricky was busy that year. In between killing his wife, leaving his band and putting on a fucking kid's pantomine.'

'Would Lipmann have known this?'

'Of course. Manzanoni would have rung Lipmann before he rung the ambulance. In entertainment you always ring the management first. Golden rule.'

'That means that Lipmann would have been able to hold something over Manzanoni for the rest of his career,' Peter theorised.

'That how good management works.' Howe laughed bitterly. 'We knew that Manzanoni wanted to leave the band for a while. Ricky's massive ego was getting too big for us. He wanted a solo career, so he wrote a musical. To us it looked like it had failure written all over it. A musical with just kids in it? Not involving Walt Disney? Total shit.' Howe paused. 'Yet...'

'Lipmann was very reluctant at first to even let Manzanoni do it. They had some massive arguments over it. Then it all suddenly changed.'

'How?' Peter queried.

'It went from fizzer to West End hit.'

'Interesting,' he observed, 'and yet Manzanoni sounds like he was in the driver's seat, rather than Lipmann.'

'That's one we could never work out.'

'And Ricky was out of the band. Lou granted him his wish. How convenient,' Howe added.

'Last question. Did you ever meet Olivia Michaels and Andrew Smith? They starred in the musical.'

'I've only heard of Olivia Michaels through her movies and I've never heard of Smith,' Bailey replied.

'We never saw it. We didn't want to,' Howe said. 'I think I would have vomited on myself if I'd seen it.'

'It was the end of a great band,' Bailey said.

'Certainly was,' Peter added quietly as he turned off the tape recorder.

'I hope our information helps,' Howe said. 'Showbiz has a habit of hiding its dirty laundry.'

Snoddy had left Peter a message about Walter Evans, sitting on his desk for him to see when he returned. Apparently, Walter had lived with his wife in Anglesea until 1985. She'd died that spring and he'd disappeared off the face of the earth. Nowhere to be found. *Great.*

That evening, away from the prying eyes of the night editor, Peter shot off a fax to Stella Reimers' personal machine. By morning, he had a reply. *Andy Smith located and contacted, but has no interest in your project. Says he was robbed once and isn't interested in going through it again. Sorry. Will keep you posted if anything else comes up. Stella.*

49

Ruby was coming in on the five-thirty Concorde flight that afternoon, from New York's JFK airport. Peter had been too long without her. Here he was, waiting in arrivals at Heathrow, holding a bunch of long-stemmed red roses and a placard saying *Welcome Back, Ruby. Every Day of the Week*. He was like a teenager in love. He was lost in the moment.

Ruby broke into laughter when she spotted him. She dropped her bag and they clung to each other, oblivious of the impatient throng of other recent arrivals, chatting, moving and rushing about them. So oblivious were they, that they didn't notice a young man, sporting a mullet and a beige suit, snapping photographs of them as they kissed.

Peter tossed Ruby's suitcase into the taxi and clambered in beside her. The roses had survived their passion relatively unscathed, but the placard had fared worse. He got out again and crammed it into a rubbish bin, as Ruby protested.

'I was going to keep that to show my children,' she said.

'Our children?' said Peter, feeling his throat tighten.

'Not necessarily,' she laughed. 'That's being presumptuous. Possibly nothing more than a memento of someone I met along the way.'

'Is that what I am?'

She kissed him again, her hands pulling him against her until he could feel her breasts rise and fall with every breath. The ride to Warwick Gardens was interminable.

Once at the flat, they made love continuously, resting briefly between orgasms, drinking Billecart-Salmon out of the bottle and eating late-season strawberries that Peter had sourced from the market. Where once he would have felt the nausea rise in his throat at the word, now he repeated *love* over and over. *The story can go to hell. I don't want the story. I want Ruby. I want her in my arms forever. Fuck newspapers.*

Ruby awakened Peter with a kiss. Her tongue slipped into his mouth for the briefest moment and then it was gone. He opened his eyes. She was virginal in a white bra and knickers. He reached out and rubbed her *mons pubis* as she tried to pull away.

'Hey, I've only just had a shower. I don't want you making me all hot and bothered again.'

'Is something wrong?' he asked. 'Only you're dressed.'

'You've got to get up,' she replied as she slipped out of his grasp.

'But I want to lie here with you.' Peter smiled. 'Forever.'

'Sorry, we're going out.'

'We don't need to go out. We have everything we need right here. Food, wine, a bed, each other.'

'We're meeting Manz and Megan at Harveys within the hour.'

'Your dad?' Peter felt his throat tighten again.

'He just rang. He wants to see us.' Ruby was already slipping on a skirt and zipping it up.

'Why? I didn't think he liked me.'

'Perhaps he wants to have a man-to-man talk with you,' she replied, raising an eyebrow. 'That might be a good thing. He hasn't done that since Seb.'

'So what exactly happened between you and Slithering Seb?'

Ruby sighed. 'I worked out after a while that he loved himself far more than he loved me. Seb only liked talking about Seb. Let me give you an example. It makes me ill to think of it. He liked to have a mirror near the bed so he could look at himself when we made love. Any position as long as it was doggie.' She paused to gauge Peter's reaction. 'You're okay with this?'

'I guess you have to love yourself before you love others. Looks like Slithering Seb never got past the first bit. He didn't twist both ways, did he?'

'Possibly, although, I didn't think of it at the time. I did get myself checked for AIDS after we broke up.'

'All I can say is he really missed out. I'm glad it happened that way or we would never have met.'

'Me too.' Ruby kissed Peter. 'It'll be all right tonight. I won't let Manz bite you.'

They arrived at Harveys at precisely nine o'clock. Peter had briefly considered jumping out of Ruby's Porsche at a set of traffic lights, but his heart wasn't in it. *What was that medical term? A sense of impending doom?*

He tried to avoid rubbernecking as Ruby led him between tables. *Not Ollie Reed again!* Megan tottered to her feet as they approached and air-kissed Ruby while still holding her glass of champagne. For the first time, Peter really looked at Megan. She was wearing a black velvet flounced pinafore with a white, sheer lace blouse underneath, her eyes lined thickly with kohl and her mouth blood-red. *Slut meets choirgirl.* He found it unsettling.

'Bubbly?' she cried, slopping some more into her own glass.

They sat down next to each other. Ruby was beaming with excitement, cuddling into him like a honeymoon bride. Richard Manzanoni's face was lined with worry, his make-up unable to disguise the deep furrows. He and Peter barely spoke, only mumbling brief greetings at each other. Peter felt the urge to run but Ruby was holding onto him so tightly that he would have had to take her with him. She noticed the tension between the men, and remarked that after a few drinks they'd be like old friends. Marco Pierre White flitted past, nodding at them as he went. Peter wished he'd stopped for a chat.

He knows something. I can feel it.

Manzanoni started with a plate of oysters, sucking each out of the shell like a vampire drawing blood for the first time in a century. Peter ordered soup instead. By the time his pig's trotter came out, he was so stressed he didn't even notice what he was eating. He could have been eating flowers off the table, for all he knew. Megan giggled as Manzanoni gave a brief rundown on his latest success. Peter sat as rigid and silent as a fence post.

'You're very quiet tonight, Peter,' Megan grinned.

'I'm enjoying the conversation.'

'Really? You don't look it. Now Ruby,' said Megan, 'let's leave the boys alone while we fix our lipstick. Shall we?'

Ruby beamed at them. As they both stood up, Peter clasped her hand. 'Do you have to?' he asked.

'You're only talking to Manz, you're not going to the dentist.' She kissed him on the cheek and was gone.

Manzanoni spoke first. 'I think Ruby and Megan are under the illusion that we're going to be having a father and son-in-law talk.'

'And that isn't the case,' Peter said dryly.

'I would rather have Ruby join a nunnery than marry someone like you. To put it bluntly.'

'That's certainly candid.'

'I'll come straight to the point,' Manzanoni said quietly. 'Of all the men in the world, she had to fall in love with a lying scoundrel. She could have had any man but she picks a bottom-dweller like you.'

Peter took a sip of his wine. *Show no fear.*

Manzanoni slammed his palm onto the table. 'Have the decency to look at me when I'm talking to you!'

'I don't know what...'

'Don't play the fool with me, Clancy. You know exactly what I mean. I received some intelligence about you today.' A pulse in Manzanoni's temple was throbbing. 'You want to know what I learned? I learned that you're not an Australian author. You're not even an aspiring novelist. Oh, no. You're a staff reporter for that low-brow rag of a paper, the *Star Gazer.*'

'And so what if I am?'

'So what if you are? You've crafted a very intricate story to insinuate yourself into my daughter's life. For what purpose, I ask myself.'

'And what answer did you give yourself?'

'I've been in this business longer than you've been alive. We're fodder for the scum of the earth that your paper appeals to. You're here to make some money off our backs. "My Summer with Ruby Manzanoni by that piece of shit Peter Clancy."'

'That's not true. I only created this fiction because I knew she'd never go out with a tabloid journalist. I would have told her the truth from the start, if I'd thought she'd have given me a chance.'

'Oh yes, and lies are such a great way to forge a relationship. There isn't a thing you can say in your defence that I would accept.' He tossed back a glass of Cabernet. 'Olivia will be very interested in what I've discovered.'

'If you could only find out where she is. She seems to have gone to ground.' Peter finished his glass of wine and called the waiter over for more. 'Before you do anything, you may want to hear what I have to say and what I know about you. Ever heard of Lou's academy?'

'No. Never,' he replied coolly.

'Really?' The waiter set down a bottle of Chateau Latour. 'Let me take you back to where it all started. I met Ruby in a bar and I told her I was an author. She was beautiful and I wanted to impress her. I'm really sorry for making up the author persona. Then Olivia Michaels approaches me out of the blue, to ghost-write a book. What can I do? I thought that should be good for several celebrity stories in the paper. She's newsworthy, as we scum toe-rag journalists say. I should be able to get away with that. Nothing too hard. But, what Olivia tells me is amazing. No. It isn't amazing, it's perverted. It's fucking disgusting. It's so disgusting that it makes me vomit.'

Manzanoni shifted in his seat, rocking the table and sending two wine glasses clattering to the floor and the waiter scurrying.

Peter resumed. 'I'm very good at my job. In fact, I'd say one of the best. I know everything about the academy thanks to Olivia. Everything. That's how good I am.'

'Olivia couldn't tell you anything. She's…' Manzanoni paused to wipe his mouth with the napkin.

'She's what?'

'She's…fragile. That's why I've had to help her at times.'

'Really? Does that involve keeping her mouth shut?'

'I don't know what you're talking about.'

The waiter returned with two new glasses. 'You were managed by Lou Lipmann. You know exactly what happened at the academy.'

Manzanoni took a gulp of wine. 'It helped young kids get a start in show business. That's all I know.'

'Come on.' Peter shook his head. 'You know it was really a paedophile ring operated by Lou Lipmann for well-known clients.'

'You're deluded,' Manzanoni replied, wiping his hands with a monogrammed silk handkerchief.

'Olivia says you stopped her being abused but you did nothing to help the other kids. That makes you complicit. And why Olivia? Why help her?'

'That's it? That's all you have to say?' Manzanoni rested back on the chair and smirked. 'You have nothing on me, you piece-of-shit hack. After I tell Olivia about you, you'll be sued within an inch of your life. Maybe I'll tell Lou too. That might produce a more interesting outcome.'

'Yes. I forgot to mention, there was also a boy in the musical called Andrew Smith. Remember him?'

'Vaguely. He was her co-star.'

'Do you know what happened to him?'

'He left the business. I don't know where he is.'

Time to take some liberty with the truth. This should unsettle him. 'Funny, I found Andy Smith living in America. It's amazing who you find. I got a great interview for the book.'

Manzanoni gulped. Peter noticed that his face had turned grey. 'Andrew was very troubled.'

'Not troubled enough to forget your involvement in Lou Lipmann's grubby little caper.'

'I had nothing to do with it. I never attended any of the parties.'

Ah, so you did know about it, even if you weren't part of it. Let's push the envelope. 'No, but you saw Lou Lipmann's fondness for pretty boys as a career opportunity for you, didn't you?'

He took a long time to answer. 'I didn't blackmail him, if that's what you mean. Yes, Lou let me out of the band. He put money into the musical and made it a success. But you don't understand.'

'Perhaps I do.'

Manzanoni drank the remaining wine and let out a loud sigh. 'Okay. How much do you fucking want?'

'I don't want any money, I just want you to be honest for once.'

'You...want me to go to the police?'

'No. I want you to be part of this book. Grant me an interview.'

'Utter madness. That would destroy my career.'

'You'd get to be a decent man for once. And as for Ruby, I'd love for her to never find out about my deception, but I can't. I want her to hear it from me, not you. When I'm ready.'

'I won't tell Ruby, that's agreed. But as for the interview... Couldn't I be an anonymous source of information?' he pleaded.

'I thought of doing that but being ethical, for once, got the better of me. It's got to be on the record. And on tape.'

'You won't get away with this. You're treading on some very big toes. You don't know with whom you are dealing.'

'I know exactly who I'm dealing with. I've already met them.'

Manzanoni looked away in resignation. 'Yes... Fine.' He was still looking away when the women returned.

'So, did you miss us? Are you two bonding okay?' Ruby smiled as she retook her seat.

'Richard?' Megan asked when she noticed he had his head in his hands.

'I'm fine.' Manzanoni looked up and gave a faint smile. 'Tired and emotional, I guess.'

'We were talking about the past,' Peter cut in. 'Seems we have much in common.'

'Really?' said Megan. 'Let me guess: you're both billionaire musicians?'

'We both love Ruby.'

'That's so sweet,' said Ruby.

'Strange, you didn't approve of Peter at first,' Megan continued.

'It's all ironed out,' said Manzanoni. 'We've reached an understanding.'

'Anything else happen?' asked Ruby expectantly.

'Peter can fill you in,' Manzanoni said abruptly, throwing down a wad of cash. 'We're off. All the sharing has upset my stomach.' He stood up and took Megan's arm. 'Come on, Megan. Let's go.' He kissed Ruby, glanced at Peter and was gone.

'I'm glad you two get along so well,' said Ruby as she hugged Peter.

'Underneath his celebrity exterior, there's just a normal bloke,' Peter lied.

'I know,' she replied.

50

'Do you want to come and live with me?' Ruby asked as she unlocked the door to her flat. 'What did you and Manz talk about while we were away?'

'In answer to your first question, I thought I already did,' Peter replied. 'In answer to the second, none of your business, Ruby Red.'

'It's my business if it's about me.' She snuggled her head into his chest and unbuttoned his shirt.

'As much as I adore you, not everything is about you.' He kissed the top of her head. Her hair smelled of honeysuckle. They sank into the sofa together and snuggled. 'Why do you call your dad Manz?'

'Oh, I don't know. It began when I was a precocious twelve year old. After I'd been calling him Manz for a while, Dad simply didn't sound right.'

'I can understand that,' Peter returned. 'He certainly doesn't have that paternal quality about him. I lost my dad when I was young. He was a true son of the Australian bush and that's how he died. I still miss him. I wish he was here to meet you. He would have liked you.'

'I'm sure my mother would have liked you, too. I just wish I could remember more about her. It seems so long ago that she died. All I have of her are a painting and a few photos. I remember she used to sing to me and tell me bedtime stories. She had such a beautiful smile.'

'Do you remember what happened to her?'

'All Manz ever said was that she'd gone to heaven. That was it. He thought I was too young to attend the funeral. I only found out the truth when I got older. Through a family friend.' She positioned a cushion under her head. 'It's not easy to know that your mother committed suicide. Why would she want to take her life and leave me? She always seemed so happy.'

'Did you ask your father?'

'Manz said that she had severe depression. She was getting treated but in the end she couldn't face life. "Your mother loved you." That was it. We never spoke about her again.'

'You've had too much tragedy and sadness in your life,' he said weaving his fingers around hers. 'We both have.'

'Please tell me that there won't be any more. I don't want to have any more. I never want to lose you.'

'Ruby Red, pain is part of life, I'm afraid. I'll do my best to make it painless for you,' he said, embracing her tightly.

51

Devrille had decided, with the bills accumulating, Peter ought to find Olivia somewhere else to stay. Peter knew Hammersmith. He quickly located a ground floor flat in a mansion block, spitting distance from the Odeon. In case there were any good concerts, he could crash on the couch, now that he'd surrendered his own room in favour of a share of Ruby's bed. Hammersmith still wasn't the Dorchester, but Carol-Lee seemed happy enough.

The final interview with Olivia. Thank God. As soon as this story is over and dusted, I'll take a holiday.

It had just started to rain as he strolled down the street, just as the mums were returning from the school run. He was glad he'd listened to Ruby and taken a mackintosh and umbrella. It was nearing nine—which was late for some—but which may as well have been dawn in the celebrity world. It all looked normal and mundane. He felt envious. The front door opened after the third ring. Snoddy's son Clyde stood in the hallway.

'Is everything all right? What are you doing here?' asked Peter.

'Mum's doing some work for Mr Devrille. She asked me to mind the girls.'

Peter was over the initial shock of discovering that Clyde's father, Devon Snodgrass, was a large, handsome man of Tobagonian descent, whom Snoddy had married nearly thirty years ago. He could only imagine that it couldn't have been easy for either of them back then.

'How are they?' Peter asked as he stepped over the threshold. Clyde closed the door. 'Are the ladies awake?'

'Awake, all right. In fact, they haven't yet gone to bed. I think they've got cabin fever.'

'It's nine in the morning.'

'You should know that celebrities run on a different time zone.'

Peter noticed Ting drifting up the hallway towards them.

'Hello. You've come to our party?' She giggled.

'Looks like you've had your breakfast cereal already, Ting,' Peter remarked.

'More than that. I love my big boy,' she said as she planted a kiss on Clyde's cheek. 'I feel like a fuck.'

Peter raised his eyebrows.

'Purely platonic, Mr Clancy,' said Clyde. 'I don't go there. I have a girlfriend.'

'I thought Snoddy would have stipulated to control their intake.'

'I tried. I really tried.'

Olivia and Carol-Lee were sitting in the kitchen drinking glasses of champagne. Ting disappeared into the bathroom.

'Hopefully you're in better shape than her,' said Peter as he pulled up a chair.

'She can't hold her booze,' Carol-Lee slurred.

'Or drugs,' Peter added.

'I've nearly gone bonkers, doing this bloody book,' Olivia remarked.

'Alicante here we come,' Carol-Lee whooped.

'Alicante? What's this all about?'

'As soon as the book's out, we're off to Spain.'

Carol-Lee poured herself another glass of champagne. 'Makes me smile to think that Fat Lou will be getting cosy with his jail-mates while we're soaking up the Costa Del Sand, Sea and Sun.'

Peter took his tape player out of his case and placed it on the table.

'Okay, Mum. I think Peter wants to start the interview.'

'I'll be in my bedroom, love.' Carol-Lee rose slowly and unsteadily from the chair.

Peter watched her teeter away. 'Looks like you're getting along.'

'Better than I expected. She drinks too much but she's a real laugh.'

'I'm glad you and she have put things right.'

'I'm glad too. Thank you for bringing us together.' She paused. 'Ruby is a lucky girl.'

'I really think I'm the lucky one. We should start the interview. The sooner we get it done, the sooner you'll be living it up in Alicante.' He turned on the recorder. 'You've spoken about the child abuse and your long and distinguished career but you haven't spoken about your love life. So I want to end the interviews with talking about the men you've loved, the men who you were close to. How would you describe your love life?'

'Love life?' Olivia laughed. 'One—no, two—words. Shambolic. Disastrous.'

'You've been associated with some famous men.'

'That certainly doesn't make your love life any better. In fact, when you're famous, your love life is worse, I think.'

'Why's that?' he asked.

'You're always under close scrutiny. The press is always chasing you. The paparazzi are always trying to catch you in compromising positions. I wouldn't know what it is like to go out on a date without some twat sticking a camera in my face.'

'Like living in a fish bowl?'

'More like a wild zoo. I've lived in a gilded cage surrounded by beasts. I wouldn't know what a normal love life is. I wouldn't know what a normal life is. What do normal people do?'

'You're asking the wrong bloke, Olivia.'

'Maybe I don't want to find out. I'm so used to fame.'

'Do you think people should feel sorry for you?'

'I don't want people to feel sorry for me when they read this book.'

'It's going to be hard not to, when they read about your childhood.'

'They might think I deserved it, that I sold my soul for fame. There's a price for stardom.'

'The public won't think that,' he replied. 'Children don't deserve to be molested.'

'Deep inside me, when all of it was happening, there was a voice that kept telling me that somehow, I'd asked for it. It was

238

my shameful secret. Since then, it's been like a dark cloud hanging over my life. When the abuse stopped, I thought my life would get better. I believed it was better. Or maybe I was told it was better? Fuck knows. Who am I anyway? Am I Olivia Michaels or am I Olivia Taylor, or Evans, wherever she got that name from? I just don't know.' She stretched out her pale legs. 'I used every diversion I could to block that shit out of my head; not only drugs and booze but meaningless sex, even over-eating at times. You can put that in the book too. I've had bulimia. I've done every fucked up thing you can think of, trying to forget that shit.'

'Did it work?'

'Of course not. It's always there. That black cloud following me around like a dog on a lead.' Olivia broke into song. 'Go away black cloud, I don't like you... I don't need your tears... I don't want your pain...'

'That's actually...good,' said Peter.

'I told you I was talented,' she laughed.

'Do you think the abuse has affected your...as you say...shambolic love life?'

'Of course. They've gone hand in hand.'

'Have you ever met the love of your life? Have they all just been failed relationships?'

She paused to light a cigarette. She inhaled deeply and answered as she blew out the smoke. 'We're getting deep and meaningful, aren't we?'

'The public will lap it up,' he replied.

'All right... The only man I've ever really loved? Ever wanted to settle down with and have babies?'

'The love of your life, to be precise.'

'There's only one guy I ever loved. Maybe ever will,' she said. 'Caine Shearman.'

'I remember him. He was in some kids' movies in the seventies. One of them was about growing up in a small town in America. *Morning Ride* wasn't it? I really related to that.'

'That's him. We were instantly drawn to each other the moment we met. He was beautiful. He was different from all the other men

I've met in my career. There was no narcissism, no bullshit. It didn't take much before we fell in love.'

'The media must have loved it.'

'They were all over us like flies. We were the hot couple of the moment. We really thought we were Prince and Princess Charming. All bollocks, of course. That moment didn't last long at all.'

'So what happened?'

'It didn't take us long before we realised why we were so drawn to each other. We were fellow travellers.'

'Fellow travellers?'

'Caine also started out as a child actor.'

'You mean he was…sexually abused like you?'

'Do I have to fucking spell it out? Of course he was. Paedophiles aren't just over here,' she snapped.

'I've always wondered about child actors. Why so many of them end up on the rubbish heap. How they're treated by adults in the film industry. What happens to them.'

'We're like lambs to the slaughter, you know that. Caine's parents peddled him to those bastards, basically. He became famous and his parents got all of his money.'

'What was Caine like when you met him?'

'He was beautiful inside and out but, like me, he couldn't keep those black clouds away. He wasn't getting work like he used to because he had grown up, so that started to affect our relationship. We were doing loads of drugs, going to wild parties. It started to take its toll. The worst thing for Caine was that he was heavily into heroin, crack, anything really. Big time. I was only doing coke. Funny.' She started to laugh. 'I sound like I was the better behaved.'

'So what happened to you two?'

'Caine snapped one night and beat me up. The police arrested him. That was it. Lou stepped in. All over,' she said sadly.

'Do you know where Caine is now?'

'He's still alive, I've heard. Someone told me once that he was living on the streets in New York, selling his arse for a hit.'

'That's awful. He was a great actor.'

'Of course it fucking is. I'm one of the lucky ones, if you could call me lucky. I should be dead. I'm not dead. Many others are.'

'It could be another book.'

She eyed him over. 'More than you bargained for?'

'The tip of the iceberg.'

'So that's my love life in a nutshell. A disaster of immense proportions. That's enough from me. You can turn off the recorder. I want to go to Spain.'

He switched off the tape recorder and slipped the tape into his pocket. Carol-Lee came out of her bedroom.

'I've been meaning to ask you,' Carol-Lee began. 'How did you get on with Andy? Did you find him?'

'Andy?' Olivia placed her glass down.

'Your old friend from the academy, Andy Smith. You remember him? You were great friends.'

'Yes I remember him,' Olivia replied coolly. 'What's this about finding him?'

'I thought it might help you with your book if Peter found him.'

'I didn't ask you to find Andy. I didn't give you permission to look that far into this. What gives you the fucking right?' Olivia yelled.

'I was only trying to help,' Carol-Lee sobbed.

'You turn up after all these years and you think you can organise my life again. You did a rubbish job the first time and now you're fucking it up again.'

Peter cut in. 'Calm down. Give her a break.'

She gazed at Peter coldly. 'So, did you find him?'

'He's living in America. I found him through a friend of mine.'

'But it's my story, my book. Right, I'm stopping this now,' Olivia exploded. 'I want my version of events, not yours. This book is never getting published. I'm going to make sure of that. I'm getting someone else to do it. You're fired.'

'But Livvie,' Carol-Lee began.

'Shut up. I want to talk to Uncle Richard. I thought I could do this on my own. And you,' she continued, 'can fuck off back to Methyr Shitsville and die for all I care. Once again, Mother Dearest, you've stabbed me in the back. Why did I ever let you back into my life? What was wrong with me?'

241

'I was only trying to do the right thing by you. Don't do this, Livvie. Don't leave me again.'

'Remember, you're the one who left me.'

'I love you, Livvie,' Carol-Lee cried.

'Shut up. You don't exist.'

Carol-Lee left the room in a flood of tears.

'Let me think,' Olivia added as she paced the room, attempting to light a cigarette. After several failed attempts to get the lighter to work, she took the cigarette out of her mouth and threw it away. Ting rushed towards her, shoved a cigarette in her mouth and lit it for her.

'Just hear me out,' Peter said as he followed Olivia about.

'You were never meant to find Andy Smith. This book was supposed to be just about me. About me. What I told you. Nothing else. You weren't supposed to find out stuff behind my back. I wanted to destroy Lou Lipmann my own way.'

'If you publish this book the way you want, all of these paedophiles are going to get away with it. This book will be discredited.'

'Keep Andy Smith and Uncle Richard out of it.'

'I can't do that,' Peter shot back. 'You need his testimony to back up your claims. If you go ahead with your version, Lou Lipmann will sue you successfully and you'll be ruined both financially and professionally. That's if a publisher even touches it.'

'Right. Then it's not happening,' she shouted. 'I want the tapes back.'

'The tapes are my property. No way.'

As he made his way up the hall and to the front door, he heard a sound like a car backfiring at close quarters. And again. He reached his hand out to take his coat off the rack. It was gone. Then he noticed that the front door was ajar. On the footpath a little further along the road was a figure dressed in his mac, carrying his umbrella, one leg twisted backwards up the front step of an adjoining building. On the wall adjacent to the body was a splatter of bone chips and brain tissue. Peter looked at it in disbelief. *Carol-Lee.*

Across the road, a figure in dark pullover and trousers, his face obscured by a balaclava, jumped into a London cab. Except it wasn't. It was an unlikely get-away car. He watched it pull away from the kerb and screech around the corner. He studied the body again. There was no doubt in his mind she was dead. And the bullet that had killed her had been meant for him.

A large pool of blood was already seeping across the footpath and into the gutter when Olivia reached the door and glanced down the road. She took one look and screamed. Peter did his best to shield Carol-Lee's body from her sight, as she slumped to the ground and beat her fists against her head.

'Clyde!' he yelled. 'Clyde? For fuck's sake.' He could hear police sirens in the distance but they sounded like they were blocks away. *We're in central fucking London. How long does it take?* Moments later the sirens were closing in. *Where are the coppers and the paramedics? Having a cup of tea and a fucking biscuit?* He felt for a carotid pulse on Carol-Lee's neck, not expecting to find one. Next thing he knew, the paramedics rushed forward. Five minutes had felt like an eternity.

Attention, finally. At last, they're here. Peter stepped away from the body and thought of home.

52

After shepherding Olivia back indoors, Clyde called Snoddy. Peter spent the next two hours at the police station, explaining over and over to an expressionless detective and his constable side-kick precisely what he'd seen. *Description of assailant? Well I didn't see the actual act, I heard it. The man who left the scene wore dark clothes. Tall, male, athletic, professional, hooded. I think I've said that twice already.*

'Do you think you would be able to identify the gunman from a photograph or a line up?'

'How? Not unless he's the only one with a balaclava permanently affixed to his face. Are you bloody joking?'

'Can you describe the vehicle?'

'It was a London cab. Black.'

'Can you describe the driver?'

'I couldn't see the driver.'

'You seem agitated, Mr Clancy.'

Peter shook his head in bewilderment. 'Wouldn't you be if you'd just seen someone with half their skull blown away? I don't think that usually happens in London, does it?'

'You're Australian, aren't you? What is the purpose of your stay here?'

'I'm on holidays. I'm supposed to be on a relaxing holiday. I heard London is a great place to unwind. Now it seems to me like a great place to get shot.'

'Would you care for a cup of tea?'

'I'd like more than that but that's a start.'

The constable left the interview room to make tea. Was tea-making in the job description? *What is it with the English?* 'My whole family was just killed in a bombing raid.' 'Have a cuppa, there's a good chap, you'll feel better soon.' *Tea and stoicism.* The constable returned carrying three mugs. Peter tried to drink it but his hand was shaking uncontrollably. *If it was a cup of coffee, it would be a cappuccino by now. Hey, that's funny. I wish I could laugh.*

The police thought he was an innocent bystander, who had been out sightseeing and happened upon the scene. To have explained his relationship with Olivia to the police would have only made him a person of interest. *You had an argument over this book you're writing? Prime suspect.* Then they would have wanted the interview tapes for sure. That would have been the end of the biggest story of his career.

After his release, he made two phone calls. The first one was to Snoddy. He asked her to help out Olivia and pick him up from the police station as soon as possible. He expected Snoddy would sort out any remaining red tape. Then he rang Ruby and got her machine. He asked her to meet him at the Savoy at seven. *Tonight's the night. Tonight, she'll learn the truth. At last, I can be me. Hopefully, she'll understand why I did it and forgive me.* His next task was to take the interview tapes to the office. He couldn't afford to lose them or have them taken off him. They were journalism's equivalent of the crown jewels.

The Rover shuddered to a halt in front of him, while he was still thinking about Ruby. *Love overcomes all adversity, doesn't it? It's the cockroach of human emotion.* He rang Ruby again on Snoddy's car phone, hoping to catch her this time. *Please leave a message...*

Minutes later, he was outside the *Gazer*. As Snoddy sped off, Peter's eyes drifted from the Black Lubyanka to the Old Bell Tavern and his feet soon followed. *That's what I need. A good, strong drink.* Devrille could wait.

53

At seven o'clock, Peter was stuck in traffic along the Strand. He was seriously doubting the wisdom of having taken a taxi, but his legs had been too shaky for the tube. He was suffering the after-effects of trauma. He was also suffering the after-effects of a three-hour stint at the Old Bell Tavern. He'd fallen off the wagon. That horse had well and truly bolted by around five that afternoon. All he had to do now was to look sober enough to be admitted to the American Bar. He knew Ruby would wait for him there for at least fifteen minutes. *I'm sorry, Ruby.* It wasn't an auspicious start.

After stumbling from the cab, he walked the last block to the Savoy. It was six minutes after seven. The London air was as bracing as a slap to the cheek. *I can feel myself sobering up with every step.*

He entered the bar a minute or two later, his eyes scouring the crowd for a glimpse of Ruby. *Ah, there she is! But...* She wasn't alone. A man was leaning over her, bending over her chair, and they appeared to be having an animated conversation. *Hey, that's my girlfriend, soon to be financier—I mean, fiancée—that you're talking to.* A moment later, the man moved away. Ruby was looking at a newspaper, distracted, and didn't appear to notice Peter.

'Hello, darling,' he said. No sooner had the -*ling* left his lips when Ruby raised her glass and flung the contents in his face. The alcohol burned his eyes. 'What? Why?'

Ruby didn't say a word. She stood up and pushed past him, without saying a word. She left the newspaper behind her, still without saying a word. As the barman was making a bee-line towards him,

Peter wiped his face and focused on the paper. It was folded around a photograph of Ruby and him, locked in an embrace, taken just outside the airport. The headline said it all. *Take A Geezer At This!* and below it, *Which Celeb's Dating A Star Gazer Hack?*

Peter looked around for the man, but he'd already left the bar. *Yuppie! Of all the gin-joints of all the towns in all the world, Yuppie had to walk into the American Bar and destroy my life.* It was too late to run after Ruby. He'd catch her up at home. He left just before the barman had the chance to reach him and toss him out.

Shame. Quite liked the American Bar. Never mind, I guess I won't be going back there in a hurry.

The liberal dose of alcohol he'd applied to himself earlier that day had numbed a bit of the pain. There would be more of that to come later, no doubt.

54

Peter must have been no more than half an hour behind Ruby, but by the time he arrived at Warwick Gardens the shadows were long gone, although the sun was still holding its own. Barely. He spotted his clothes and the rest of his belongings sitting in a heap at the top of the stairs leading to Ruby's front door. The heap was ordered and neat. He took it to be a bad sign. *Only a person who's already detached would fold clothes so neatly and place them in a mound out of the rain.* Then he took it to be a good sign. *Maybe part of her still cares about me.*

He tried ringing the intercom, but nobody answered. He was tempted to use his key, but sense got the better of him. Life was certain to improve in the morning and he'd be sober by then.

It was as he collected the bundle and descended the steps that he spotted Yuppie once more. This time, Yuppie was snapping shots of Peter carrying his bundle, revelling in Peter's sadness, sniggering at his pain. Peter could have knocked him out with a single punch, but he simply didn't have the energy to care. His life was ruined already. *A sodden man doesn't fear the rain.* As Peter ambled away, the door of a Silver Spirit a little further up the road swung open. He was barely aware of its presence. A Silver Spirit was hardly a remarkable sight in Kensington.

He heard Lou Lipmann's voice before he saw him.

'You fucking little toad. You twisted little maggot. I'll teach you to mess about with my talent.'

Peter spun around. Lou was waddling down the road, unaccompanied. *Can it get any better?* At the end of Lou's arm dangled a gun.

It just did.

Peter kept walking away from him, keeping as close as possible to the fences and buildings. He could easily outpace Lou, but he'd hardly outpace a bullet. He glanced back. Yuppie was still snapping, but now he was torn between taking photos of Peter or Lou.

'Look at me when I'm fucking talking to you!' Lou bellowed. 'I'm going to finish off what Malcolm couldn't. These days, you gotta do everything yourself.'

Lou was already out of breath and Peter was stepping up the pace. A moment later, he heard the distinctive ping of a ricochet. *What the fuck?* He stopped momentarily and swung about. Behind Lou, still at a distance, a pair of constables was running in his direction at full pelt. Lou was swaying side to side. *Is he drunk?*

Lou placed the gun between both paws and fired off another bullet as Peter braced. He was still a reasonable distance away, nothing at all for even an amateur marksman, but Lou had evidently not kept up target practice. The first shot had been an accidental discharge. On the second shot, the recoil almost knocked Lipmann to the ground. As he scrambled to keep himself upright, he discharged a third. It glanced off the light pole and hit Yuppie in the chest.

Yuppie collapsed silently as Peter, hidden by the portico of a building, watched in horror. He thought about running back to help, but he'd be running back to almost certain death. As the police drew closer, he turned and kept walking, the fading twilight his only ally. Yuppie or not, there was a code of conduct between journos. He'd left an innocent man behind. His conscience weighed him down like a diver's belt.

By the time the constables reached Lipmann, Peter had disappeared along Kensington High Street. He rationalised that since the police were at the scene, if there was anything that could be done for Yuppie, they were better qualified to do it. Quite frankly he didn't know if he could handle another shooting.

He took the District line to Hammersmith and walked to the safe flat. He didn't know if anyone would be there, but he had a key and nowhere else to go. The police had gone and the only evidence of Carol-Lee's death was a patch of paint on a building down the road that was a bit brighter than the rest, after her remains and the London grime had been washed away.

He rang the bell before he entered, but no-one answered. He unlocked the door and put down his bundle, thankful that his life in London could be summed up by an armful of clothes. The drink was wearing off and he was already feeling dreadful. Wherever Snoddy had taken Olivia, it wasn't there. He was alone with a barload of booze and Olivia's stash of cocaine. He flushed the cocaine down the toilet. He'd had more than enough drama for one day.

He poured himself a large glass of Courvoisier but didn't touch it. He'd had some pretty awful days in his life, but this ranked among the worst. It was quite possibly the very worst. *Supremely bad. One death, possibly two. Two attempts on my life. Ruby gone. Olivia gone. Andy won't play ball. Nowhere to live and by next week, no job and no visa. On the plus side, Lou's almost certainly in jail.*

Struggling to one of the bedrooms, he pulled off his clothes and dropped them onto the floor as he went. The bed smelled faintly of Carol-Lee and it nearly made him cry. Her things were everywhere. He was asleep even before his head hit the pillow and he dreamt of rats. At about three in the morning, the telephone rang.

'Hello?'

'Tell me you're asleep and I just woke you.'

'Stella?'

'Yes it's Stella. Who else would call you up at this time?' Peter was so groggy he nodded off. 'Wake up you lucky sonofabitch.'

'How did you get this number?'

'Waddayathink? I can find ghosts for you at the touch of a button, but I can't locate the great Peter Clancy? I asked your boss. He thought you might be there. And let me tell you, he was none too pleased about being called up at home, either.'

'So, what's so important that it couldn't wait till breakfast? Yours, by the way, not mine?'

'I've been working on a puff piece in the Catskills.'

'Great. How nice for you. Can I go back to sleep now?'

'No. Listen. Anyhow, I was in the Catskills, like I told you. A friend of mine and I thought we'd catch ourselves a show while we were there.'

'Ah ha.'

'Well, we went and saw a stand-up comedian. From England.'

Peter was about to start drumming his fingers. 'Ah ha.'

'Okay, okay. Get this. His name was Wally. Wally Evans. I began to think: Wally, Walter. English. Show biz. Could it be?'

'For fuck's sake put me out of my misery.'

'He was. The Walter Evans. From England via Anglesea, Wales, all the way to New York State.'

Peter was wide awake and sober. 'He's our man?'

'He's our man.'

'You asked him about the films?'

'Was Jesus Christ a Jewish Rabbi? Of course I did.'

'And he'll co-operate?'

'You betcha. Buy him and the wife a ticket. He always promised her a trip to Old Blighty.'

'Wife?'

'After his first wife died, he came Stateside for some R and R. Met some gal and five minutes later, he's hitched. Give the guy a green card, and he's playing comedy clubs in the Catskills. Go figure.'

'I'm onto it,' said Peter. Dawn was about to crack over the City of London. 'Thanks, Stella.'

'I know, you owe me. Remember, one way roads extend only so far, my friend. One day, I may actually get to collect.'

After the worst day of his life, he saw a glimmer of hope on the horizon.

55

Devrille was scowling as he read the first of the interview transcripts. Peter couldn't tell from Devrille's expression if he was impressed or not. Every so often, Devrille let fly with an expletive. Ten minutes later, Snoddy arrived with news that Olivia was staying with her but Ting had disappeared.

Devrille put the transcript down. 'Good work, Snoddy, she'll be safe with you and the boys,' he muttered distractedly and turned to Peter. 'And you've transcribed every interview?'

'Every interview, every word. That's what I've been busy doing when I wasn't here.'

'And here's me thinking that all you were doing was Ruby Manzanoni. Let's see what we've got. Two key witnesses, although one's dead. Interviews with ex-members of Manzanoni's band. We have a lot to run with.' Devrille grinned. 'I remember you said once that you didn't want Manzanoni mentioned. Don't you want him as your father-in-law any longer?'

'I don't think that's my call to make,' said Peter. 'I've always had a hunch he knew what was going on. Granted, he helped two of the kids involved to end the abuse, but that was only for his own end.'

'We could suggest he murdered his missus, although we probably won't be able to prove it. I wouldn't want to rely on the testimony of two very aggrieved former band members. Manzanoni is going to get a good mention, nevertheless,' said Devrille.

'Your Miss Ruby isn't going to like her father exposed, and that's putting it mildly. She'll probably want to punch you in the balls,' Snoddy added. 'I would.'

'She's not going to be happy, I know.' He winced. 'I don't know how she'll take it.'

'You could leave your name off the story and I could give it to someone else. Are you willing to do that? You have to choose between your career and protecting others. That's easy if you don't have a conscience. Very difficult, however, if you do.'

'This is my baby. I don't know what to do.'

'*Crise de conscience*,' said Devrille. 'It's the eternal dilemma between being ethical and not. What will you do to get the story? How far will you go? It's especially difficult when you're doing the wrong thing for the right reason.'

'Does the end always justify the means? I'll let you know after I have another crisis of conscience.'

'Make your crisis quick before I give this to someone else.'

'Don't you bloody dare.' He turned to Snoddy. 'How is Olivia holding up?'

'At home, you mean? Well, it's not the Brady Bunch, I'll tell you. It's hard keeping her off the champers and cocaine.'

'A pity we haven't found any other victims. Olivia said a foster home was involved, but she didn't know the name of it,' said Peter.

'Don't worry about that too much. When this story gets published I'd wager that an awful lot of people will be coming out of the woodwork and others will be wanting to disappear back into it.' Devrille resumed reading the transcript. 'I have to tell you, JB, I had my doubts,' he began. 'This isn't good.'

Peter's mouth dropped open. *This isn't good?* He had no words.

Devrille raised a hand. 'It isn't good, JB, it's fucking brilliant!'

'So, you're in?'

'Subject to us locating a credible second source prepared to go on the record, the *Gazer's* all aboard.'

He glanced at Snoddy, who nodded in return. She unfolded a sheet of paper, written in Carol-Lee's jagged hand. 'You asked Carol-Lee to make out a list of names before she died,' she said. 'I found this when I was cleaning out the Rover. She must have meant to give it to you and forgot.'

Peter glanced at it. 'It's a list of men's names. Some that she knew about, some she recognised after the event. Regular party-goers, every one of them. And it'll make your hair stand on end.' He passed the list across to Devrille. Then he stood over him so they could both see the piece of paper.

'There are at least twenty names here.' Devrille examined the names more closely. 'There are several politicians here that I know. Lord B? He's the chap…who goes on about porn and looks like a toad.'

'Yes, the same,' Snoddy whispered. 'He's a big anti-pornography campaigner. What does he say? *Britain must not shame itself.*'

'What a contradiction.'

'Makes you sick, it does.' Snoddy poured herself a whisky and two others besides. She took a long drink and passed the others around. 'Habit. Pure habit,' she said.

'Of all the people I would never have suspected.' Peter sighed.

'Who's that?' asked Devrille. 'I wouldn't have suspected most of them. Although, I have heard rumours, but they were only rumours.'

'Larry Sidney, the man who plays Percival in the kid's show.'

'Disgusting isn't it? He's an institution in this country. All the kids adore him,' Snoddy replied.

'What a betrayal. I bet he used his fame to groom these poor kids.'

'This is going to be the biggest story in the last ten years.'

'What's this?' Peter said, ignoring Snoddy's remark.

She peered over Devrille's shoulder. 'Beside their real names are nicknames. They're like code names if you want to call them that.'

'It must be what they called each other.'

'One of these politicians is called Mr Whippy. Lord B is Mr Cuddly.' Peter paused to finish off his drink. 'Fucking sick fucks.'

'And Larry Sidney is Mr Chuckles. They've all got nicknames, like demonic cartoon characters or something.'

'I've seen enough,' said Devrille. 'Let's get working on this tonight.'

Peter folded up the piece of paper and put it aside.

'I may have found you that source you've been asking for and maybe, just maybe, some primary evidence. But it'll cost you two tickets New York to London and five nights at the Ritz.'

'Why does it always end up costing me money?' Devrille's scowl turned into a frown. 'Go on, then.'

'I've located Walter Evans.'

'I know that name. Why do I know that name?'

'He was an actor.'

'That's it. Yorkside something.'

'Terrace. That's right. Well,' Peter continued, 'I didn't tell you earlier that the Suicide Lord sent more than just a note to Olivia as his final act of contrition. He sent a load of films to her as well.'

'Films?'

'Live action. Films of the acts in question. Apparently, the elite members of his dirty little club liked to watch as well as to participate.'

'Pornography?'

'If you will. As soon as she saw it, Carol-Lee was scared. She and Olivia needed protection from Lipmann and the others. Those films were the only thing that implicated the entire disgusting ring. But she was smart; once she realised that the perversion went all the way to the top, she never told a soul that she had the films. She contacted the only person in the world that she trusted and who might help her keep the films safe. Walter Evans.'

'But why him?' Devrille was engrossed.

'Because he's Olivia's biological father.'

Devrille looked away.

That's right, Devrille, you old skinflint, this information alone could sell you and the sheik millions of papers. 'Turns out that Walter kept his word and placed the films into a bank vault for safekeeping, some fifteen years ago. Then he left Britain about five years ago to live in America. He still has the key and access to the safe deposit box in the vault. The films are still in there, right here in London. He's prepared to fly here and hand them over to us. One condition: nobody ever knows that he's Olivia's father, including Olivia. He has a family, you see.'

'But you said two tickets?'

'He and his American wife. She wants to tag along for the ride.'

Devrille rolled his eyes. 'Does she know?'

'No. Nothing.'
'But she wants to come along?'
'Yes.'
'Bloody wives.'

56

The Evans' tickets booked, Devrille wanted Peter to get the articles ready for typesetting, with a view to going to press the moment Walter arrived with the films. Peter went straight to his desk, to Willy Prager's great amusement.

'Been gone a while,' he said. 'So long, that I've had time to miss you.'

Peter ignored him and typed furiously.

'Must be working on something important. Let me in on the secret?'

'Sorry, Willy.' As Willy retreated, he resumed battering his keyboard, reading over his notes and cutting and pasting vast pieces of his transcripts. Word by word, sentence by sentence, he was coaxing them into a series of coherent investigative pieces. The first day's splash and the next two odd pages would be on the paedophile ring generally, followed by Carol-Lee's shooting death on page six. Devrille wanted to publish the paedophile allegations, while her death was still hot in the news. The shooting had been today's headlines for the other papers. The *Star Gazer* would be giving it a context and uncovering the real reasons for her death in a day or two, on page six.

The following day's edition would be on the academy. It would name Lou Lipmann, but no-one else. Not yet. The third piece would name the other paedophiles. It would build tension. Peter was confident that there would be enough evidence to name them all. No-one would be spared. The headline and grab would be: *Exposé*.

Shocking Evil. Inside Lou Lipmann's Academy. Olivia Michaels Tells All: 'Some of the People You Love and Trust Abused Me as a Child'.

As Peter drank espresso after espresso, couriered to him by Snoddy from the French bakery down the road, his post-Ruby brain fog lifted. By the third espresso he had suppressed the pain he had been feeling in his heart; by the fourth, he could barely remember his own exhaustion. He was in the saddle again, though it felt more like he was hanging on tightly to the horse's mane.

Snoddy looked on for a while but eventually she crashed in a spare chair. By six the following morning, the office was all but deserted and the articles were almost ready to go. Peter backed them up onto a floppy disk and placed it, along with the tapes, in a paper bag and pushed it to one corner. Then he slumped forward in his chair and lay his head on the desk. He was amazed to see Devrille, a few minutes later, hovering over him.

Please don't wake me up yet.

Devrille was tapping on Peter's keyboard, accessing his files. He was animated and ecstatic. 'It'll be ready for tomorrow's evening commuters. By tomorrow night, you'll be the most famous hack in London.' He cast his eye over the first draft on Peter's screen. 'And in the halls of power and celebrity, you'll probably be the most hated. How does that feel?'

'I like that,' Peter slurred without lifting his head from the desk. 'Hated and famous. I like that. You may not like what I have to say but you're going to know I said it. I like it.'

'And this is going to put the *Gazer* on top of the mountain,' said Devrille, 'where we belong. No longer the laughing-stock of London's papers. The *Gazer* will be the fucking boss... Shit, I want to celebrate.'

'Celebrate?' Peter said. 'Give me four hours' kip and I'll be ready to celebrate with you. Aren't you tired?'

'There's no time to be tired, old chap,' Devrille smiled. 'I don't need strong coffee to stay awake. There are better ways, you know...'

'I think I know what you mean,' Peter replied. 'No thanks. None of that for me. I've seen what it did for Olivia.'

'As you prefer. All the more for me.'

57

Time all but stood still from the minute Peter had put the articles to bed until the moment Walter and Bobbie-Jean Evans arrived from JFK. Peter had crawled back to the safe flat, which Devrille had told him could be his home until the lease was relinquished at the end of the month. Then he slept for almost twenty-four hours. He thought of Ruby the instant he woke up. He tried to call her. She had changed her telephone number.

Snoddy agreed to collect Mr and Mrs Evans from the airport and deliver them directly to the Ritz. The following day, while Bobbie-Jean was seeing the sights, Peter arranged to collect Walter from his hotel and take him to Barclays Bank in Regent Street. From there they agreed to go straight to the *Gazer* and hand over the tapes, but Peter diverted to the Old Bell Tavern for a quick drink. Peter liked Walter, who was down to earth and uncomplicated. At the Bell, they chatted about Walter's childhood in London during the blitz and discovered they had a mutual regard for wartime fighter planes.

At the bank, Walter had taken the film canisters and placed them into a nondescript canvas bag. He now positioned the bag at his feet. Every few minutes, as they shared pints of Newcastle brown ale and a ploughman's lunch, Walter's hand reached out and felt for them. Peter couldn't settle down and enjoy any of it: the scent of the pickled onions clung to his nostrils. Today, it seemed particularly strong. *Maybe it's nerves.* In the back of his mind, as nice as Walter seemed, Peter worried that he might have a sting in his tail.

Before they left the pub, he asked Walter if there was anything else he could do for him. He didn't want to mention the possibility of paying money for the films.

'Other than making certain that those bastards pay their dues, there's nothing I can think of.'

'Are you sure? Expenses, perhaps?'

Walter shook his head. 'It's enough if this helps the girl sort her life out,' he said. 'I couldn't be there for her and Caroline. It's the best I can do under the circumstances.'

'All right, then. Thank you, Walter. Olivia may seem like a mess to the rest of the world, but let me reassure you, your girl's a beautiful, kind human being. One day, the world will get to know her as she is, and not as she's portrayed.'

'The press has been harsh on her, that's for certain. It's dog-eat-dog. No-one cares who's caught in the middle.'

'True.' Peter recently felt it as keenly as any of the others. He had no right to have expected better treatment from Yuppie than that which he himself had meted out to everyone else. For all the pain he'd caused, Peter regretted bitterly that Yuppie had been shot. Ruby hated him and he grieved alone. 'I'll take you next door, now. Mr Devrille wants to meet you and thank you personally.'

'Right-o.'

While they lingered for Devrille to finish an important overseas telephone call, Walter and Peter watched the television in the waiting room beside his office. Moments later, Lou Lipmann's face flashed on the screen.

Celebrity agent Louis Lipmann has been charged with murder, as journalist Cuthbert Small lost his battle for life today in Guy's Hospital. Police would like to speak to a passer-by who was seen carrying a load of washing, apparently on his way to the laundromat, and who may have witnessed the shooting. The man is described as Caucasian, aged between twenty-five and forty, around six feet tall, with an athletic build and brown hair. If you or someone you know meets that description, please contact...

'Hey, said Walter, 'that description could be you.'

Peter looked at his hands, while Walter took another look at the screen. Lou was being led away in handcuffs. He looked as oily and evil as usual, but this time without his habitual Havana in his smirking, bulbous mouth. *The Devil in a Savile Row suit.*

Suddenly Walter piped up, 'I remember him, you know. Lou Lipmann. By God, he's aged a lot. Bloody agent to the stars? From what I've heard, he's a bloody thieving wanker! And by the way,' he told Peter quietly, 'he's on those films.'

Peter was about to ask him how he knew that and had he ever watched the films, when Devrille came out and shepherded them inside.

'Care for a drink, Mr Evans?' asked Devrille, as he lined up the glasses like soldiers on parade. 'A glass of champagne before Michael Guthrie arrives?'

Walter put the bag of films on Devrille's desk. 'Just one glass will do me.' He was staring at the bottle intently.

Poor Olivia, seems that she gets it from both parents.

'Who's Michael Guthrie?' Peter asked as he lifted a flute off the desk.

'Michael Guthrie QC. He's going to be making sure that it's all legal. The *Gazer* doesn't need any nasty surprises.' Devrille opened the bag. 'Are these the films?' he asked. 'Good God, they don't half smell.'

'Been in storage a long time,' said Walter. 'All yours now.'

'Seems to me that Walter's just ensured that your arse is well and truly covered.' Peter tossed a look at Walter, who chuckled. He had understood the context. They had bonded.

'Still, it pays to be safe,' Devrille retorted. 'I don't want the paper sued.' He checked his watch. 'Unless he's detained at court, he's expected here at one.'

'He's trustworthy, isn't he? Not on anyone else's payroll?' asked Peter, testing the limits of Devrille's willingness to justify himself to a subordinate.

'He's silk, for goodness sake, of course not.' Devrille laughed. 'That's absurd. Besides, we went to school together. An Old Boy would never do that.'

Guthrie appeared at precisely one, just as they were finishing their second glass of champagne. Added to the pints of ale, the champagne had worn away much of Walter's natural reserve. Guthrie was a winter's morning: sallow-faced, pinstriped, cold. He could only manage an imperious mutter when he was introduced to Peter and Walter. Then he followed Devrille into his inner sanctum, the holy of holies—a private ante-room off Devrille's office that no-one was permitted to enter—*to look at the transcripts*. It was always locked. Peter suspected the articles of interest had travelled a lot further than his desk.

'He thinks his shit doesn't stink,' Walter observed.

'One doesn't shit, old boy,' Peter mocked in an upper class accent. 'Shitting is strictly for the lower classes.'

'So,' said Walter. 'Is this going to finally make you a big name journalist?'

'It's not about that. It's mostly about justice.'

Walter eyed him as if he was playing the role of store detective and Peter was the novice shoplifter. 'Oh, really?'

'Truly. Of course, it doesn't get any bigger than this. It'll be all over the news tonight. But I haven't done it for my career. I could earn a living writing about Madonna's intimates and never have to leave the office.'

Walter looked relieved. 'I believe you,' he said. 'I hope you can handle it. Don't let all that fame go to your head.'

You're speaking from bitter experience, aren't you? 'I'll be fine. I'm sure people will let me know if I'm getting too full of myself.'

'I'm certain they will.'

Devrille opened the door to his inner office and shouted, 'Clancy! We need the interview tapes. Go fetch them.'

Peter wandered to his desk just as Willy Prager trundled in, takeaway coffee in hand, a bacon sarnie and a bag of chips dangling from his arm in a plastic shopping bag.

'I've been wondering what you've been up to. Devrille said you were working undercover,' he said. 'By the way, you look like a torn bag of shit.'

'Thanks, Willy. And you look like a used toilet roll.' Peter laughed. 'I'll tell you all about it after I've recuperated in the Algarve. But you're looking especially good this afternoon.'

'Okay,' said Willy, 'so, what's really going on?' He opened the bag and handed the chips around. Peter grabbed a handful.

'The investigative story I've been working on is, as we speak, getting the final check over by a QC in Devrille's office.'

'What story?'

'Only the biggest one this paper has ever done, Willy boy.'

'Is this anything to do with Olivia Michaels' mum getting shot?'

'You'll find out soon enough.'

'I just checked the messages. Olivia was at her funeral. Who would have thought this would happen in London?'

'This is going to be a big news day, Willy. My story is going to be the splash.'

'It will lead the funeral?' Willy said as he munched on his chips. 'Bullshit.'

'This story's huge enough to go out and get drunk on for a week. That huge.'

'Big news day all right. Someone rang in from St Thomas's that Ruby Manzanoni, the fashion designer, had overdosed,' said Willy as if he was talking about the weather.

'Ruby?' Peter leapt out of his chair, heart thumping. 'Is she...' He was too afraid to ask.

'She's lucky to be alive. Her father found her. Apparently it was serious, not a cry for help. She overdosed on pills.' Willy watched Peter's reactions. 'I almost forgot. Didn't you know her?'

'I met her in a bar. She's a lovely, sweet girl.' He glanced at the clock. He wanted to go straight to the hospital and beg her for forgiveness, plead for another chance. He would have done it, except for the story. He had to wait for Guthrie.

'Sounds like it will be buried back in the paper. Better for her reputation, I guess, no-one reads that far back.'

Willy's head suddenly swivelled around as he strained to watch two men approach. Peter's eyes followed. Behind the men in dark suits trailed four uniformed police officers.

'What now? Who are these two? It's a flipping circus here today.' Willy moaned. 'As if I haven't got enough to do. I haven't even got enough time to enjoy my lunch. Fuck it.' He threw the remains of his bacon sandwich on his desk, adding to the ever-growing pile of rotting food and empty coffee cups.

But the suited men didn't stop at Willy's desk. They didn't make eye-contact with Willy at all, not even when he left his seat, stood up in front of them and extended his hand. They dodged him instead and kept their eyes fixed on Peter. *Oh, shit.* Peter moved towards the men and stopped just short of Willy's desk.

'Are you Peter Clancy?' the taller of the two asked. He positioned himself between the first man and his only exit.

'I am,' said Peter.

'I'm DCI Robilliard and this is DI Curtis.'

They both flashed their identification badges at Peter. He couldn't have distinguished theirs from the one in his cunning kit. The steely stare and the four constables behind them seemed authentic enough. 'Who are you and what do you want?'

'Scotland Yard.'

'You're joking? This is an office prank? Right?'

'Do you see us laughing, Mr Clancy?'

'Am I being arrested?' he asked. 'If so, I'd like to know what for and why.'

'Please, Mr Clancy, would you kindly identify which of these is your desk and come with us.'

'My desk? Why?'

'We have to execute a search…'

Peter interrupted. 'Where's your warrant, then?'

'Mr Clancy, Mr Guthrie's already been served with the warrant. Would you please co-operate, sir.'

Peter glanced at his desk. It was still tidy as a result of his absence. He pointed to it. 'This one.'

'Thank you.'

Willy Prager was goggle-eyed and open-mouthed. Peter cast him a lingering look as he followed the detectives. They led him towards Devrille's office, while two of the constables remained behind to conduct the search of his desk.

'You're going to see Mr Devrille?' he enquired. 'Do I have to be there?'

'Yes. We need to talk to both of you.'

He entered the office after them. There were several more constables in the office, and a tower of boxes along one wall. *How did I miss all this? I was only gone for twenty minutes max. How on earth did they get in without me noticing?*

Devrille was sitting away from his desk, ashen-faced. The effects of the champagne and whatever else he had ingested appeared to have worn off. Walter was in one corner, with the air of a spectator at a play. Next to him stood Guthrie, looking uncomfortable.

'I say, do you think this will take long?' said Guthrie as the constables began piling things into boxes. 'I'm expected back in chambers, you know.'

'Well,' said Robilliard. 'That's a matter for you, isn't it? You can be here to support your client, or you can leave.'

'I'd rather you stayed,' said Devrille quietly.

Peter looked at Devrille. 'What's this about?'

'It seems that they're investigating the *Gazer* for offences under the *Computer Misuse Act 1990*,' he replied. No sooner had the words left Devrille's lips when two more men, similarly attired, entered the room. One man had a receding hairline and bat ears. The other man was shorter, with unsettling, piercing blue eyes.

'I'm Agent Barnes and this is Agent Pascoe,' the balding man said. 'Who's in charge of this investigation?'

'I am,' said Robilliard, lifting his arm. 'And you are?'

Agent Barnes removed his identification badge from inside his jacket and flashed it in Robilliard's face. He studied it closely. 'MI5,' Barnes announced coolly as he snapped the badge shut and returned to his jacket.

'But this is my investigation,' Robilliard began.

Peter could tell that Barnes wasn't impressed. *Boys, please, don't squabble in front of the punters. Will one of you do something? I have to leave. I have a hospital to visit.*

Barnes showed his identification badge to Devrille and Guthrie.

'Is this legit, Michael?' asked Devrille.

'It appears to be.'

Devrille was seething. 'What brings the spook department to the *Star Gazer*? I don't think we've outed any cross-dressing spies lately.'

Barnes looked at Devrille as if he were no more than a buzzing mosquito. 'Under the *Security Service Act 1989*, we are stopping the potential publication of a story that could expose this country to outside security breaches. We are also seizing materials gathered to aid in its publication.' He pointed to the constables. 'Stop that, immediately.'

Robilliard was busy making a telephone call, at the conclusion of which he signalled to the constables that they should stop what they were doing, pack up and leave.

Guthrie bristled. 'I say, I'm Michael Guthrie QC. You can't just wander off the street and stop the publication of a newspaper story. And which story, precisely, are you talking about?' he asked indignantly. 'This is the height of arrogance. I should warn you, I'll be complaining to Sir Anthony Woodward about this. He's a friend of mine, if you want to know.'

Barnes handed Guthrie a bundle of documents. 'The story in question is the one the *Star Gazer's* intending to publish about an alleged paedophile ring,' he replied. 'And to answer your question on the limit of our authority: yes, we can.'

'This isn't anything to do with the Soviet Union, KGB, CIA or IRA, or whatever else. It's a story about paedophiles. How does an exposé on a bunch of filthy paedophiles breach national security, you tell me?'

'We are not at liberty to disclose anything further, sir,' Pascoe responded coldly.

'So you must have had us under surveillance.' Peter pushed past Pascoe and stepped into Barnes' line of vision. 'How would you know all that, otherwise? Have you been watching me all along? Did you look on when an innocent woman was killed? Were you bugging me?'

'I won't be commenting on how we conduct our business. We do our job,' Barnes smirked, 'as we think fit.'

'Great fucking job you have, shutting down the free press so you can protect the guilty. I thought this was England. Why don't you go and catch an IRA terrorist instead?' Peter muttered.

'Sit down, Clancy,' Guthrie ordered. 'Don't make matters worse.'

Peter shook his head in disgust and sank into a chair at the desk.

'We are seizing all computers and documents related to the story. To withhold anything will result in criminal prosecution.'

'It's all here,' Devrille said sadly as he pointed to the transcripts, his computer and the films.

'We'll need your computer too, Mr Clancy,' said Pascoe.

'Okay,' Peter muttered as he rose slowly from the chair.

Peter stood in stunned silence while Pascoe unhooked his computer's hard drive. The constables had already gone. From the look of his desk, they had taken nothing with them. Willy Prager and a few of the others were looking for answers. Most were happy to wait to be informed by management, in due course.

'What's going on?' Willy probed. 'Does it have to do with the story I don't know anything about?'

'Yep,' Peter said bluntly, 'you can pull it. The spooks have just shut it down.'

'Spooks? Like…'

'James fucking Bond,' Peter growled.

'I've never heard of this happening before,' Willy commented. 'Why?'

'I can't say.' He observed as Pascoe checked his desk and took the hard drive away. He watched as a procession of computers and boxes exited Devrille's office and left the building. Then he saw Walter Evans wandering aimlessly about.

'Ho there,' he called. 'Walter.'

Walter seemed pleased to be found. Peter steered him back towards his desk.

'Well, you don't expect to see that every day,' he said.

Peter poured him a mug of whisky from his emergency supply. 'Sit here. I'll take you back to the Ritz in a little while.'

'Have you been sacked?' Willy asked.

'Probably.'

'I wonder how Johnny's taking it?'

Peter wished he'd reserved some of the whisky for himself. 'I'm done with the *Geezer*. I need a rest. A long rest.' He pushed a couple of empty coffee cups into his wastepaper basket and looked over at Willy's desk. 'Since I've already started, do you mind if I clean some of that up for you, Willy?'

'What? That?' Willy shrugged. 'Knock yourself out.'

Peter threw out the remains of Willy's bacon sarnie, the chips and a week's worth of disposable coffee cups and sandwich bags. Then, when Willy was distracted, he picked up a larger, heavier paper bag. He felt for the interview tapes and disk. *Still there.* He transferred that bag and its contents into an empty shopping tote he'd found in one of the drawers of his desk.

'Go home and have a good sleep,' suggested Willy. 'You might feel differently after that.'

A dishevelled Devrille emerged from the hallway, like an angry rodeo bull emerging from its pen. He was flushed with anger. He noticed Peter holding the carry bag. 'Where are you going, Clancy? You're not resigning are you?' he shouted. 'You can't just run off and leave me with the mess that you caused.'

The other journalists scarpered, leaving Willy, Peter and Walter to witness his rage.

'I'm resigning all right. I should have done it before all this happened,' he replied calmly. 'By the way, I didn't cause any mess. I did my job above and beyond what was expected.' Peter shot back, 'Maybe, you should have thought this story might cause a problem. Remember, you're the man in charge, you're the owner-editor.'

'I'm going to fucking destroy you, Clancy,' Devrille yelled. 'You'll never work in this country again. You're a washed up, useless hack. I should have given this story to someone else. You were out of your fucking depth.'

'Suits me just fine. I'd sooner clean toilets, than do what you do,' Peter replied quietly as he stepped forward. 'And, just so you know, I've always hated you calling me JB. I've never, ever been a Joh's Boy. And I'm certainly not a John's Boy, you sanctimonious piece of shit.'

Devrille blocked his path. 'I'm not finished yet.' He shoved Peter against the desk.

'Oh, you're finished all right. I've been battered and bruised because of you. Twice, Lou Lipmann's tried to kill me. I've been nearly run over. I've lied and cheated. I've lost the woman I love. I almost sold my soul to do this job. And for what?'

Walter wasn't staying quiet this time. 'Mr Devrille, you're a bully. I've worked with directors like you. Leave him alone.'

'Fuck off. Don't take the moral high ground with me. Parents are meant to protect their children. Where were you when your daughter needed a father? Where were you when Olivia Michaels was being traded around by those perverts, like she was a commodity?' Devrille laughed. 'Not anywhere to be found. Nowhere.'

Willy leapt in from the sidelines. 'Bastard,' he yelled as he swung a wild punch that connected with the side of Devrille's jaw. 'Don't you ever talk about Miss Michaels like that.'

Devrille was spun around by the force of the blow and fell heavily across the top of a desk, scattering papers, pens and a computer keyboard.

Peter rushed forward and checked Devrille's state of consciousness by grabbing the back of his hair and raising his head. 'Stone cold,' he remarked, as he lowered Devrille's head to the desk. Billy Bunter had flattened the Dark Lord with a single blow. 'Good punch, Willy. Never thought you had it in you.'

'Neither did I. I've been wanting to do that for a very long time. I don't even care for Olivia Michaels particularly.'

'You know what this means, don't you?'

'I'm going out with a bang,' Willy smiled, 'and not a whimper.'

'Come on, Walter,' said Peter. 'We'd better get out of here before Johnny comes to. Fortunately for you and the missus, your accommodation's pre-paid. On the other hand, I'd better get my stuff out of the flat, before he evicts me.'

Peter slung his bag over his shoulder and walked slowly down the corridor with Walter following closely. The other journalists had returned to their desks. As Peter and Walter passed along the corridor, the journalists pounded the desks with their fists. The noise was deafening. Some of them cheered.

'What are they doing?' asked Walter. 'It's like a football match.'

'They're giving me a send-off. Nice custom isn't it?' *The English are really funny cattle.*

58

Peter hailed a cab at the front of the Black Lubyanka and asked the driver to make two stops, first at the Ritz and then at St Thomas's. Then he charged the trip to the *Gazer*.

He'd go back to the flat in Hammersmith as soon as he'd cleared things up with Ruby. He doubted that locking him out of the flat would be uppermost in Devrille's thoughts at the moment. He was confident of a few hours of grace at least.

He could have dealt with the pain of losing Ruby if it hadn't all been for nothing. All the lying and conspiring had amounted to nothing. No story. No justice. He could only pray that Lipmann would be jailed for a very long time for murdering Yuppie. Peter's barometer was so frigged that he even found it hard to feel bad about that. It might just as easily have been him who had been killed while listening into private conversations, rummaging through rubbish bins, and taking elicit photographs and publishing them. In fact, in a sense, it had been him.

As the cab negotiated the London traffic, Walter turned around to Peter. 'Thank you for the best day I've had in years,' he said.

'Really? It's certainly something to tell Bobbie-Jean.'

'Ah,' Walter replied sadly. 'She'd never believe me.'

Peter gazed out at the scene beyond the cab's window. Everyone except the tourists was in a hurry to be somewhere else and the tourists were intent on recording it all on their cameras. 'I'm sorry you lost those films,' he said. 'I doubt any of those maggots will be charged now. My story's dead in the water and so, it seems, is Olivia's book.'

'Bloody untouchable, they are.' Walter hesitated. 'Not all is lost, though, is it? I saw you take things off your friend's desk.'

'My friend? Oh, you mean Willy? Well, I still have my interview tapes with Olivia and Carol-Lee. I did all the hard work and the contract between Olivia and me had nothing to do with the *Gazer*, so by rights they're still mine. I still have my articles and the transcripts and I'll rummage around the flat when I get back, and see if there's anything left there. I guess I'll have to let Olivia know that her book's off. Shame about the films being seized. They'd have made all the difference.'

'No, they wouldn't have.'

Peter was puzzled. 'What do you mean?'

'Couldn't you smell them?'

He thought about it for a while. 'It wasn't the pickled onions, was it?'

'Is that what you thought? So you smelled something like vinegar?'

'It was strong.'

'It was, wasn't it?' said Walter. 'I've always been interested in both ends of the camera, not just the acting end. I've been a gaffer. I've done editing, directing, you name it, I've done it. I'm also big into film conservation. When a film's degrading it has a distinctive smell.'

'Vinegar.'

'Correct. Those films were done for. I doubt the films could be viewed any more.'

'Yet you were happy to let us all believe that you had something worth a trip to London.'

'Well, until I inspected them, I couldn't be certain what I had there. No harm in fulfilling your wife's dreams at the same time, is there? I wasn't harming anyone.' Walter smiled. 'Now I think I just may be able to help you and the girl.'

'In what way?'

'Now, I always knew that those films would go off one day. I saw the fear in Caroline's eyes the day she handed them to me and the bruising on her face. I knew her life and the girl's were worth noth-

271

ing if I didn't keep those films safe, so I decided to preserve them. Not long before I left for America, I copied them all onto video. At first, I watched what I was copying, but it made me so sick, I couldn't. I still checked from time to time that it was all there. I believe I've got the lot.'

'You have a copy?' Peter was astounded. 'Of everything?'

'Everything.'

'Where?'

'I took them to the US with me. They're there. In a flameproof safe in my house. Right next to Bobbie-Jean's jewellery.'

Peter sat opened mouthed for a while. 'And you'd be willing to share them with me?'

'Not here, but if you came to the USA, I would.'

'You met my friend, Stella Reimers? The journalist?'

'Yes, of course. She's a lovely lady. Bobbie-Jean took a real shine to her.'

Ruby aside, he had no real reason to stay in England any longer. He stopped to think. *I can keep in contact with Olivia, no matter where I go.* There was a fork in the road ahead. 'I've decided that I'll be off to Washington DC, as soon as I can get a flight. Would you mind if, once I get there, I looked you up?'

'Mind? We'd be very happy if you did. You and Stella. She has our contact details. Always welcome.'

As the cab pulled up outside the foyer of the Ritz, Peter added, 'Maybe I'll get to finish Olivia's book now. Maybe, we'll get those bastards after all.'

'If my videos help put those predators in jail, I'll die a happy man.' Walter opened the door and swung out a leg.

'Can I ask you one last thing?'

Walter nodded. 'Of course.'

'Why don't you ever call Olivia by her name? Why don't you call her your daughter?

Walter closed his eyes, as if Peter had opened an old wound. 'I lost that right nearly thirty years ago. I'm afraid it's too late.'

'You're wrong, you know,' Peter replied. 'You and she are blood. It's never too late.'

59

It was as the taxi pulled up outside the main entrance to St Thomas's Hospital that Peter noticed that his palms were clammy. The hospital was huge; it was a lot busier and a lot bigger than he'd expected.

I have no idea why I've come here. I have no idea where Ruby is or how to find her and no idea what I'll say to her, if I do find her.

He rushed through the garden, past patients enjoying the last of the afternoon sunshine before the thick clouds hanging over Westminster blew in. Some of them wore dressing gowns as they chatted to visitors, while others had a solitary smoke, away from the disapproval of the nurses, most of whom seemed to smoke themselves anyway. Eventually, he found his way to the north wing of the hospital and to the information desk.

'I'm looking for Ruby Manzanoni?'

'I'm sorry, sir, you'll have to enquire with our media department.'

What the? Do I have tabloid reporter written across my forehead?
'But I'm a personal friend of hers.'

'Really? Well you'd be the fiftieth person who's told me that today. I'm terribly sorry, sir, I can't assist you.'

'But I am. Can't you call her up and check?'

'No, I can't. There's a strict policy here about that.'

'Then, how can I contact her?'

'Well, since you're her friend and all, I'm sure you already know how to contact her, don't you? Good day, sir.'

Peter was almost angrier about being refused access to Ruby, than he was about not seeing her. He actually felt a little relieved that he couldn't see her. He thought he'd send her flowers instead, and write a note that she couldn't resist.

He found the hospital's florist and picked up a card. In his habitual scrawl, he wrote: *Please forgive me Ruby, I never meant to hurt you. I should have told you I was a scumbag journalist, but I was scared. I should have trusted you.* Then he tore it up. In its place, he wrote: *Ruby, I love you. I always will. Peter.* He stood in line with his selection, immediately behind a woman in a Hermes scarf and a dark, impeccably tailored coat. She was tall and thin and smelled of roses. *I know that scent. Jean Patou. Joy.*

As the woman made her purchase and moved away, Peter called out softly, 'Megan?'

Megan turned and looked. She wore oversized sunglasses, but Peter still detected the bruise on the arch of her brow that her make-up couldn't conceal.

'Oh, it's you,' she replied.

'How is she? The truth.'

'She's on the mend and I'm sure she'll be fine in the long run.'

Peter smiled. 'Can I...'

'She doesn't want to see you, Peter.' Megan pulled him away from the counter. 'Please leave her alone.'

'But we're in love.'

She shook her head and sighed. 'Look, you don't understand. You can't understand and you were never meant to. You were meant to be a little diversion, nothing more. She was stung by Seb and you were supposed to be the light relief.'

This wasn't the woman he had met at the Manzanoni manor, the one who asked him if he yodelled and thought his mother-tongue was German. 'Who are you, Megan?'

'Never you mind who I am. Who were you? You lied to them. There's no way back, no apology they'll accept, no atonement, no forgiveness. He'll kill you if he sees you. That's not a threat, it's a prophecy. Get out. Go, while you still can. Forget the Manzanonis. You have no fucking clue, Peter, not a single one.'

'And what about you, Megan?'

Megan turned around and giggled. 'Me?' she asked, naively. 'Whatever could you possibly mean?'

60

Peter was relieved to find his key still opened the front door of the Hammersmith safe house. The flat had remained empty since Carol-Lee's death, with the exception of Peter's overnight stays, and only Olivia's personal belongings had been removed. *God knows where she'll end up now that Devrille has no further use for her.* He could only hope that Snoddy might have enough compassion to keep her off the streets.

He telephoned British Airways and enquired after flights to Washington. He was assured that there would be seats available for this evening's flight. He telephoned Stella next and left her a message. Then he packed his clothes into a single suitcase and put on his best suit, the one Ruby had sourced for him from Savile Row at a celebrity discount. He rubbed the fabric between his finger and thumb. Impeccable.

He checked and rechecked the cupboards and drawers for anything he might have misplaced. In Carol-Lee's bedside cabinet, he found the photograph album and scrapbook she had cherished and another, smaller book. He placed all of them into the duffel bag he'd be taking on board with him. Once he'd looked at them, he intended to return them to Olivia. *As soon as I'm settled over there, I'll finish writing your book, Olivia, that's a promise.* He had just enough funds to pay his way for a month or two. If he was careful.

Unfortunately, careful no longer included taxis, so Peter struggled his way to Heathrow by train.

He bought his ticket at the sales office, passed through customs and immigration, window-shopped his way through duty free, and settled down for a wait at the gate.

'Would Peter Clancy please make himself known to British Airways staff at the service desk immediately.'

What now? What more can possibly go wrong?

He picked up his duffel bag and strode up to the desk, ready for a fight. Fortunately, the woman at the desk was far too much of an English rose to argue with.

'Might I have your boarding pass please, Mr Clancy?'

He was about to ask her why, but thought the better of it. Faith wasn't his strongest suit. *Have faith. Something good will happen.*

'Thank you, Mr Clancy.' She tore up his boarding pass with a smile.

So much for faith.

'I don't understand,' he began.

She smiled again. 'Your new boarding pass, Mr Clancy. You've been upgraded to first class. Please feel free to make use of the Club Lounge.'

He wanted to yell out, *what the fuck, truly*, but he refrained. 'Thank you,' he replied, taking the boarding pass.

'Enjoy your flight, Mr Clancy,' she said. As he turned to leave she added, 'Nice suit, by the way.'

On his way to the first class lounge, he encountered a mob of newly arrived Australians, waiting for a connecting flight. He hadn't heard the accent for a while and to his unaccustomed ear, they sounded like a flock of cockatoos. 'Good old Collingwood forever, they know how to play the game...'

Did someone say Collingwood? Did I hear them singing the club song?

He instantly made a bee-line for them.

As he approached they changed tune. 'We are the champions...'

He singled out one of the group, a young, swarthy man with a chinful of stubble. 'Who won the premiership?' he asked.

'Where have you been, mate,' came the reply, 'Siberia?' He pointed at Peter. 'Hey, this guy's just asked me who won the Grand Final.'

One of his mates approached Peter, evil and alcohol glinting in his eye. 'Who do you barrack for?'

'The Magpies,' said Peter without hesitation.

'Fucking oath. They won the fucking Grand Final!'

Where had he been these past few months? He'd missed seeing the first Collingwood Premiership victory in his lifetime. *Missed it, I didn't even know it had happened!*

His disappointment was tempered a little by the sheer joy and excitement of travelling first class.

They know my name. No noisy children. No smelly armpits in your face. No chair reclining onto your meal while you're trying to eat it. This is the life!

He settled into his seat with a glass of champagne and took out the smaller of the three books he had collected from Carol-Lee's bedside. Peter looked at the smooth, vinyl cover, now cracking with age. It was covered in hand-drawn flowers and hearts. He opened out his tray table and rested the book on it. He sprung open the clasp and read: *Olivia Taylor's Diary 1974.* As Peter opened it, glittering stars and flowers cut out of crepe paper fell out onto the table. He gathered them together in a heap and put them aside.

DD

25 December 1974

Hello! You're my Christmas present. I promise to write in you every single day of my life from now on. From today onwards I'll tell you everything that happens to me. You're my own, true friend.

Before the plane took off, he stowed away the table and began reading the unbelievably boring daily insights of Olivia Michaels aged thirteen. As it banked, he read how she'd won the child lead in *Children of the Dark* and how excited she had been. As it levelled out to cruising altitude, he learned of her romance with Tinker. The entries were more of the same; her happiness when she saw Tinker, her sadness when he wasn't there, lots of hearts and flowers drawn in margins and dreams about the future. *But who's Tinker? Was he Andy Smith? One of the other children in the play?*

He read on.

DD

16 May 1975

Tinker finally invited me to stay at his house. No-one was home and we slept together in the same bed for the whole night! I can't believe it! He kept telling me how much he loved me and how one day, when I was old enough, we'd get married. If only…

Peter re-read the last line of the entry: *If only he didn't have to raise Ruby.* The diary fell out of his hands onto the table like a lead weight. He flipped through the pages. There were a few more entries and a page where Olivia had practised signing: *Olivia Taylor, Olivia Michaels, Olivia Manzanoni, Mrs Richard Manzanoni* over and over. There was no doubting Tinker's true identity.

'That lying bastard,' he muttered to himself. 'I knew it. I bloody knew it. Manzanoni's one. Andy probably knew it. Olivia was protecting him and didn't want to say. She loved him. Fuck.'

He gathered the stars and the flowers and slipped them into the inner plastic sleeve of the diary. He put it away with Carol-Lee's treasures. He was on his way to Washington DC. He had connections with a journalist employed by arguably the finest broadsheet in the world. He had Olivia's diary, his interview tapes and Walter's videos. He knew his work was only just beginning.

THE END

Printed in Australia
AUOC02n1854130315
266357AU00006B/6/P